Anna Legat is a Wiltshire-based author, best known for her DI Gillian Marsh murder mystery series. A globetrotter and Jack-of-all-trades, Anna has been an attorney, legal adviser, a silver-service waitress, a school teacher and a librarian. She read law at the University of South Africa and Warsaw University, then gained teaching qualifications in New Zealand. She has lived in far-flung places all over the world where she delighted in people-watching and collecting precious life experiences for her stories. Anna writes, reads, lives and breathes books and can no longer tell the difference between fact and fiction.

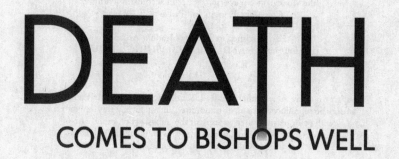

DEATH

COMES TO BISHOPS WELL

ANNA LEGAT

ACCENT

First published in 2021 by Headline Accent
An imprint of HEADLINE PUBLISHING GROUP

4

Cataloguing in Publication Data is available from the British Library

ISBN 978 1 7861 5794 2

Typeset in 10.5/13pt Bembo Std by Jouve (UK), Milton Keynes

Printed and bound in Great Britain by Clays Ltd, Elcograf S.p.A.

HEADLINE PUBLISHING GROUP
An Hachette UK Company
Carmelite House
50 Victoria Embankment
London EC4Y 0DZ

www.headline.co.uk
www.hachette.co.uk

DEATH

COMES TO BISHOPS WELL

Chapter One

'I'll tell you this for nothing, Sam – you need to get out more. Look at me, old man!' Richard beamed from the height of his stool. His elbow was propped on the edge of the bar, his right foot on the rung of the stool, his left, firm and assertive, planted flat on the floor. He had pulled back his shoulder blades and thrust his chin forward as if he were posing for a portrait. He was several years Sam's senior. The cheek of calling Sam old!

'Yes, I'm looking. What am I supposed to be seeing?'

'My vibrant and unbridled youth.'

'I see . . .'

'I'm glad you do!'

The hint of irony bypassed Richard, but Rhys, the barman, exchanged a bemused glance with Sam. He swept past them, casually wiping the counter and collecting a few empty glasses along the way. An ex-full back, he had a boxing-glove textured body, heavily padded with raw muscle. A dense tangle of tendons, veins, and sinews teemed beneath his rolled-up sleeves. He was young and strong. Had it not been for a neck injury, he would still have been on the pitch instead of manning the bar at Bishops Well Rugby Clubhouse. By comparison, Richard came across as an old man, whether he cared to admit it or not: his frame was hollowed and his skin leathery and wrinkled, the hue and texture of tea-soaked parchment. But he knew how to carry himself with bravado.

'I look youthful,' he proceeded to expand his point, 'because I don't hang on to the past. I catch the moment, here and now!

1

Carpe diem, old man! *Carpe diem!*' He slapped Sam on the arm and squeezed it with his bony fingers.

'Yeah,' Sam agreed distractedly and took another long and pensive swig from his pint glass. He jolted as he caught his own reflection in the mirror behind the spirit bottles lined up on the shelf. He looked a washout, which was precisely how he felt. Nevertheless, his own face took him by surprise. It was blotchy, unshaven, and swollen from another restless night. His hair, once thick and black, seemed faded and dusty, as if he had scattered ashes over his head.

'How long has it been now – eighteen months?'

'Nineteen months.'

'It's time to move on, for pity's sake!' Richard leaned forward and gripped his arm. 'You're bloody well coming - I won't let you off the hook, not this time! This is my last birthday bash, I have decided, and that is final. Sixty-eight, past your average retirement age, and that's it. After this one, I'm well and truly retired from birthdays. Last chance!'

'I really don't think so. You know I'm not good with people I don't know. I'll only feel rotten.'

'Bring someone you *do* know.'

Sam emitted a derisive snort. He had left the people he knew behind him, in London.

'In fact, I can think of someone just perfect for the occasion. That charming little neighbour of yours – she'll be fun.'

'Maggie Kaye?' Sam found the idea preposterous. He hardly knew the woman. Their dealings had been limited to him buying one half of her house, a pleasant enough and straightforward transaction.

'Yeah, Mystic Maggie! I know her old man, Eugene. Even he doesn't know what to make of her, but one thing is for certain: you won't be bored. She'll have plenty to say – she always does. I have it on good authority that she even talks to the dead – she might get a direct line to Alice and bend her ear. I wouldn't put it past her!'

Amused by his own joke, Richard slapped Sam again – this time on his thigh – and gave a jolly loud guffaw. Sam didn't join him. He wasn't in the mood, especially now that Richard had managed to bring Alice into this. Two years and four months . . . it felt like only yesterday.

Richard sighed. 'Just do it for me, Samuel. I'll need you there. You're my oldest friend here – I don't have many, old or new, come to think . . . I'm better at making enemies.' A false note rang in his laughter. 'Seriously, Sam, I want all of the people I love to be there. You're one of them. You know you are. You're sat deep in here, in my soul!' With his typical Slavic exuberance, Richard thumped his chest. It reverberated with a hollow sound. 'I want you all together, raising a glass to my good health. That's not too much to ask, is it?'

Sam sighed in reply.

'Even the scorned wives are coming.'

'Mary?'

'Oh yes! And Dotty, all the way from Florida. I pray to God I recognise her face.'

'It's been a good few years . . .'

'It's not that. Yes, she may be a few decades older since I last clapped my eyes on her, but it's what she's done to herself in all those years.'

'What has she done?'

'All the bloody surgeries and implants she's been through. She's made of silicone or whatever it is she pumps into herself. A friend of mine said she looked like a puffer fish. At least I've got a pool.' He laughed again, then quickly pulled a supplicatory face. 'Be a good sport and come . . . Come, for old times' sake.'

'I'll see. I can't promise –'

'Good! I'll take that and I'll drink to it!' Richard raised his glass, swivelled the honey-coloured brandy with panache, and downed it. He banged the empty glass down on the bar and gestured to Rhys for another round. His eyes wandered aimlessly around the half-empty bar and halted abruptly. He twisted his lips with dismay. 'Hell, not him!'

Henry Hopps-Wood was ambling into the bar from the restaurant end of the clubhouse.

'Richard! Samuel! Good to see you!' Henry arranged his face into a poor impression of a smile. His face muscles struggled to stretch his small, tight lips. He sailed towards them and shook their hands, Richard's first. 'Birthday wishes are in order, I hear. Many happy returns!'

Richard murmured something remotely resembling a grudging thank you.

'Vera and I are coming to your bash. Wouldn't miss it for the world . . . Especially Vera!'

'Who told you?' Richard's question sounded like a grievance.

'Penny, of course. Oh, have I just put my foot in it? It isn't one of those surprise parties, damn it? You do know you're having a party?'

'Yes, I know. I just wish she left the guest list to me. It's my bloody birthday!'

Henry stared, his nose out of joint, but Richard merely went on steaming with frustration, expelling grunts of discontent.

'Whatever do you mean?' Henry demanded as soon as he recovered his voice.

'Do I have to make myself any clearer? I can, you know! I bloody well can, but you won't like it.'

'Why don't you try me?'

The staring competition between the two men was turning nasty. Finding himself between them, Sam felt decisively squeezed. He groaned inwardly and spoke with a put-on joviality, 'Richard, you devil, I almost took you seriously!' He slapped the old boy on the back and laughed.

On reflection, Henry laughed too, insincerity rattling in his throat. 'You got me there, damn it!' He turned on his heel and hurried away in the direction of the exit, from which he then promptly retreated to finally find his way to the gents'.

'I wasn't joking,' Richard told Sam. 'He's a damn snake in the grass, Hopps-blinking-Wood! Hopps . . . Slithers, more like!'

'What's brought this on?' It was common knowledge that Richard, a confirmed Tory, had campaigned for Henry in last year's

4

election, staking his reputation and fame to unseat the Lib Dem incumbent and successfully getting Henry elected. Penny, Richard's third and present wife, was still driving Henry's PR wagon and ghostwriting his speeches, so far as Sam was aware. They were in each other's pockets – one happy family.

Or were they?

'Don't get me started! He is a bastard through and through. I know things ...'

'Know what?'

'Bah! Don't ask! It's nothing.' Richard looked atypically downcast, but only for a few seconds. He downed his brandy, which Rhys had just placed before him, in one go and exhaled. The alcohol seemed to lift his spirits. 'Who knows,' he raised his brow thoughtfully, 'he might yet regret gatecrashing my birthday do. If he insists on coming.'

'What are you getting at?'

'We'll see ... We have to keep our politicians accountable. For all their sins.' The mischievous spark returned to Richard's eye. He glanced at his watch and sprung from the stool. 'Damn it! Have to run! I'm already late.'

'Where are you off to?'

'Bristol.'

'Oh?'

Richard turned and tapped the side of his nose. 'Meeting a lady, an old flame of mine. A blast from the past, you could say. So much to catch up on, old man, so much to catch up on!'

At that point, Henry emerged from the gents' and the two men collided with each other. Neither of them looked too pleased. They eyed each other with thinly veiled hostility. Finally, Henry blinked first and stepped aside to let Richard through.

Sam left the clubhouse a few minutes later. In the car park, he ran into Frank Savage.

'Richard – is he inside?'

'You've just missed him.'

'Is he heading back home?'

'Bristol, I believe.'

'Bristol?'

'That's what he said.'

Frank cursed under his breath. He was a broad-shouldered ex-military man who had been working for Richard in the loose capacity of bodyguard-cum-Man Friday for some fifteen years now. Where exactly Richard had found him was a mystery, but Frank was his most loyal employee and confidant. It came therefore as a surprise to Sam that Frank didn't know Richard's precise co-ordinates at this very moment.

'He said he was picking up a lady. A "blast from the past" is how he put it.'

'Dorothy – Dotty, his ex?'

'He didn't say who.'

'Only she's already arrived!' Frank appeared flustered, his trade-mark military disposition unable to keep frustration at bay. He ground his teeth, 'She's not only arrived, but she's also full of shit, if you get my meaning – wants an explanation why Richard is avoiding her. The answer is staring her in the face – she's a cow. She's always been a pain in the arse apparently but she's got worse with age. *And* she's only just got here. What did she expect – a red carpet and a guard of honour?'

'Well, yes . . . quite ridiculous . . .' Sam bumbled just to say something supportive. Frank was in a state.

'You'll never guess who brought her from Heathrow.'

'You?'

'Tuppence!' Frank often used Penny's full name, pronouncing it with a lethal dose of venom. 'Of all the sad suckers out there, snotty Tuppence drove all the way to Heathrow to chauffeur Dotty about. She was the only one at home when the old bat rang – couldn't think of an excuse.'

'That's decent of her.'

'She didn't look decent from where I was standing. Pissed off, more like.'

'You can't say no to Dotty –'

'I would've killed to be a fly on the wall in that car with them two driving back to Bishops. Two hours of sheer bloody-mindedness. The moment she let the old bat out of her car, Penny took off without a word – like she had to be somewhere urgent. Left me alone with Dotty. Not an experience I'd like to repeat, not even if they paid me double. The way she spoke to me, I was minded to tell her where to go. The woman's mad as a hatter, I tell you! But what the hell is she *doing* here? That's what I'd like to know!'

'Richard did mention she was invited to his birthday bash.' Sam was finding this comedy of errors mildly entertaining. 'They must've got their timings muddled up.'

'They sure as hell did! The "bash" isn't for another two weeks.'

'It looks like you're stuck with her till then.'

Leaving Frank with that thought, Sam departed. Home was within walking distance of the clubhouse and he enjoyed strolling down the steep cobbled streets of Bishops Well.

Bishops was a quaint market town. Sam had once made the mistake of calling it a *village* in front of a few deeply patriotic locals. He had narrowly escaped a lynching. He'd had to endure a long lecture about Bishops Well's proud past. None other than King John himself had granted Bishops Well (then known as Westonbury) town privileges in 1211. These included a Thursday Market (which continued to this day), as well as 'quittance from tallage, stallage, lastage, and payage'. The town's propitious location halfway between Bath to the north and Salisbury to the south had made it an attractive pit stop for travelling merchants and pilgrims. In its heyday Bishops had boasted four inns and six taverns, now reduced to a mere two public houses, the Rook's Nest and the Watering Hole. In the neighbouring village of Parson's Combe stood Parson's Combe Inn, the only local establishment offering overnight accommodation. It wasn't bursting at the seams, due to the fact that only a handful of visitors passed through the area nowadays, and even fewer took respite within the town's walls. There was a puritan faction of Bishopians who didn't regard the humble hamlet of Parson's Combe as part of Bishops; they offered their exclusive patronage to the Rook's Nest.

Sam would always remember his first encounter with Bishops Well's eccentricities when he had visited and fallen in love with the place. He had been forced to leave his car in a muddy country lane on the periphery of town, since the High Street had been taken over by revellers. Driven by curiosity, he had joined the crowd of bizarrely dressed druids and faeries. Beating drums, shaking giant rattles, and chanting in an eerie combination of menace and drunken rapture, they had flooded the streets from all directions and headed towards the Market Square. There they had set up an enormous bonfire and begun tossing straw effigies and spitting mouthfuls of ale into the flames. This ritual was accompanied by unrepeatable cursing and beseeching the Devil to return to hell his Saxon spawn. When the raging flames started to lick the arms of the stone cross, the mob broke into a frantic dance and its now jubilant chants reached their crescendo. At that point, Bishops' only fire engine had emerged and put an end to the spectacle.

The revellers had retreated to the Rook's Nest for more celebrations. Sam had followed, keen to establish the meaning of the madness he had just witnessed. Over a pint, or two, of the home-brewed ale, he had discovered that the good people of Bishops Well who considered themselves the direct descendants of Ancient Britons had just celebrated the demise of their Saxon oppressors. When he had pointed out that the Saxon oppressors had simply been replaced by the Normans, he had been advised that patience was a virtue. The Normans would get their comeuppance soon enough.

'One thing at a time,' Terrence Truelove, the publican, had said, offering Sam his next pint on the house. Sam had become instantly besotted with the place. The more he had found out about it, the greater was his infatuation.

A valiant attempt had been made after the Great War to revive the town by linking it by rail to the rest of the world. Today the derelict train station stood forlorn and drowning in weeds at the end of a defunct line. A local farmer used the buildings for grain storage in harvest season. There was an operational bus service, however. The parish activists fought tooth and nail to keep it subsidised for the benefit of Bishops' citizens. Bishops' postie, John Erwin (who also drove the fire engine!) had taken over the bus driver's role on a part-time basis ten years ago. Ever since, he had enjoyed the status of national treasure, even though he never kept to any particular schedule and would frequently misappropriate the bus in order to deliver post in bad weather.

Architecturally, Bishops Well was steeped in history and quite averse to change. The wheels of time seemed to have become derailed en route there and progress had never made it to town. Bishopians resolutely rejected all attempts at modernisation and stuck to maintaining their thatched roofs, inglenooks, and chimney stacks in their original condition. The Market Square boasted Bishops' very own circle of stones – three still standing and the fourth laid across like a sacrificial altar – apparently predating Stonehenge. This ancient Celtic relic housed at its centre a blackened, ten-foot-high stone cross – blackened undoubtedly by centuries of Saxon-cursing fires. Inadvertently, Bishops Well managed to project an image of diversity and tolerance in this perfect blend of its pagan and Christian leanings. Local lore had it that beneath the cross was a spring well. A splash of water from that well could heal leprosy, as it had done in the early fourteenth century, miraculously restoring Bishop Anselm's health after he had contracted the disease on his pilgrimage to the Holy Land. It was then that the town had been renamed Bishops Well. However, no one had been able to verify the presence of the well, never mind its healing properties, as the considerable bulk of the stone cross could not be shifted or in any way tampered with.

The Grade 1 listed edifice of Bishops' Tudor Town Hall stood side by side with the recently erected Community Hall. Across the Market Square was a seventeenth-century arcade, affectionately referred to as the Old Stables. It was home to a stylish café-restaurant, a butcher's shop still run by the descendants of Robert

Kane, who had established it in 1701 (if the plaque over the door was to be believed), and a bakery whose owner, appropriately named Angela Cornish, was famous countywide for her pasties.

The Old Stables arcade vied for attention with the Rook's Nest, the town's oldest public house. Cobbled streets sprouted from the Market Square like arteries from the town's beating heart. The High Street served as the main aorta carrying traffic through the village – sorry, *the town* – and across a charming single-lane bridge over the River Avon. It continued towards the rolling hills of the Commons Green where the Folly stood, and beyond where the rival town of Sexton's Canning sprawled like an ugly grey toad.

To many Bishopians, Sexton's Canning's relentless expansion was a travesty. A place that had begun as a small hamlet of farm workers had over the centuries overtaken Bishops Well in size and significance. It had encroached upon Bishops' outer confines, gradually absorbing the villages of Little Ogburn, Lower Norton, and even parts of Parson's Combe. But Bishops Well held its own in the face of adversity and successfully resisted being appended to the south-western outskirts of its bigger neighbour. It had to put up with Sexton's Canning hogging all of the county's primary amenities, such as libraries, leisure centres, hospitals, and shopping centres, as well as a busy train station, the County Hall, and the police headquarters. Bishops Well may have defended its sovereignty but it had to yield to Sexton's supremacy. Bishopians found that fact irritating: since when should a bishop bow to a sexton! Instead of grumbling, though, they resolutely maintained a stiff upper lip and got on with their exciting lives.

And life in Bishops Well was brimming with excitement. Apart from the Thursday Market, summer and winter fetes were held with many noble charities in mind. The list of worthy causes was as long as the High Street. Bishopians were particularly fond of all things old. The past was never far from a Bishopian's mind. Every important – and unimportant – historical anniversary was noted in the Parish calendar and wholeheartedly commemorated in the residents' unique way. The most powerful force to reckon with in

Bishops Well was the AA – Bishops Well Archaeological Association, that is – and that spoke volumes about the town's priorities. A large number of other exotic societies with a limited level of usefulness called Bishops Well their home.

And, since last November, so did Samuel Dee.

He had decided to relocate there after a few weeks of intense introspection following the anniversary of his wife's death. Rather than spending a second painfully lonely Christmas in London, without Alice, he had decided to shut the door on his old life and move somewhere where the memories of Alice could not find him. Their children, Abi and Campbell, were grown up and had left home. There was nothing to keep him rattling around his and Alice's old London haunts without her by his side, and bumping into people who knew him as Alice's other half. It would never be the same without her.

That was when he had remembered the mad little town of Bishops Well. It would be a perfect hidey-hole to afford him peace of mind and anonymity, he had decided, and started packing.

Anonymity hadn't been fully accomplished, as, a couple of months into his brand-new life, he had run into Richard Ruta at the Thursday Market. Sam had totally forgotten that Richard resided in a country estate, ironically named Forget-Me-Not, a couple of miles south of the town. Sam had visited Richard there before, notably swinging by Bishops Well on that one memorable occasion, but had somehow failed to make the connection when placing the offer on his new house. Now, he was glad of that. In the end, having just one old friend around couldn't be that bad, and in the main, it wasn't.

Sam's new home wasn't that new. It was a subdivided old vicarage called Priest's Hole. The blackened name plaque hung over the archway of the original front door, and the Roman numerals chiselled into it indicated that it dated back to 1645. According to the property deeds, the vicarage hadn't actually been built until 1849, but word had it that the foundations remembered the days of the Civil War, when the then Royalist rectory was plundered and

11

burned down by marauding Roundheads in search of easy pickings. Religious differences may have had something to do with it, too.

Priest's Hole sat snug and comfy, nestled in the churchyard. With its sharp belfry, St John's church towered over the priest's living quarters like a mother over her babe. The house backed on to the cemetery.

Sam appreciated that aspect of his neighbourhood: it was dead quiet. Blossoming nature held together the crumbling tombstones. Squirrels and blackbirds rustled the treetops which twitched and rippled with incessant activity. Sam's garden blended well with the graveyard: it was wild and overgrown, and utterly untamed. Over the four-foot stone wall was his neighbour's garden. Maggie Kaye occupied the other half of the old rectory building. Her garden, a mirror reflection of Sam's in shape and size, teemed with colour, erupted with scents, and buzzed with life. If Sam's garden was a yang, Maggie's was a yin. In all its hyperactive vitality, it must have kept all the dead souls in the cemetery wide awake.

Maggie was doing her best to keep the ghosts on their toes. With her around, nobody stood a chance of resting in peace. She spent most of her waking hours in the garden, tending to her vibrant bushes, deadheading and, frequently, to Sam's initial disbelief, entertaining herself with part-mumbled, part-hummed monologues.

More than six months into their neighbourly co-habitation, the initial disbelief had worn off. By now, Sam was used to Maggie's bizarre ways. In fact, he had warmed to her. She had become a welcome reminder that life went on somewhere on this planet, regardless.

As he stepped out of his kitchen door onto the weed-infested patio, a mug of steaming coffee in hand, he was delighted to find his neighbour waving to him. She was leaning over the fence, a big smile gracing her face.

'I was expecting you to pop out any second now, and look – wasn't I right?'

This was how she would often start a conversation, and it

explained why people called her Mystic Maggie. She was always one step ahead of you. He raised his mug to her and said hello, and for the sake of neighbourly harmony, added something about a lovely day. The bees were buzzing over Maggie's flowerbeds, while an occasional stray wasp droned competitively in Sam's nettle patch. The sun felt warm on his face. This was as good an opportunity as any to ask his neighbour to accompany him to Richard's damned birthday bash.

Chapter Two

I was sitting in the garden, sunning myself on a bench and contemplating the hidden health benefits of Jaffa Cakes, when she appeared. At first, I heard the swing creak. Ever since I could remember, that swing would creak whenever someone sat in it. It was a sturdy plank of wood suspended from the tree on two rusty chains. Over the years the wood had been polished to smooth perfection by our bottoms. My sister Andrea and I used to fight over that swing when we were little girls. Being older by nearly two years, I would invariably win the contest and plant my even then sizeable backside on the wooden seat, demanding that Andrea gave me a push. But she wouldn't because she was sulking, her little mouth downturned and wobbly. So I would let her have the first go. But it would be on my terms, you see, because I had won and could afford to be magnanimous. I would push her and then she would push me, and the swing's rusty chains would creak.

So when I heard it creak again, my happy childhood memories fluttered in and I peeked over the fence, half-expecting to see my little sister sitting in it, knees wide apart, clutching the chains and waiting to be pushed. But, of course, it wasn't Andrea. It was my neighbour's dead wife.

She had sat in the swing, rested her head against the chain, and was indulging in a faint to-and-fro movement, the swing rocking lazily like a pendulum, her dress air-lifted.

I said to her, 'You look like a happy camper. Your hubby's coming out to play, isn't he?'

She didn't answer – they never do.

She peered dreamily into space, smiling. She looked twenty, not a day older, even though she must have been at least in her mid-forties when she died. But even in death people can be vain and will try to look their best. Especially women. I would be the same, I imagine. Given a choice, I too would go for my twenties looks. I was slimmer then, wobble-free, crow's feet-free, and carefree. I was boyfriend-hopping like an Easter bunny on Duracell because after my first heartbreak I had decided that true love was for the birds. And I still had a sister –

But I digress.

I saw my neighbour's dead wife on the swing, and that told me he had to be nearby. She – I believe her name was Alice – would never turn up in the garden to keep *me* company. She only had eyes for him. I don't think she could see me, or if she could, she was ignoring me. I, on the other hand, could see her as plain as day, in all her ghostly glory.

Did I mention that I can see the dead?

I realise I sound demented, like I stole a line from *The Sixth Sense* and ran away with it, but it's true. I can see them. The dead.

I wasn't born that way. It took the disappearance of Andrea for me to cross that line. I looked for her everywhere, and after I had exhausted all of her hunting spots here on earth, I moved further afield – into the realm of the dead.

I was alone in my search. No one else was worried, because Andrea had been a wayward young thing, footloose and fancy-free. She had not kept in touch at the best of times, but in the end would always find her way home. Especially when she needed cash. So everyone assumed that she had upped sticks and left for some exotic island in the Pacific, and that sooner or later she would be back. Dad had said more or less exactly that and told me to give it a rest. Mum had told me not to fret, Andrea would turn up. I didn't believe them. It was typical of Andrea to disappear, but it wasn't like her not to come back when she ran out of funds. I started visiting all kinds of charlatans and necromancers, spent a fortune on

15

mediums, and consorted with the so-called white witches (they are the good ones, as opposed to the rest of them who can be real cows).

To this day, I cannot pinpoint the person responsible for nudging me over to the other side. The dreams had come first: vivid, convoluted nightmares crowded with faces made of wet clay, stretching and coiling in turn, reshaping themselves as they reached out to me, and through me, and out, while I could do nothing to stop them, screaming soundlessly with my mouth wide open, gasping for air and missing on every breath. I can only compare that experience to drowning. I know that sensation intimately from the day when, as kids, we had been apple-bobbing at Halloween and it was my turn. I had been doing well but then my stupid big brother Will, for laughs, had pushed my head into the bowl and held me down for what seemed like for ever. The apple I had been holding in my teeth slipped out and water raced into my lungs. It felt like it swelled in every organ of my body and burst out through my eyes and ears. They had pulled me up and had to pump my chest. Apparently, the whole episode had only lasted a few split seconds. When I had come round, it seemed to me that I had come back from the dead. And that was exactly how I felt when all those years later I woke up from those nightmares.

And then they stopped.

On that night when I screeched out of another nightmare, my mouth grasping in the dead of night for the word *help*, I stared right into the eyes of a figure sitting at the foot of my bed, curling a lock of hair around her finger, peering into space. I said, 'Excuse me?', which was the first thing that sprang to my mind. I think I must have been feeling a bit defensive – protective over the privacy of my own bedroom. She didn't respond. Like I said, they never do. She got up and walked into the wall, or rather, through it. After that, the nightmares had stopped but the dead kept turning up, uninvited as they were, because none of them was Andrea. Remember, all I had wanted when I had started meddling with the dead was to find my little sister.

But I stray again. I do this all the time: I talk too much and fly off on a tangent.

Going back to that warm and sunny May day, true to form, Samuel Dee, my neighbour, the dead woman's husband, strolled onto the patio of his garden, a coffee mug in hand, and shouted a cheery hello in response to my friendly wave. I told him I had been expecting him, but he didn't ask why. Instead, he pointed out to me the obvious fact of the weather being rather pleasant, and then, out of the blue, said, 'Richard Ruta is having a garden party – it's his birthday – a birthday bash. Saturday week. I was wondering – would you like to . . . would you like to come?'

'Oh . . .' It isn't like me to be stuck for words, but I was. I adore Richard Ruta and I love his films. In the late eighties, his films were my religion, and he a distant and unattainable deity. If anyone had told me that one day the deity would descend from heaven and move to Bishops, I'd have been struck dumb. So, when he married my old pal Mary and the two of them moved from London to make their home at Forget-Me-Not, I went dizzy with disbelief – and rather green with envy. Seeing Mary on the arm of my idol was a little bit too much to take. I had felt betrayed by my friend and cheated on by my – imaginary, as it were – lover. I had found a polite excuse not to be one of Mary's bridesmaids and left town for a couple of miserable weeks in Wales. It had rained all the time. When I had returned home, I could not bring myself to visit Mary and her God-husband, so I had drifted further and further away, worshipping the man from a safe distance and watching his turbulent life with the same fascination as I watched his films.

Unsure about my ambiguous reaction, Samuel felt obliged to explain, 'I've got an invitation for two – myself *plus one*, you see . . . I don't know anyone else in these parts. I thought you might – Otherwise, it'll go to waste.'

'We can't let that happen,' I regained my power of speech. It was time to grow up and face my fears. 'I'd love to come, thank you!'

'Good, then, hmm . . .' he replied, absently, turned on his heel and stole back indoors. Alice rose from the swing and she too disappeared from sight. I could safely assume that he wasn't coming out again, so I returned to deadheading the roses.

That evening, I climbed up to the loft and rummaged through the woodlouse-infested coffer where I kept old videos and DVDs. I could swear that I saw a mouse's tail trailing away under the floorboards as I stumbled from the ladder, but I stifled a scream and pretended it was a shadow. The tail *might* have belonged to a rat. I wasn't going to investigate – it was long gone by the time I switched on the lights. I knelt by the coffer and began my search. I was looking for a Richard Ruta box set. It dated back to 2001, since Ruta had not directed any new films in years. He had burst on to the scene in the eighties. I remember watching it on telly: the story about the famous Polish director and his notorious defection to the West. In those days, he looked like a Greek god: dashing and devilishly handsome, and full of disarming attitude. That was my heyday, too – the best days of my life; I was young and full of ideas; I designed my own outfits from Mum's net curtains and bedsheets; I had my first wet perm, and Andrea was still living at home with us, far from trouble.

His films had shaped the generation of decadence and excess. They were different. Alien. Intriguing. They were iconic, and they had set trends for years to come. His adaptation of *Tristan and Isolde* had opened the floodgates to guiltless extra-marital affairs and spelled the end of the Seventh Commandment. My favourite was *Into the Bargain*, a tale about an aspiring actress who sells her soul to Lucifer for stardom and throws her own body *into the bargain*. It was deliciously immoral. And horrifying. Ruta had the knack for leading you to throw caution to the wind with wanton abandon, for which in the end he would make you pay the weight of your heavy soul in gold. I loved his films. I had seen each of them on the big screen, and later, when DVDs replaced video tapes, bought the whole box set as soon as my pay cheque had cleared.

At last, I uncovered the box set at the bottom of the coffer and, triumphant, raced down the ladder and down the stairs, to the sitting room to push the first DVD into the player. A bottle of Pinot Grigio had been cooling in the fridge since the afternoon. I fetched it and poured a glass, which misted satisfyingly. I retrieved the deliciously salty, steaming popcorn from the microwave as soon as it pinged. Finally, full of anticipation, I curled up on the sofa to indulge in all my guilty pleasures: eating, drinking, and having dirty thoughts.

It was on the second glass that my finger could find no more particles of salt at the bottom of the bowl, and I became disillusioned with my viewing. Even though the storyline was a cracker, the acting was overcooked, the makeup grotesquely overdone, the hair too big, and the clothes ... God help us all who wore them in those days! Sometimes it is best to leave the ghosts of the past in the past where they belong. I switched to the TV and flicked between channels. I caught a repeat of *Wallander* and rejoiced. With his cool Scandinavian understatement, Wallander was the antidote my mind (and body) craved. He would go down well with a cheeseboard and a bunch of grapes, I concluded, and trotted to the kitchen to plunder the fridge for a wedge of Brie and a slice of cheddar.

Chapter Three

Sam had not worn a tie since Alice's funeral. He had to dig deep into the boxes to find his old collection. The fact that he had not labelled the boxes when moving home did not help with his search. Neither did the fact that most of them remained packed and sealed, for he only bothered to open them when necessity called for it. Which wasn't often. In his new sedate life in the West Country, Samuel didn't need much: a sturdy pair of wellies to negotiate muddy ruts, a waterproof anorak to brave the incessant drizzle, and a kettle, for obvious reasons. Everything else that had seemed indispensable in London was superfluous here in the deep country. Particularly the ties.

It was late and the tie was proving elusive. Sam decided to settle for a Ted Baker shirt with a bold print. He only knew it was Ted Baker because it had been a gift from Alice and she had been particular about things like that. In Alice's day, this shirt had been well-fitting; now it hung on Sam without definition. Without Alice, even his clothes had lost the will to live.

Had he not invited Maggie, and had she not accepted, Sam would have changed his mind about going to Richard's party. This morning, he hadn't risen from bed in the highest of spirits and they only sank deeper as the day went on. But as things stood, he had to pull himself out of the depths of self-pity and knock on his neighbour's door.

Maggie opened the door on the first knock. Bright-eyed and bushy-tailed, a bejewelled clutch bag in hand, she smiled at him and, true to form, said, 'Ha! I knew you were at the door.'

'Am I too early?'

'No! Spot on. I was expecting you at this very minute.'

'I hope you were. I did say I'd collect you at half-two.' Sam couldn't hide his bemusement. 'Shall we go?'

Maggie stepped out and locked her front door with an iron key, which was far too big for her tiny bag, so she hid it under a terracotta pot full of yellow pansies. Sam was obliged to roll up his sleeves and tilt the pot, which weighed a ton. A family of deeply traumatised earthworms wriggled out as he did so.

Maggie fussed about getting into the passenger seat of his Jag, making irrational noises about there not being any space for her to squeeze in despite the ample leg room. She insisted on taking the back seat. Sam, though puzzled, relented. They were running late.

Forget-Me-Not was a Georgian mansion of creamy Bath stone. Built on elevated foundations, it loomed over its surroundings. Triple French doors led out on to a terrace where an outdoor pool took centre stage. From that level, stone steps led down to the garden. They were guarded by statues of a stag standing on one side and a lion lying on the other. At the bottom of the steps was a gravelled courtyard, which was encircled by a perfectly manicured, Versailles-type garden with box hedges, a snail-shaped maze curling and unfurling in the middle, a symphony of colourful early blooms, such as clematis, and topping it all, an array of forget-me-nots scattered in large ceramic pots.

When Sam and Maggie arrived, the garden was already full of extravagantly dressed individuals, strutting and posing around the pool, air-kissing and bursting with peals of staged laughter. It was a bohemian crowd: artists, actors, film-makers, and film critics. Those people knew how to put on a show. And they knew how to make everyone who didn't belong in the show feel painfully out of place.

Maggie intercepted a white-clad waiter carrying a tray of champagne glasses on the palm of his hand. She grabbed two and passed one to Sam. 'Let's get smashed,' she recommended.

It was as good an idea as any. Sam took a tentative swig, secretly hoping for a pint of lager.

Someone tapped Maggie on the shoulder. It was an elderly gentleman with a head – and ears – full of thick white-speckled hair. Maggie spun on her heels and threw her arms around him.

'Dad!'

'You look surprised! I bet you didn't foresee us being here. A small malfunction in your sixth sense wiring?' he teased, a glint of mischief in his eye.

A small older lady added, 'We certainly didn't expect to bump into you. On second thoughts, how come you *are* here?'

'I know, I know … Isn't it funny? My new neighbour invited me.' Maggie flipped her wrist in Sam's direction. 'It's all down to him I'm here. But you haven't met him yet - this is Samuel Dee.'

The elderly gentleman's eyes and the eyes of the little lady on his arm settled on Sam. They seemed to be assessing how good he was at plumbing and changing light bulbs – two qualities required of any half-decent neighbour.

'Samuel is the man who bought the other half of Priest's Hole. He moved in before Christmas.'

'Yes, you did mention …' her father agreed, but looked doubtful. 'She did, didn't she, love?'

'It goes to show you never visit. When was the last time?' Maggie turned to Sam, 'They only live down the road.'

'My knees gave up a long time ago, and your mother's been off colour since … Since when, love?'

'Never mind,' Maggie sighed theatrically. 'Samuel, meet my parents.'

'Eugene,' Maggie's father shook Sam's hand. He had a firm grip.

'I'm Irene,' said the mother, her eyes warm and liquid like runny honey. 'Nice to meet you.' She couldn't hear Sam returning the pleasantry as she was gripped by a bout of coughing. She looked apologetic when they stopped. 'Please excuse me. I've had this nasty cough since Christmas. I can't shake it off.'

'That's right – since Christmas! When she starts, she can't stop – on and on she goes.' Eugene gave a mocking impression of a nagging cough.

'Mum, you need to have it seen to –'

'Don't fuss, Maggie. This is a party. I want to enjoy myself, if you don't mind.'

'Still . . .'

'That's our Maggie!' Eugene stepped in, 'Once she's wound herself up about something or other, you can't convince her otherwise. She'll bang on about it until the cows come home. And beyond!'

'I only want –'

'I hope you're coping. Never a dull moment being her neighbour, I imagine.' Eugene winked.

'Well . . . yes . . . I mean, no!'

'What's that supposed to mean, Dad?'

Eugene was saved by Henry Hopps-Wood.

'Well, hello there! So glad to see some familiar faces! I was beginning to think I came to the wrong do. Such an awkward crowd, don't you think?'

Henry strode into the middle of their small circle, like a heron on stick legs. His wife dragged her feet behind him, wearing a hopeless, fish-out-of-water expression. The two of them were well-matched, Sam thought: he with his unusually elongated neck and a small head with a pinched nose and beady eyes, she long-limbed and narrow-shouldered, with a long face to go with her long body. She stood with her feet wide apart, looking distinctly uncomfortable in high heels. Her dress hung too low on her to be knee-length and sat too high on her calves to qualify as full-length. Vera Hopps-Wood was not a picture of confidence. She clearly was a trousers and wellies kind of gal.

'Sam, you must meet my wife. Vera, darling, this is that barrister I told you about, Richard's old friend from London, Samuel Dee.'

'No longer a practising barrister. I've left the Bar.'

Vera smiled at him sweetly. 'I'm pleased to meet you.' Her voice was raspy and her cadence clipped as tightly as a bonsai tree, but her tone was warm and her manner genuine. Unlike her husband's. Sam replied that the pleasure was all his.

Henry's attention had already drifted away, and he was waving to another couple. 'Over here, Alec, Vanessa, over here! Come and join us! Over here!'

Alec waved curtly back – it looked more like a salute than a wave. He was tall and bulky, with a thick neck and sloping shoulders, and possessed a military spring in his step. By contrast, Vanessa was short and corpulent with a well-pronounced midriff and even better-pronounced breasts. As much as he charged forward, she rolled next to him like a soft ball of cotton wool.

As they approached, the man's cleft lip became inescapable. Hard as he tried, for a few troubling seconds, Sam could not take his eyes off it. It seemed to crack the man's face into jagged fragments, like a broken mirror. Alec Scarfe turned out to be the Detective Chief Superintendent of Sexton's Canning CID, a position on the local society ladder high enough to hold Henry's attention for a few minutes. Vanessa was his charming wife.

The small circle of locals had now grown in size – and confidence. They appeared to be on friendly terms – at least outwardly – and formed a close-knit group. Their conversation wandered off towards the activities of the Bishops Well Archaeological Association, of which most, if not all of them, were members. Maggie dominated the discussion by musing out loud about draining some remote swamp where an ancient Celtic village was rumoured to be buried. More champagne was requisitioned from the white-clad waiter to whom Maggie had taken an instant liking.

The champagne swivelled inside Sam's head, which was unaccustomed and hostile to this sense-numbing beverage. He was dreaming of a cool, life-saving pint of lager, when Maggie enquired, out of the blue, 'You would be interested in joining us, Samuel, wouldn't you? Aren't you into digging up old pottery and laying ghosts to rest?'

'Can I borrow Sam for a minute?' Penny Ruta floated to his rescue from nowhere, hooked her arm into his and, with a regal smile tolerating no resistance, led him away.

Penny was Richard's third wife. Hers was the sort of breezy, flawless beauty which radiated and shimmered like gold dust. She wore a figure-hugging red dress which emphasised her sensually curving spine. The perkiness of her round buttocks contrasted delightfully with her effortlessly flat stomach. Maggie instantly drew in her belly, but that didn't last, and as soon as she breathed, it bounced back out. Watching Penny lead Samuel away, she felt helpless. Her companion was lost to her. There was no getting the man back. She would probably have to walk home.

Vera Hopps-Wood noticed her discomfort. She whispered into Maggie's ear, 'Yes, I wouldn't trust her as far as I could throw her. A lethal weapon when it comes to men. Can you blame her? She's half Richard's age. The girl wants to have some fun before it's too late . . .'

'And with looks like hers, who could say no? Anyway, the poor man could do with some harmless entertainment. He's not over his wife. Well, his wife isn't over him, if you must know.'

Vera peered at her strangely but didn't probe her for clarification. People rarely did. Instead, she said, 'That's why, you see, I'm grateful Henry gets his kicks at Westminster. All he does all day is play with his toy soldiers, planning his next manoeuvre. And talks to the mirror. Another glass of bubbly?'

'We have to find somewhere to sit.' Maggie felt legless. This would be her fifth glass.

They found a garden bench tucked away amongst the rhododendrons. The white-clad waiter was on hand to produce two more glasses of champagne.

Vera unstrapped her high heels and pushed them under the bench. 'What a bloody relief!' she purred. She was enjoying herself, safe in the conviction that her husband had nothing to fear from the lethal Penny Ruta. She nevertheless kept a watchful eye on him as he chattered away with the Scarfes, probably poring over the ins and outs of the pleasingly low local crime statistics. At the same time, she was dishing out gossip on other guests. Maggie only pretended to listen. Her head was swimming in the bubble bath of champagne.

'That's Edith Brenmar, Penny's London agent,' Vera commented on the arrival of a flat-chested, skinny woman in her fifties, who joined Penny and Samuel in the courtyard.

Maggie pricked up her ears. 'Oh, I didn't know Penny was an actress – I've never seen her on screen.'

'You wouldn't have. She isn't an actress, my dear, she's a writer: a playwright, apparently. I say *apparently* because I've never seen anything written by her actually performed in the West End.'

'Maybe she isn't that good at it,' Maggie offered helpfully.

'Evidently not.' Vera's long face cracked open in a grin, and then quickly resumed its scowling expression. 'She helps Henry with his speeches – sometimes . . . Though, personally, I think it's a waste of time and money. I don't think she understands politics. She's just a girl . . . I hear she's writing – or has written – a memoir about her life with Richard. Henry mentioned it the other day. Well, I say, good for her. She'll make a tidy living out of it – riding her husband's fame.'

'Oh, there you are, Edith darling!' Penny flicked a lock of her gleaming black hair and beamed at her agent. 'Sam and I were just talking about *Life with a Legend*. Well, Sam was giving me his advice – legal advice. He's a barrister.'

'Well, not any more, strictly speaking.'

The two ladies air-kissed and Edith extended her hand to Sam in such an imperial way that he had to fight the impulse to kiss it. He succeeded. Disappointed, Edith withdrew her long-nailed fingers. 'What sort of legal advice?'

'Privacy laws, I suppose. Injunctions . . .'

'Injunctions?' Edith looked alarmed. She had high hopes for the memoir. It could be a nice little earner for her struggling agency. She had fought hard to secure a deal for Penny, made promises and concessions, and had a fat advance cheque from the publisher in her drawer, waiting to be cashed.

'I've been thinking about it – the book is about real people, some of them real bastards. They may have reservations. I was worried they could try to stop the book from coming out – the truth from coming out . . .'

'And? What's the verdict?' Edith prompted.

'As long as there's nothing defamatory and no falsehoods, there's nothing anyone can do to stop me!' Penny raised a triumphant eyebrow.

'I'd strongly recommend you see someone who specialises in this area to check that,' Sam tried to point out. It was hard to get out of the habit of adding a string of disclaimers to his opinion.

'Why would I do that, darling, when I've got you!' Penny planted a kiss on his cheek and glided away. She had lost interest in the matter and in Sam. He was free to return to his *Plus-One*.

On their umpteenth glass of champagne (they had lost count), Maggie and Vera remained firmly embedded on the garden bench, watching the world go by. Their eyes followed Penny as she strolled towards none other than Henry himself. An interesting scene ensued that both ladies followed with bated breath.

At first sight, all was well. Seeing Penny approach, Henry grinned and opened his arms to greet her.

'There she goes, the *femme fatale*,' Vera hissed, slurring her words.

Penny threw her head back and stabbed her finger into Henry's chest. She was saying something to him, repeating the stabbing gesture with menace. Henry's face dropped and his lips shrank in a scowl. He tried to say something, but Penny wagged her finger at him, and laughed. He grabbed her wrist and pulled her towards him. He tried to guide her behind the hedge, but she wrestled her arm out of his grip and walked away. Her tight little backside wiggled as she looked back at Henry over her shoulder and – incomprehensibly – waved her middle finger at him.

Maggie and Vera exchanged glances: Maggie's bemused and intrigued, Vera's furious.

Someone else caught a glimpse of that scene.

Richard had just emerged from the house with an older woman on his arm, shadowed by Frank at a discreet distance. She was using a walking stick, but carried herself with elegance and her step, though slow, was self-assured. Her hair was long, blonde, and somewhat younger than she was. Judging by her rabbit-in-the-headlights expression, all her facial muscles were embalmed in Botox. Richard looked dapper in his white summer blazer, a cravat, and a panama hat. Though he was smiling benignly while chatting with Dotty (for this was she, his first ex-wife), his gaze paused on Penny and Henry, and a steely expression crept into his eyes. He peered at the pair for a fraction of a second, then promptly restored his full attention to his companion. He patted her hand that was clutching his forearm and said something amusing. Dotty guffawed.

'Should I get you another drink, ladies?' Sam appeared by the garden bench occupied by Maggie and Vera. He had vanished briefly to answer the call of nature and had missed the entire spectacle.

'That'd be great!' That was Maggie's personal opinion. Judging by Vera's stony expression, she'd had enough of the booze, and of the party altogether.

'Henry and I are leaving,' Vera said icily.

'Surely not before dinner is served?' Having witnessed nothing untoward, Sam was baffled.

'I'm not hungry!' Vera stood up and swayed unsteadily, looking hapless with her bare feet and haunted eyes.

An awkward silence fell upon the trio.

It was very fortunate indeed that at that moment Richard caught Sam's eye and gave a mock salute from the rim of his panama hat. He shouted a jolly, 'Ahoy!' and, leaving Dotty in the care of the omnipresent Frank, hurried towards them. Dotty shaded her eyes and looked after him longingly. Left alone with her, Frank looked terrified. He pointed at a marquee, only a few yards away, and she nodded. Slowly they headed there.

Meantime, Richard was flashing his white-toothed grin at Sam and the ladies on the bench. That smile must have cost him several thousand pounds in dental work. 'So you managed to convince your beautiful neighbour to join you! Good man, Samuel, good man!' He tipped his hat to Maggie and Vera, 'Ladies. Glad you could make it.'

'Such a lovely day,' Maggie pointed out enthusiastically.

'Lucky me! That's one thing money can't buy in this country – decent weather . . .'

'Happy birthday, Richard,' Vera felt compelled to add.

'Where did you lose your loving husband?' There was a note of sarcasm in his tone. 'Never mind, I'm sure Samuel is looking after both of you ladies.'

'Oh, he is!' Maggie exulted, and Vera gave a tight-lipped smile.

Richard wasn't listening. He turned to Sam, 'Not to detract from the festivities of the day, but I'll need to catch you about something, old man. The sooner, the better.' His eyes rested on a small package Sam was holding. 'Is that for me?'

'A small birthday gift. Cuban,' Sam handed him a metal box that looked sufficiently exotic to contain Cuban cigars.

'Oh, you didn't!' Richard snatched it. He was delighted. 'Thank you! People have been spoiling me rotten of late – all the things I can't resist. Nothing like good old friends who know my guilty secrets! People have come from the ends of the world and showered me with gifts – indulging me, reminding me I am – well, was once – loved. It is humbling.'

'You twisted a few arms, I must point out,' Sam smirked.

'Only a little . . . but shhh, let it stay between us.' Richard winked at him. 'By the way, it isn't the right time now, but I need to see you next week – I've got a couple of tweaks to my Will to talk over with you. Two weeks ago I discovered that –'

His words were drowned in a commotion coming from the direction of the swimming pool.

Chapter Four

A man carrying a bucket charged at Richard. He tore down the steps from the terrace, yelling abuse. Clearly, he was not on the guest list. In a pair of greasy jeans and a dirty T-shirt, he was also not dressed for the occasion. He was fast. By the time Frank, who had his hands full entertaining Dotty in the marquee, realised what was going on and set off in pursuit of the intruder, the man had bellowed, 'Murderer!' in Richard's face and hurled the bucket at him together with its content. Red liquid – paint or blood – stained Richard's white clothes. He wiped it from his face and shook it from his fingers onto the grass.

Frank had finally caught up with the man and tackled him to the ground. Though his arms were locked behind his back and Frank's knee bore down between his shoulders, the man was still glaring at Richard, 'Arrest him! He's got blood on his hands! Murderer!'

Richard held his glare. 'Escort Mr Nolan to the gate, Frank,' he said with astounding calm.

Frank lifted the wannabe assassin to his feet and, holding him by both the scruff of his neck and his right arm, which was bent backwards and looking painful, started leading him out. Nolan let himself be led, knowing that he stood no chance against Frank's bulk. But he still had a lot to say, 'Happy birthday, you dirty old bastard! Leila never made it to her twentieth. Thanks to you!'

'Goodbye, Mr Nolan.' There was almost perceptible irritation in Richard's voice.

'I won't let you get away with it! Hear me? Let me go! Keep your filthy paws off me . . . You're in on it too! Don't think I don't know!' Nolan was trying to wriggle his way out of Frank's vice-like grip, in vain. But he did manage to twist his body to face Frank and spat at him. His saliva hit Frank on the chin.

'There! Take that!'

Frank showed no anger. He frogmarched Nolan up the stairs and they disappeared through the French doors.

They were watched by the entire gathering of partygoers in a stony silence. Penny appeared by Richard's side. As much as his face was smudged with stage blood, hers was white as a sheet. She was trembling from head to toe.

'All right, love?' Richard asked. She didn't seem to hear him. She thrust her champagne glass into his hand, and fled.

'What, in God's name, was that all about?' Dotty caught up with the rest of the crowd on the lawn.

'I do apologise for this . . . interruption,' Richard addressed everyone with a grisly smile: his dazzlingly white teeth were cutting through the red paint as if he had just torn into the arteries of a living animal. 'Please give me a second to change into something less . . . red, and then we can resume the celebrations.' With a youthful spring in his stride, he took two steps at a time, hot on his wife's heels.

Abandoned, the guests sought temporary shelter and alcoholic sustenance in the marquee. Dotty appeared to be the only one who had never heard of Dan Nolan and his daughter, Leila. Vera Hopps-Wood was only too happy to enlighten her:

'Fifteen . . . no, um, let me think . . . must be eighteen years ago now. Time flies . . . Leila died in that swimming pool on the terrace. It was one of Richard's famous birthday bashes –'

'One of the wilder ones –'

'Yes, it was his fiftieth, I think. He put on a grand show, good old Richard . . . Nothing like the rumours had it – orgies, drugs, sex with minors, Sodom and Gomorrah . . . but not far from it.'

'Those were different times, darling,' Henry pointed out. 'That was 2000 – we were still getting our heads around the new millennium. There was this vibe in the air that the end was nigh.'

'It may still be closer than you think,' Vera shot him a cutting glance.

Henry responded with a hurt one. 'Whatever do you mean?'

She snorted and said nothing.

Mercifully, Alec Scarfe stepped in to continue with the story. 'Some people took it literally, and it was a bloody wild party to end all parties. But, that aside, Leila Nolan's death was an accident. There was a thorough police investigation – everyone who'd attended that damned party was given the third degree. No stone was left unturned. The Coroner's verdict was unequivocal: accidental death. Leila had had too much to drink. She was only a young lass – nineteen, I believe. She tripped, banged her head on the edge of the pool, slipped in, and drowned. They found her in the morning, floating in the pool. By the time the ambulance arrived, there was no hope . . . It must've happened some time after midnight. By then everyone had gone home or was inside, sleeping it all off, totally oblivious . . .'

'No witnesses then?'

'She was alone. No one saw anything.' Henry assured them authoritatively.

'With a house full of people! That's convenient,' Dotty snorted through her nose, venting her doubts.

'People were paralytic, I'll have you know! We had no idea, not until the next morning!' Henry retorted.

'You were there that night?'

'Naturally,' he shrugged, 'we come to all of Richard's dos. Anyway, like Alec said: there was no evidence of foul play, no drugs – contrary to popular belief. There was nothing untoward in Leila's bloodstream except alcohol. The girl just got drunk and fell. Tragic, but nobody's to blame.'

'The girl's father begged to disagree,' Eugene said grimly. 'He went mad with grief. What father wouldn't?'

Vera nodded, 'He drove everybody mad. All of us! Hired a private detective, tried to dig up dirt on Richard, on everyone ... Haunted us, literally! It was harassment, plain and simple, but we humoured him because he was a grieving father. He even brought a private prosecution against Richard-'

'Which failed – naturally.'

'That was when he stopped, and disappeared.'

'It was after his wife left him. Debbie.' Maggie remembered. 'She'd had enough, couldn't take it anymore. He was scratching her wounds, not letting her heal. He wouldn't let Leila go either. Poor girl was held down here, watching her father torture himself and her mother ... She couldn't break away and pass on –' Maggie checked herself, looked apologetically at the baffled faces around her, and promptly changed the subject. 'Poor Debs! She'd gone to live in Australia. I thought Dan might've followed her there. I didn't know he'd come back until I saw –' Maggie bit her tongue.

'Nobody knew. We don't keep tabs on grieving fathers,' Alec closed the account.

Chapter Five

From the moment Samuel ushered me to his car where I found Alice reclined in the passenger seat and refusing to vacate it, I knew this party would be a catastrophe. It was downhill from there. I wasn't at all surprised when Dan Nolan gatecrashed it to add a splash of colour to Richard's white outfit. If you think that was the point when the party reached rock bottom, think again.

That was only the aperitif. The main course was yet to come.

In fact, my new best friend, a white-clad waiter with an unlimited supply of beverages, turned up on the top terrace and sounded a gong. Dinner was to be served.

We climbed the stone steps. Dotty was lagging behind us and instructing Frank to hold her steady. Frank looked like he had swallowed something bitter and got it stuck in his windpipe. When we reached the top step, we all looked like Frank. Confronted with that swimming pool, we had all been reminded of the young woman who had died there. Everyone's mood took a nosedive. Mine plummeted even lower.

There was the pool with Richard's panama hat floating in it, circling amongst swirls of oily red paint. Being oil based, the paint had not sunk. Instead, it formed rings of crimson on the surface, rings which rotated and spun, reflecting the sunrays in erratic flashes. I had the impression that I had found myself in the middle of one of Richard's surreal cinematographic experiments, typical of his seventies output back in his native Poland. I had watched one of those on YouTube recently. An iconically beautiful young woman starred in it: sinuous body, long, dark hair and expressive pale eyes. I had seen her in a few other shorts directed by Ruta. It was in Polish, but there was hardly any dialogue. The drama was captured in her body language and her eyes. Towards the end, she tied a band over her eyes and started walking towards a lake, shedding her clothes along the way until all she was wearing was the blindfold. She waded into the lake, disturbing its stillness, and walked on, deeper and deeper. Her long hair splayed across the surface. The last frame was a close-up of the blindfold as the woman completely submerged herself, generating only a very faint ripple which the camera followed across the surface of the lake until it became still again. Looking at Richard's swimming pool now, I was reminded of that film, and that beautiful but tragic woman brought to mind poor Leila.

Unlike in the film, the surface of the swimming pool was rippling and churning without the slightest intimation of a breeze in the air. I don't know how everyone else interpreted the relentless whirling of the blood-red rings of paint, but I could see where their velocity came from. A young woman sat on the edge of the pool. Her toes were dipped in the water, and they twirled faster and faster in a bizarre toe waltz. I recognised her from the newspaper clippings of eighteen years ago and from the framed photograph in her parents' home when I used to visit her grieving mum Debbie to offer moral support. The girl was Leila Nolan.

The long-dead Leila Nolan.

I should have guessed she was entering the scene – or at least a dead person was coming – because Alice had vanished. They – the apparitions – never rain on each other's parades. If there is one, there aren't any others. I suppose they don't like sharing the attention. My attention, because, of course, no one else can see them.

I watched Leila for a little while, hoping for a clue or the tiniest of hints of what might have happened to her all those years ago, but she wasn't co-operating. They never do. She was just playing with the rings of blood paint, the surface of the water in the pool rippling gently. Maybe there was no Leila with her feet dipped in the

35

pool. Maybe I was imagining her. Maybe it was the small breeze that made the water ripple and made the circles of paint twirl? That would be a perfectly rational explanation which I would be prepared to accept had I not known better. Seeing is believing, as the saying quite correctly goes.

'Maggie, are you joining us?' Samuel roused me from my reverie. I followed the crowd.

We flocked into the dining room. The mood was subdued and not at all celebratory. I wished we could skip the dinner and go home. I, for one, had lost my appetite and would have been happy to forsake the pheasant for baked beans on toast followed by a Jaffa Cake. The decadent world of Bohemia had suddenly lost its appeal.

Still, there were good manners to reckon with. We sat at the table, peering at each other timidly and exchanging innocuous remarks about the weather. It was a long table accommodating twenty guests. They were allocated by name. I landed with Samuel on my left and a gentleman on the other side who introduced himself as John Whitby, dean of the London Film School. He was tall and narrow-shouldered, wore thick-rimmed glasses, and had longish fair hair in a state of disarray. Across the table from me sat Alec and Vanessa Scarfe, he with his cleft palate scar and she with her life-affirming smile. Next to the Scarfes sat Vera and Henry, he self-assured and brusque, she distinctly long-faced. Vera shared her elbow space with the literary agent, Edith Brenmar, who in turn, was flanked by a well-known actor, whose face I recognised but whose name escaped me. My parents were on the same side of the table as me, and as much as I could feel their comforting presence, I couldn't quite see it unless I leaned forward over the table and craned my neck. Which I wasn't going to do, because the absolutely fabulous Lena Wolski was in the way and I was hopelessly starstruck. You may remember Lena from *The Avengers*, one of John Steed's razor-sharp and gorgeous assistants. She was the idol of my early puberty: clever, flat-chested, and with an upturned nose between a pair of round, bluer-than-blue eyes.

There was an empty space to Henry's right and only then did I realise that I had not yet seen Mary. Considering that he had invited his first ex-wife, I would have been surprised if he'd left Mary out in the cold. I may not be as close with Mary as we used to be as kids, but we aren't strangers. As far as I know, she and Richard are on civil terms. After the divorce, she had moved out of Forget-Me-Not but stayed in town. In fact, she lives in Pond Lane, in Richard's cottage, rent free. I think that was part of her divorce settlement.

I was sure she had been invited. You simply could not *not invite* Mary. She is such a darling – sweet and loving, and she doesn't hold grudges. If she had been invited, though, she would've been at the party. I was intrigued by her absence and made a mental note to investigate fully. I would have to orchestrate bumping into Mary at the Thursday Market. I could drag her to the Old Stables Café – she would never say no – and we could have a good natter over a slice of Victoria sponge and a nice cup of tea, by the end of which I would know everything there was to know.

While I was contemplating the absent Mary, Dotty had finally made it to the table, assisted by her walking stick and a fanfare of huffs and grunts. Some five minutes later, Frank dived into a seat beside her. She instantly grilled him about how long it would be before we would have the pleasure of Mr and '*the current*' Mrs Ruta's company, to which Frank threw his arms in the air and said curtly, 'Search me!' I thought Dotty would beat him with her walking stick – she looked none too pleased, but she only peered at him down her nose and ostentatiously turned her back on him.

My neighbour, John Whitby, was babbling excitedly about Richard's return to the world of cinema. 'Through the back door, as it were,' he added, 'since he won't be directing, as such.'

'Producing, then?' I enquired politely to show interest in the matter. Frankly, I didn't care. I just wanted to go home.

'No, he has no interest in executive or financial nuance. Not Richard! No, he will deliver a series of lectures at the London Film School, training the next generation –'

'Wow!'

'You've no idea how long it took to persuade him to step behind the lectern!'

'I couldn't begin to imagine,' I agreed.

'Let's just say – decades.'

'You don't say! You must've been pretty chuffed when he finally surrendered.'

'Delighted, my dear lady. Delighted! He's joining the faculty this October. I still can't believe it! I certainly can't wait.'

John was looking forward to that prospect almost as keenly as I was looking forward to dinner being served and this whole party being over. *And where the hell are our hosts?* I echoed Dotty inwardly.

At last they obliged. Richard and Penny entered the dining room. Richard was all joy-to-the-world, 'My humble apologies for keeping you waiting!' He eased himself into his seat and banged on the table an open bottle of what looked like red wine. I didn't recognise the brand; the shape of the bottle was unusual and the lettering on the label was in a foreign language. Richard poured himself a glass. He was pure boisterous elegance. He had discarded his ruined clothes and replaced them with a smart dinner jacket. Only a smudge of red paint in his hair bore testimony that the incident in the garden had really happened. Strangely, going by Richard's nonchalant demeanour, it almost looked like everything that had happened had been planned right from the start. Only Penny wasn't in on it. She took a seat to his right, still scowling and biting her bottom lip. The colour of her lipstick went nicely with the hue of red in Richard's hair.

At last, the dinner was served and the general clamour of conversation resumed. Alec Scarfe and Samuel entertained themselves with their take on the last week's politics, which I found immensely un-entertaining. I listened half-heartedly, my attention drifting away to Edith Brenmar and the actor whose name still eluded me.

'Oh, believe you me, it'll be a bestseller. I've read a few extracts – no holds barred ... It's right up there in the kiss-and-tell genre,' Edith was saying in an excited half-whisper. I was in no doubt she was talking about Penny's memoirs. She lowered her voice, and added, 'I wouldn't be surprised if they decided to go their separate ways.'

'Richard and Tuppence?' The actor feigned disbelief.

'Well, don't quote me on that, but you don't kiss and tell if you intend to stay married to someone.'

'When is it out?'

'As soon as I get my hands on it. There's already a bidding war raging between two major publishers.'

'It'll be interesting.'

'Explosive!'

The actor pulled a face and I instantly knew where I had seen him – a few years ago in *Downton Abbey*! His name, too, was coming to me slowly, but it hadn't quite made it when Richard rose from his seat and clinked his glass with the tip of his knife. He was going to give a speech. While waiting for the last of the table conversation to subside he topped up his glass from the bottle he had brought with him. He raised the glass to his wife, who saluted him back with silent reticence, and then to all of us at the table.

This is more or less what he said. I'm trying to be as accurate as possible here because in his words that evening, I am convinced, lurked a clue to his death.

'A toast to all my friends – those who made it here and those who couldn't!' On that cue we all raised our glasses. 'Thank you all for the gifts you bore me . . . you know what I like!' He took a swig from his glass. 'Thank you for putting up with an old git like me.' He ignored a few voices of dissent and downed his glass in one go. 'Fine Tokaji, the finest I've had in years!'

'Oooh, I'll have some too, Dicky,' Dotty demanded and passed her glass to Richard over the table. 'You got me started on Tokaji, remember?'

'How can I forget?' Richard winked at her. 'Those wild nights . . .'

They both giggled like two naughty teenagers. Richard dispensed a rather meagre drop of his precious Tokaji into Dotty's glass and returned it to her with the added bonus of a kiss planted on her hand. He poured himself another generous glass, swirled the dark red liquid inside it and had a sip. 'Sixty-eight years! Where did it go? God knows! It made me think ... catching up with the past, or rather, should I say, the past catching up with me-' He paused, looked around at us. We were smiling lopsided smiles, wondering what the hell he was getting at. Shaken by Dan Nolan's accusations, was he about to make a confession? I followed his gaze towards Penny. She was pale, tight-lipped, and shook her head slightly as if warning him off.

'Sooner or later we all have to face up to our past, don't we, darling?' He winked at her, and at last she smiled at him. She was beautiful, I thought for the umpteenth time. 'Tuppence is writing a book about it, about the past – our past - warts and all! No one'll be spared, I'm told – not even me,' he gulped more of his wine. For a split second, I fancied, his eyes stabbed at Henry, and he repeated, 'Warts and all ... Oh well, I'm looking forward to it. Not sure everyone else is,' he chuckled. 'So join me in a toast – to all the years gone by!'

We raised our glasses and drank to it. It was such a clever toast, I thought: drinking to the past. That way no one felt left out. We all have a past to reflect on.

Richard put his empty glass on the table and refilled it for the third time. He drank it. 'In case you were wondering, Tuppence and I ... we've decided ... we are ...' He was slurring; he appeared seriously drunk. His fingers fumbled with his cravat, trying to loosen it. 'We have no secrets with each ... with ...' He staggered and had to grasp the edge of the table to regain balance. 'We've a ...' he mumbled a word. I could hardly make out what it was – *a pact?* Richard wouldn't clarify it. He grasped his chest, rubbed it violently and appeared to be choking.

'Water? Do you want some water?' Frank ran towards him, reaching out to him just as Richard leaned forward and threw up across the table. The few people closest to him gasped and scampered away in disgust, while he tumbled to the floor, taking with him his plate and cutlery as he pulled down the tablecloth.

'He's passed out! He's drunk!'

'Oh dear, what a shambles!' exclaimed Dotty.

We all flocked to the head of the table to gape. Frank was kneeling next to Richard. He slapped him twice: fore- and backhand; the slap resonated in the room. 'Someone, call an ambulance!'

Penny rushed towards them. She stared down in horror and had to lean on the table before she herself lost her balance. As she leaned, she knocked over the wine bottle. It rolled, spilling its contents which dripped down onto Richard's face. He didn't as much as flinch. His eyes remained wide open and didn't blink despite the wine drops splattering into them.

'He's dead,' someone said, 'My God, the man is dead!'

I had no doubt about that as I watched him – his dead self – rise away from his body and stare at it with mild disbelief. Within seconds, he shed decades from his appearance: his skin became smooth and translucent, his shoulders sprang back up, and that daredevil half-smile, half-sneer he used to flash in the eighties made a return. He stepped away from his body, examined his nails, and straightened his cravat. He did not look at his mortal remains or at anybody gathered in the room. We seemed to hold no interest for him. He turned on his heel and walked away into the dusk without a second glance.

Chapter Six

A few seconds of shocked silence were superseded by a flurry of clamour. It started with gasps and exclamations, and a couple of entreaties for divine intervention, after which mobile phones were whipped out and thumbs began dancing on touchscreens.

Detective Chief Superintendent Alec Scarfe soon put away his phone and stepped in to control the crowd. 'Let's remain calm,' he bellowed in a clear state of agitation, 'and don't touch anything! Everyone, let's move to the sitting room. The police are on their way. Come along, madam ...'

He tried to give Dotty a hand, but she pushed him away.

'Frank, where's my stick?' She was trembling from head to toe, blinded by the shock – her hand gripping her walking stick. 'Frank, give Dicky a nudge ... He's playing his moronic tricks again! Where's my stick? I'll do it myself! Frank!'

Frank was deaf to her calls. He was kneeling, motionless, by Richard Ruta's body – a pillar of salt. Penny picked herself up from the floor. She had a bewildered look in her eyes as she stared at her dead husband. Her breathing was rapid and shallow until it steadied and her expression morphed into something inscrutable.

'This way – to the sitting room,' Scarfe insisted.

The guests shuffled along, exchanging looks of horror. Gently, Sam took Penny's arm and led her away from the scene.

'Frank, give Dorothy a hand, will you?'

Frank did not budge. His fingers closed Richard's gaping eyes.

Eugene Kaye was obliged to assist her, leaving his wife to deal with another bout of coughing on her own.

'Mum,' Maggie passed a tissue to her mother.

'It's the shock ... Thank you, Maggie. Don't worry about me.' She looked apologetic for drawing attention to herself.

'Mr Savage!' The superintendent asserted authoritatively, 'I won't have the scene tampered with. Please, do not touch the body.'

At last, Frank heaved himself to his feet. 'Sorry, I couldn't let him ... I ... Sorry. Yes, sir, you're right.' He followed the rest of the party, being the last one out of the room. Tears glistened in his eyes.

The ambulance arrived first, then the police. Scarfe left the room to talk to his officers. The final confirmation of Richard Ruta's death came when the paramedics departed without a patient on their stretcher and the ambulance was replaced by a Forensics van. Men in white overalls took over the dining room. Dread spilled over the guests sitting in the room next door when the realisation dawned that one of them could be a murderer.

'It was a heart attack, surely?' Vanessa asked Alec as soon as he returned briefly to assure everyone that his team were doing everything in their power to secure the evidence and to let them go home as soon as humanly possible. He expressed his gratitude for everyone's patience.

'What else could it be?' Maggie looked to Samuel for an answer.

'Let's hope it –' Sam had no idea what to say. Richard had been flamboyant and irresponsible, a womaniser and frequently a churlish fool, but none of that qualified him as a candidate for murder. And he had been a friend – a good friend, through thick and thin.

Time flew at first but now it was dragging. It had been more than an hour since Richard's death. Cooped up in the room like convicts awaiting transportation to the colonies, the guests started whispering about their innocence, the effects of their trauma, emotional exhaustion, and their desire to *bloody well* go home. Emboldened by each other, those voices grew in volubility.

'They can't keep us here indefinitely!' Henry pronounced. Like everyone present, he was deeply distraught by the events. Blisters of sweat had beaded on his forehead and temples and were beginning to run. 'Superintendent! How much longer are we to be detained here for? We have the right to know.'

'You're not detained. My Senior Investigating Officer is on the scene and she'll be –'

'What do you call it then – if not detention?'

'Well –'

'Can we at least be briefed about what's going on? Our friend is lying there, dead!'

Alec Scarfe was sweating too. He looked besieged and as confounded as the rest of them. 'I'm very sorry. My officers are doing their best to get to the bottom of what happened to ... You'll appreciate I can't comment, even if I could – I mean, I can't.'

'Then why can't we be allowed home? Everyone's in shock. Are we actually suspects?'

'I hope not,' Lena Wolski spoke in solidarity with Henry. 'It could've been natural causes. A heart attack, for example. Did you notice how he clutched his chest?' She demonstrated the action, her painted nails digging into her prominent collarbone.

It was at that precise moment that Dotty did the same thing: she clutched her chest, her body rippling as she tried to draw a wheezy breath. 'Frank, get me to the hospital!' she gasped. Her eyes bulged. Then she passed out.

The same ambulance with the same paramedics arrived for the second time at Forget-Me-Not, this time to collect Dotty. Everyone watched her, attached to a drip, unconscious and limp, being wheeled out of the room and whisked away to the hospital with a fanfare of sirens and flashing blue lights. The stupefied guests moved away from the windows and flopped onto whatever seats they could find because their legs were no longer able to support them.

When Maggie's mother had another bout of coughing, all eyes scanned her suspiciously for signs of chest-clutching. The air was thick with fear.

'Sorry,' Irene Kaye apologised, 'I can't seem to be able to shake this off – not since Christmas ...'

Henry wiped his sweaty forehead with a hanky. 'Is it hot in here, or is it me?'

'Alec, you don't mind if we open the windows?' Sam tried to think and act rationally. The room was stuffy. Body heat was rising to unprecedented levels. They needed air.

'Yes – I mean, no! Please do ... Let's do.'

The two of them pushed the sash windows open. A soft breeze of sobering May air swirled in.

'Have we been poisoned?' Vera was fanning herself with her hand. It looked like a rather futile effort. Her face was flushed red.

'I must take my wife home,' Henry dashed to her side. 'We're going. You can't keep us here. This is scandalous!'

'Sit down and shut the fuck up, Henry! Let them do their job!' Out of the blue, Penny came to the Detective Chief Superintendent's rescue. She stood up abruptly but didn't appear angry – just determined to put Henry in his place. Henry's lower lip trembled and he gave her a deeply hurt look, but he had enough presence of mind to put his arm around Vera and whisper reassurance, 'It won't be long now.'

Penny ambled towards Sam. A little smile quivered on her lips. Behind that smile anything could be hiding: grief, horror, pain. Sam sensed her vulnerability – or perhaps he was able to imagine it. He knew how it felt when the world came crashing down on you. He had felt it when they had come to tell him Alice was dead.

'Shall I get you a glass of brandy, Penny?' he offered.

'Yes, I need a stiff drink. Thank you. Make it a double.'

Sam poured her a generous glass.

'Get yourself one, too. Let's get drunk, Sam darling! Richard wouldn't mind. He'd probably join us!' She laughed. Her laughter sounded sinister.

Sam didn't know how to take it so he occupied himself with pouring his own drink and downing it in one go. Others in the room peered at the two of them with a mixture of disdain and envy. They could all do with a drink. If they only dared.

A small fair-haired woman burst into the room. In her washed-out jeans and worn T-shirt, she was ostensibly under-dressed for an officer of the law. Her face was white as a sheet, her eyes encircled with dark rings. *Busy night out?* Sam mused. Despite her appearance, she acted like someone who – at last – had a plan. She swept the room of sweaty bodies with her eyes and located Alec Scarfe. She headed towards him without acknowledging anyone else in the room.

'Sir! I have a speculative cause of death from Dr Almond.'

Sam, and everyone else, held their breath and pricked their ears. Conscious of the stir she had caused by her dramatic entry, the woman lowered her voice to a whisper. Despite her efforts, Sam caught the word 'poison'. He wasn't the only one to hear it. A few alarmed looks were exchanged amongst the guests. The police woman continued out loud.

'Forensics are still securing evidence. We'll start by taking fingerprints for elimination purposes and interview everybody here before we can let them go. I've got Webber, Macfadyen, and Whittaker raring to go.'

'Tread carefully, DI Marsh.'

'I always do, sir,' she said, but judging by her raised eyebrow, Sam deduced that the opposite was true.

Chapter Seven

It took me a while to fully comprehend why I had ended up in a sealed Plexiglass cubicle in the isolation unit at Western National Hospital, surrounded by people wearing astronaut suits.

But I get ahead of myself. Let me go back to the party – well, the aftermath of it.

We were all to be processed by the police. DI Marsh was the Senior Investigating Officer, Alec Scarfe had informed us as soon as she had entered our confinement room. She looked rather peaky. Well, peakier than usual. She has a dishevelled appearance as a matter of principle and there isn't much to her in terms of stature, but that evening she definitely looked the worse for wear. I already knew DI Marsh – not to speak to, but she was a familiar face. I had seen her on many occasions in Bishops Well. She would visit Michael Almond and stay overnight. This had not gone unnoticed, and I for one was quite excited for him. Michael Almond had been what you would call a confirmed bachelor. A girlfriend had come as a surprise. A girlfriend in the shape and form of Ms Marsh was a bit of an enigma. She wasn't very sociable. Until Richard's unfortunate birthday bash I had learned nothing of her background, and had no idea of the fact she was a detective. A detective inspector at that! She certainly didn't look it – she lacked the gravitas.

I was one of the privileged few guests DI Marsh chose to interview herself. I had never been interviewed by the police before so I headed for DI Marsh's Operational HQ in the library on shaky legs.

It is an unkind thing to say, but I must confess I did not like the woman in conversation. She struck me as abrupt and inattentive. Under her judgemental glare, I found myself feeling irrationally responsible for everything that had happened. She peered at me with narrowed eyes for a tortuous half-minute, then told me to sit down. It wasn't an invitation – it was an order. I perched meekly on the edge of my chair and put my hands neatly on my knees where they could be seen. I identified myself timidly, my mind racing through all of my past parking tickets and the expiry date on my passport.

'What is your relationship with the deceased?'

'With Richard?' I sought clarification. The word *deceased* sounded vague and awfully impersonal.

'Are there any other bodies in the house I'm not aware of?'

'Well, Dotty – that's his ex-wife – she seems –'

'She's still alive. Can we not stray, Miss Kaye? It's been a long day for all of us.' Her eyelids drooped slightly and it looked to me like it was through sheer willpower that she was keeping herself awake. The unhealthy hue in her complexion was zombie-like. Her lips were bloodless. 'Your relationship to Mr Ruta . . .'

'I don't have any. We live in the same village . . . town. I sort of know him – of him . . .'

'How did you end up on his guest list?'

'My neighbour – I am his plus one. He invited me to accompany him. I quite looked forward to it. Richard Ruta is – was – my absolute idol.'

DI Marsh rolled her eyes. In slow motion. Her eyelids were too heavy to allow her eyes much room for manoeuvre. 'OK, OK,' she slurred, as if it was too much effort for her to open her mouth. The volume was gradually draining from her voice. I could hardly hear her next question.

'Did you notice anything . . . Do you want to tell me anything?'

'About the incident with Dan Nolan?' I suggested helpfully.

'Anything apart from that?'

I started telling her about Richard's speech. Something was

48

niggling me about that speech. I had the impression that he intended to tell us something important. DI Marsh didn't seem to listen. Her eyes were out of focus. She tugged at her collar and muttered something about needing air.

Then she passed out.

It wasn't anything dramatic. She just swooned in her chair, her head falling backward, her mouth gaping.

I raised the alarm.

The rest is a blur of raging insanity. This time no ambulance arrived. In its place, a string of vans snaked into the driveway. People clad in white protective gear and gas masks hurried out of the vans. They carried white cases and stretchers. Some started setting up a cordon around the whole estate. Others spilled into the house and began shouting at us about this not being a drill, about this being a real-life emergency, and to remain calm. Easier said than done! When a helicopter landed on the lawn, followed by another two, we all hit the panic button. This was too much for even the most laidback in our midst. This was nothing short of an alien invasion.

Clearly in shock, Lena Wolski suddenly remembered her combat training from *The Avengers*. She screamed blue murder and with a high kick attacked the first man whom she perceived as trying to neutralise her. It took two people to force her onto a stretcher and carry her – screaming and kicking - to the helicopter. The rest of us followed obediently. Even Henry was too dumbfounded to protest or demand an explanation. We were petrified. We thought we were about to die. Like Richard.

After a helicopter ride with a gang of *astronauts* who refused to utter a single word to us, we were led through a sealed temporary tunnel leading from our aircraft directly to the Contagious Disease Isolation Unit. There, we were separated. My clothes, shoes, and even my clutch bag had been taken away from me for safe disposal. I was told that meant immediate and irrevocable incineration. I found myself alone and scared shitless in my Plexiglass cubicle. I was too scared to cry – I was too scared to realise that I was scared.

I was in a state of shock. I was watching my stomach, expecting it to start swelling and for an alien form to burst out of it with a deafening screech.

It took ages for somebody to finally come and explain to me that what I had been subjected to was an 'emergency response to the suspected use of a chemical weapon'. Given what had happened in Salisbury recently, it made sense.

If their explanation was supposed to assuage my fears, they had failed miserably. They couldn't – or wouldn't – tell me what kind of chemical weapon and what my chances were of coming out of my cubicle alive. They didn't know how long this whole nightmare would last. They wouldn't let me see my elderly parents. All in all, they were acutely unhelpful.

I lay in my cellophane-wrapped coffin, listening to the medical gadgets beeping out my last few seconds, snippets of my short but, in the main, happy life flashing before my eyes, drifting into what I imagined was an induced coma from which, I reconciled myself, I would be mercifully ushered into death. Lights out.

Chapter Eight

Living in Bishops Well, Sam had developed great fondness for the Rook's Nest's toad-in-the-hole. It was the chef's signature dish, featuring sausages sourced exclusively from local farmer Harry Watton. It went perfectly with the home-brewed ale Rook's Nest was famous for across the whole county. In Sam's opinion, the combination was a match made in heaven. He had no culinary skills beyond poaching an egg for breakfast, opening a tin of soup and heating it up for lunch, and ordering a takeaway or booking a table for one for dinner. When the fancy took him he would make an effort and travel to Sexton's Canning for an Italian or Thai, but in the main his everyday haunts were the Rugby Clubhouse and the Rook's Nest. The other pub in town didn't serve food. It was called the Watering Hole, and by all accounts it was just that – a hole.

Tonight, he was tucked at a small table by the wall, enjoying toad-in-the-hole with a cold pint of lager. For company he had the *Sexton's Canning Herald* spread in front of him. The news of Richard's death and the nerve agent scare were still rattling about on page three. He skimmed through those and moved swiftly to the sport section where life seemed to go on regardless. Bishops Seniors had beaten Parson's Combe in a one-day cricket fixture on Saturday, thus qualifying for South West Over-Fifties Games. Sam had been promising himself to join Bishops Seniors for months. He did enjoy a slow-brewing game of cricket and in his heyday had scored a few centuries. He used to be a brilliant batsman, and his bowling hadn't been that bad either.

Sam's musings were interrupted by the arrival of Michael Almond in the company of a tiny waif of a woman Sam just about recognised as Gillian Marsh – the detective inspector who had so spectacularly been taken ill shortly after Richard had died that all of the party guests had ended up being evacuated into quarantine. She was even slimmer now but seemed to have a bit more colour in her cheeks.

Without noticing Sam, they took a neighbouring table. Terrence Truelove was on hand in no time to ascertain that they were expecting company, and to take their drinks order. For DI Marsh, Sam noted, it was just plain orange juice.

Sam wasn't one to eavesdrop or gossip, but he was bored and found himself tuning into their conversation. He was likely to find out more from those two than from the papers. After all, Gillian was a copper and Michael a forensic pathologist who worked for the police.

'The first time you came to visit and didn't wear any protective gear, I was bloody relieved,' said Gillian.

'Relieved? Why? What horrors did you expect?' Michael asked.

'What do you think? In your line of work, you dressed in your overalls and hovering over a person can only mean one thing – they must be dead.'

'Stop fooling around, Gillian. You need to start taking it seriously.'

'Didn't you say it was a false alarm? There's no chemical warfare on the go.'

'No, but you passed out!'

'I know – I don't have to be reminded. I didn't have breakfast that morning, that's why.'

'You have acute anaemia – severe iron deficiency.'

'I know what anaemia is.'

'Then you'll know that you need to start looking after yourself. Your lifestyle is a bloody joke. You can't sustain yourself on coffee and long hours at work. You've been signed off and you'll be staying with me until you're good to go.'

'But I'm not dying, am I?'

'God almighty, you do put everything on a knife-edge! I bloody well hope you're not dying and I hope you have a long life ahead of you – though, God knows, you will be keeping me on my toes all the way to my grave, which is fine – I know what I've signed up for. But, right this minute, you can't just carry on the way you were. You need treatment and a long respite.'

'Don't be stupid, Almond. I told you I didn't have –'

'Breakfast. You did say, but that won't do. They won't have you back at the station, anyway. Mark will be handling the case while you're convalescing. You don't need to worry about anything.'

'But I do! Webber's not ready to be in charge – certainly not in charge of a murder investigation!'

'He'll be fine. And don't you go telling him he's no good,' Michael sounded dead serious. 'They should be here any minute. Try to be nice for a change.'

'Who's coming?'

'The whole crew. They all want to see you, hug you –'

'Spare me the hugs!' Sam couldn't see Gillian Marsh's face but he could imagine her rolling her eyes. 'So, while we're waiting for the crew, appraise me of the situation. Cause of death?'

'I told you, I will not –'

'Go on, Michael, don't make me beg. I just want to know.'

There was resignation in Michael's voice but he proceeded to explain, 'We found a large concentration of aconite in a wine bottle and traces of it in Richard Ruta's and Dorothy McCain's glasses.'

'Is she dead?'

'No. She only had a few sips – not enough to kill her. She's recovering.'

'OK . . . so what the hell is aconite?'

'It's a type of alkaloid toxin. Not your traditional poison, like arsenic or cyanide, not something that would naturally spring to mind when you're contemplating killing someone. It comes from the highly toxic root of monkshood – quite a common plant in some parts of the country. Mountainous areas, like Snowdonia for example.'

'I know it. It's a herbal remedy. My gran swore by it – perfect for toothache.'

'Yes, probably. But it's also known in medical circles. It has its benefits – slows down the heartbeat and soothes the mind, to put it in layman's terms. It's used to help patients suffering from panic attacks, PTSD, people on suicide watch … serious psychological disorders. Its extracts are added to a number of widely used tranquillisers.'

'Was Richard Ruta suffering from any psychotic condition? Could it be an accidental overdose?'

'Not likely, going by the concentration. In its medical form aconite is thinly diluted – you'd have to ingest quite a lot of it … It can't have been an accident.'

'Easy to get hold of?'

'If you're a clinical psychiatrist, or a patient, someone with a severe nervous or psychological disorder – but not so easy for your everyday Tom, Dick and Harry. It isn't commonly used these days. Of course, if you know what you're doing you can extract it directly from the plant.'

'Right, I know where to start.'

'No, Gillian, you're not –'

Michael was interrupted by the arrival of *the crew*. Sam observed them from behind his newspaper with fascination. There was a young man with the figure and hairstyle of a Sumo wrestler, who Gillian referred to as Riley while the others called him Jon. Another one was a man about Sam's own age. He had a bulbous nose and bushy brows, and appeared to be a man of few words, his greeting a mere, '*Good to see you back, ma'am*', whereafter he sat down with his back to Sam and said no more.

'Thanks, Whittaker.' Sam noted that Gillian had a tendency to address people by their surnames, like a sergeant major at boot camp.

The only other woman among them was fit and athletic, probably in her mid-thirties, with a bouncy ponytail. With a tearful look in her eye, she leaned over Gillian and took her into her arms.

'No hugs, Macfadyen! Keep your grabby hands to yourself!'

Seeing the third man smirk and wink at Michael, Gillian quickly put him in his place too. 'What are you grinning about, Webber? I want your full report on my desk by tomorrow morning.'

'I'm sorry, I can't tell you anything.' Webber sounded genuinely sorry about it.

'Who has the seniority in rank here?'

'It's not that, Gillian. It's all out of my hands. MI5 are in and they aren't in the habit of sharing intelligence. I'm just a figurehead SIO.'

'Why? What's it to do with them? It's our murder.'

'Come on, Gillian, catch up. Everyone thought it was another one of them Russian nerve agent attacks, like in Salisbury. We still don't know otherwise. The poison used might not be the most sophisticated one from the arsenal of chemical weaponry –'

'It doesn't qualify as a chemical weapon. Small-scale domestic tincture. It only affects those who ingest it directly. It would take some doing to wipe out a city using aconite,' Riley chuckled.

'So, I ask again, why are MI5 involved?' Gillian persisted.

'Maybe because that guy, Ruta, defected to the West?' Riley seemed to be the font of all knowledge. 'I looked him up online. He defected from the Soviet Union in the eighties. It was big. He used to be a big name in films.'

'He defected from Poland. He was Polish, not Russian.'

'One and the same thing. They were all Eastern Bloc.'

'You don't know shit, Riley, do you?' Whittaker broke his silence.

'And you do?'

Things were heating up. Sam took the last swig of his lager and left. Strolling home, he pondered the significance of what he had just overheard. He could have interjected to clarify a few details about Richard's defection. After all, he had been a junior barrister on the team which represented Richard at his asylum hearing. Then again, attorney-client privilege still applied, despite the lapse of over thirty years.

55

Chapter Nine

The phone rang the moment I crossed the threshold. That gave me an almighty jolt. It sounded like an air-raid siren. I really have to do something about that nasty ringtone. I picked up the receiver with trepidation as if there was a possibility that it had been sprayed with Novichok. I held it away from my ear and my lips and when I emitted a wary, 'Hello?'

'Maggie?'

'Oh, Dad, it's you!'

'Who did you expect? Jack the Ripper?'

'I don't know. I'm on tenterhooks. After that chemical weapons alert I'm still jittery.'

'False alarm. They've overreacted big time.' Dad didn't sound particularly reassuring. An undercurrent of anxiety trailed in his voice. 'We wanted to know you made it home all right.'

'Yes, I just walked in.' I flopped on the settee and kicked off my shoes. I was wearing my party attire – coming out of quarantine, it felt surreal to be dressed in high heels and a low-cut top. 'Are you two OK? How's Mum taken to her hospital incarceration?' Mum hates hospitals; they remind her of our mortality. That doesn't surprise me, considering the way the NHS is heading these days.

'That's the thing – she will have to go back for X-rays and the like.' The anxiety in Dad's voice was more pronounced. 'They were not happy with her chest. That cough, you know. It's been going on since the end of last year.'

I could hear Mum scolding him in the background, telling him to stop nagging and making me worry over nothing – what a fuss-pot he was. 'High time she had it checked. It's probably nothing, but still, it'll be good to put your mind at ease.'

'You think?' He sounded livelier.

'Definitely. It looks like a silver lining to her compulsory hospital trip. She wouldn't have seen the doctor otherwise.'

'Right you are!'

We said our goodbyes and rang off.

The thing I had been missing most while confined in hospital was a long hot bath. After the *Ten O'Clock News*, I filled the tub to the brim with steaming water topped with a frothing foam of eucalyptus bubbles. When I closed my eyes and submerged myself in water, the image of Richard's panama hat gliding across the red-dyed surface of the pool sprang into my head. I burst out in panic, spilling water over the edge of the bathtub and soaking my slippers. I shouldn't have left them so close to the bath. I was better off keeping my eyes wide open. I looked at the ceiling and contemplated the macabre events of that momentous Saturday. Who had killed Richard Ruta? Which one of his guests – his friends – was capable of murder, and why?

I stayed in the bath, musing and pondering, until the water turned cold and my skin wrinkled. I stepped out of the bath and shivered. It was May – lukewarm and fuzzy – but I was cold. The chilling effect of Richard Ruta's death clung to the air like frost. The best remedy for chills and anxieties is a hot water bottle. I had it bundled away under the stairs, waiting for winter to come. I fetched it, filled it with boiling water from the kettle, and carried it to bed. I curled up on a stack of three pillows, cradling the hot-water bottle to my chest, and thinking. My head was cracking open. Sleep was proving elusive despite the late hour.

'It could've been suicide,' I said out loud, and continued to dissect that thought inside my head. I tried to remember Richard's exact words. It was something about the past catching up with him. Maybe he was planning to make a confession before he died but misjudged his timing. It had to be something big. He was going to confess to the killing of Leila Nolan. He was going to clear his conscience and die. He couldn't face the courts, a lengthy and in his case very public trial, the press swarming on him, his life's legacy tainted – a big fall from grace. The greater the man, the greater his fall, as the saying goes ... So he decided to take an easy way out. Except that it all went to custard and he died before he had the chance to unburden himself. That had to be it. I couldn't imagine any of the guests at the party were capable of murder. And what motive could any of them – any of us – have? No way. There was no murderer in our midst.

Thus reassured, I slowly drifted into the fog of a righteous slumber.

The following day, I shared my findings with Mary. I had totally forgotten my plan of running into her at the Thursday Market with the intention of interrogating her about her snub of Richard's birthday bash. As it happened, the following day was Thursday and my fridge required re-stocking. I grabbed my bag-for-life, which I had made myself from old linen curtains I had no heart to throw away. The fabric was sturdy, virtually indestructible like all things made in the fifties, and the pattern was adorable – flowers of the meadow. That pattern went hand-in-glove with the theme of my dress, which was also lusciously floral.

Our Thursday Market is attended religiously by all true Bishops Well citizens. One can purchase anything one desires at the market, from a handcrafted baby cradle to a plot at the cemetery. There is fresh produce and merchandise, all locally sourced (after the *Made in China* labels have been steamed and carefully removed). Cows, alive or in a tenderised ready-to-cook format. A hog on a spit with a home-grown Pink Lady apple in its mouth. West Country ice-cream made from Cornish cream. Gucci knockoffs and black market pre-release DVDs. Freshly cut flowers, and Wadsworth beer delivered by horse-and-cart, frothing with white foam before it is even poured into a glass. Wholesome and bursting with life!

Since the day was bright and sunny, most of the stalls were set up in the square. On rainy, wintry, and otherwise trade-hostile days, indoor facilities are used. There is plenty of room in the arcade and the now disused Corn Exchange barn. But this Thursday was too nice to cower indoors. The stalls teemed with colourful awnings and rowdy traders shouted over each other, extolling the superiority of their produce. I didn't have to be told whose cheese I liked best and headed directly for our local organic dairy farmer and cheesemaker, Vernon Leitch.

I don't mean to sound unkind, but Mr Leitch was looking more and more like one of his blue cheeses. Since I saw him two weeks earlier, the tiny mesh of broken veins on his cheeks had acquired a distinct blue tinge. I enquired after his health out of concern.

'Ooh, I'm in ruddy health, Miss Kaye!' he assured me. 'I hear you've been in a spot of a health scare yourself.'

'Have I?'

'At that fancy film-maker's party – getting poisoned, I hear!'

'Oh, that! It wasn't me who got poisoned, Mr Leitch. Thankfully!' I exhaled with exaggerated relief.

'But you got taken to hospital, I hear.'

'It was precautionary.'

'That's what I'm sayin'.' He patted the side of his nose and winked.

'I don't know what you mean, Mr Leitch.' I honestly didn't.

'Well, have you been properly *decontaminated*, is what I mean.'

'There was no contamination, I assure you!'

'So you're good to go, then?'

'Yes,' I answered, still not entirely sure what he was trying to tell me. 'May I have half a pound of your gorgeous cheddar, Mr Leitch?'

'You certainly may, Miss Kaye.'

I waited patiently as Vernon Leitch cut a wedge of his prime cheddar and weighed it on his ancient scales. He fluffed a bit, adding and taking chunks away so that I had a perfect measure of half-a-pound exactly. I also had plans to replenish my stock of Rum & Raisin Fudge Extravaganza, which I purchase from my old friends and master fudge-makers, Jane and Kev Wilcox. I never made it to the Wilcoxes' stall, as I was intercepted – by Mary. We exchanged exclamations of delight and wishes of good health, and naturally, the subject of Richard's death came up.

We decamped to the café to discuss it in detail over a cup of tea and a slice of cake. The Old Stables Café is my favourite spot for socialising. You can still smell the horses there, even though it has been centuries since the last horse called the place home. The satisfying sense of communing with stallions has been created by the paraphernalia strategically distributed around the tables and hung on the walls: saddles, whips, and horseshoes galore. The rustic solid oak tables have been custom-made to fit perfectly into the caves and crevices the building has to offer. The chairs, trust me, tend to adjust themselves to your bottom the moment you take a seat. Every bottom, great or small, of every shape and size, will find itself at home in one of those chairs. They have been curved to please and to keep customers seated for ever – and of course ordering more tea and cake.

Mary and I planted our bottoms in those magical chairs and took a couple of minutes to allow our tea to brew before we poured it and took our first respective sips of Earl Grey and Darjeeling.

I raised the hypothesis of suicide.

'Nonsense!' Mary shook her head with uncharacteristic vehemence. She is a timid creature. She used to be a makeup artist. Richard had discovered her on the set of one of his blockbusters as she was busy slapping makeup on Dotty. He had divorced Dotty and married Mary, all within a year. It had been Mary who had introduced him to Bishops Well. Mary must have been his antidote to Dotty: Dotty being brazenly glamorous and not afraid to flaunt her enhanced assets, Mary quiet and genteel. To this day, she wore not an ounce of makeup, her skin tight and clear. You would never suspect that she had already crossed the threshold into her fifties. She knew how to age with grace – unlike Dotty. I like Mary. You couldn't find a gentler soul for all the trying in the world. Yet, she repeated with great force, 'Utter nonsense!'

'Oh?'

'Richard would've never killed himself. He was a Catholic. Through and through. Suicide is a mortal sin for those people. You kill yourself, you go straight to hell.'

'Surely, he didn't believe that. Such a worldly man ...'

'Oh yes, he did. Trust me, Maggie: Richard would not have killed himself. Don't forget, I lived with the man for ten years. He loved life. He loved himself. He was conceited – would've never blamed himself for anything, never mind taking his own life in contrition. That'd be the day!' Mary's cheeks were blushing faintly.

I sighed heavily. There went my theory: up in smoke. My cake was dry. I pushed it away. 'Then the only other possibility is Dan Nolan,' I proclaimed and went on to appraise Mary of the unfortunate details of Nolan's attack on Richard. 'You should've seen how badly they treated him. Like a common trespasser. Frank literally dragged poor Dan across the terrace and threw him out. After all that man has been through ... it just wasn't right. If I were him, I might have done it, too.'

'Done what?'

'Killed Richard, of course! If I believed Richard had murdered my daughter, I'd ... I'd ... I'd have ripped his heart out.' I couldn't believe what I was saying. I didn't mean a word of it. I couldn't kill anyone. I am not a killer. And then there was the matter of my victim coming back to haunt me. Literally, in my case.

'How would Dan have done that – how would he have put poison in Richard's drink?'

'Well, he sneaked in without anyone noticing. He might have, equally undetected, squirted poison into that bottle of wine. Through the cork, you see ... with a syringe. He wouldn't even have to open it.'

'Any random bottle he could find? Risking the possibility of poisoning other guests? Not Dan. Definitely not Dan. It's not like him. Yes, he's still furious. Yes, he hasn't forgiven Richard. Yes, he wanted to make a statement. You can understand that, can't you? He wanted to remind Richard of Leila, wipe that stupid smirk off his face ... He couldn't bear Richard's smugness. *I* can't bear it!'

Mary was now thoroughly flushed. Her English rose complexion was in full crimson bloom. I had never seen her so agitated before.

'Is that why you didn't come to the party?' It dawned on me that, deep down, Mary must have hated Richard. If she were capable of hatred, that is. He had dumped her for a younger woman. Unceremoniously banished her from his grand mansion and within days installed her successor in title into their marital bed. He had been flaunting Penny right in her face ever since. She must have hated that. Hated him.

'No, Maggie. I would've gone to his silly little party, if only to show I hold no grudges.' Mary spoke softly. She was back to her gentle, timid self. 'I didn't go because I knew what Dan was planning. I didn't want to witness it. It wouldn't give me any satisfaction seeing Dan humiliated, as I was sure he would be. I told him it'd be pointless, that it would only hurt him to bring it all to the surface again. I told him it would be water off Richard's back –'

'You told him? You spoke to him about it?'

'Yes, exactly, we spoke about it a lot. We're still talking about it.' Mary nodded earnestly, her round-eyed innocence for all to see. 'I've been keeping in touch with Dan – all these years we stayed in contact. We were there for each other. I was recovering from my marriage breakdown, he, from Leila's ... He's been living in the Shetlands, did you know?'

I could only shake my head and gape.

'Yes ... He only came back to Bishops last month. I'd better tell you – you're bound to find out sooner or later. He's been staying with me. It's not what you're thinking. I have a spare room. Anyway, I couldn't say no even though I don't really approve of what he did at that party. It was childish, but that's how Dan deals with pain.'

I was still gaping.

'Don't stare, Maggie!' she snapped. 'He only chucked paint at Richard! He didn't murder him.'

Her last point, I thought, was debatable.

Chapter Ten

Sam had to collect his car. It was still at Forget-Me-Not, parked in the gravelled courtyard alongside several other vehicles whose owners, like Sam, had been evacuated from the estate by helicopter and then returned to their homes in ambulances. The police tape had been removed and the gate stood wide open. He contemplated sneaking in unnoticed, starting the Jag, and driving off. He wasn't in the mood for company. He had successfully avoided any eye contact when negotiating the back streets of Bishops Well, steering clear of the Thursday Market. He strode purposefully down the narrow country lane leading to Richard's estate, seeking refuge in the roadside hedge whenever a car tore by. But, by the time he was sitting in the driver's seat of his car, his conscience got the better of him. It wouldn't be right to slink away without so much as a word of condolence and an offer of support for Richard's widow. He turned off the engine and went in.

The place looked a mess. Nobody had bothered to tidy up after the police had had their way with it. The windows were still open; the airborne net curtains shimmered in the sun. Sam traversed the sitting room. Glasses with unfinished drinks languished on the sideboard. Cushions lay dented and crumpled on the sofa. He stepped out on to the terrace. Rings of red paint had drifted towards the walls of the pool and clung to them as the weak breeze made the water lap against them. Sam experienced a sense of déjà vu: he had seen this scene once before, eighteen years ago, the same eerie stillness after the storm, the same dread. As Richard's lawyer, he had been cleared by the police to visit the scene soon after Leila Nolan's death, in order to reconcile his client's statements with the evidence in situ. Both then and now the whole place looked as if it had spun out of its owner's control and turned on itself.

He stepped inside having resolved to leave without talking to anyone after all. In the dining room he discovered a figure slumped over the table, sitting in the chair that Richard had occupied on that fateful Saturday afternoon. The man sat with his elbows on the table and his face buried in his hands. It was Frank. He was crying.

Awkwardly, Sam tiptoed past him in an attempt to spare Frank the embarrassment of a stranger witnessing his grief.

'Sam, come and sit with me!' Frank called out to him. He wiped his face with the back of his hand. He was drunk.

'I was just collecting my car – I thought to offer my condolences to Penny.'

'She's not here. Gone to her mother's, in London – straight from the hospital. She's being looked after.' A note of sarcasm rang in Frank's voice. 'Come and sit down. Have a drink with me.'

If anyone needed looking after, it was Frank. He looked dirty and dishevelled. His eyes told a story of many a tear. Sam squeezed his shoulder and picked up a chair from the floor to sit next to him.

'How are you holding up?'

Frank threw his head back and snorted. 'A bit shitty, as you can see.'

'I'm sorry.'

'You must be the only person who knew Richard longer than me.'

'I suppose.'

'D'you reckon the KGB finally caught up with him? They've been taking out traitors one by one of late. Just as we thought they'd forgotten.'

Sam was flabbergasted. He had been sure he was the only one who knew about Richard Ruta's past as a spy during the Cold War. Samuel Dee had been the young lawyer, fresh from law school, who was part of the team representing Richard in his naturalisation hearing: a lifetime ago. It had been held behind closed doors as national interests were at stake and top secrets had to be guarded. It was during that short but poignant court hearing that young Sam had learned about Richard's earlier career as a spy for the Polish Security Bureau, which in its turn fed information directly to the KGB. Richard had used his relative freedom of movement while attending international film festivals in the West to explore the countryside, take photographs of military targets, and map the location of power stations and key industrial objects of interest. Posing as a harmless artiste, he had made contacts with high-ranking civil servants, politicians, and military personnel. At the hearing, Richard divulged every bit of intelligence he had gathered in his spy career in minute detail. Sam had duly signed confidentiality papers and had never spoken to a soul on these matters.

As far as the general public was concerned, the story was much more palatable. The renowned Polish director, alumnus of the prestigious Lodz Film School, Richard Ruta defected to the West in November 1981 to continue, uncensored and undeterred, his flourishing film career. He had come to London for a cultural event, his visit duly sanctioned by the communist government in Poland. It had been just weeks before the military regime had declared martial law and the state of emergency. He had got away in the nick of time. Just weeks later no one would be allowed to leave the country. He had arrived with all pomp, had dinner at the Polish embassy, then went straight to the nearest police station and asked for political asylum. He was as he stood. He had no money, nothing. The communists had frozen his bank account and later confiscated his home in Poland. They blocked his communications with everyone he had left behind, family, friends, colleagues. His letters were being intercepted, his phone calls listened to. He was penniless and quite without a hope. But he had his talent, and the rest would be history. History slightly belied since nobody, Sam had been led to believe, would ever know the whole truth.

'How did you find out ... about Richard?' he asked Frank.

Frank shrugged his shoulders. 'How indeed! Richard employed me to cover his back. When I retired from the Royal Marines, I was thirty-six. I was looking for work. A friend of a friend, Major … let's not mention names, put me in touch with Richard. He had to explain why he needed his arse protected. I wouldn't have walked into it blindfolded. I had to know what I was getting myself into. If I was to have a decent go at it, I had to know.'

'I see.'

'Though,' he swept the dining room with a contemptuous gaze, 'look what a shitty job I've done! Richard is dead, and I let it happen.'

'You couldn't have –'

'Yes, I could. I should have. That was my fucking job – keeping him safe!'

Sam didn't know what to say to that. He remained uncomfortably silent.

'I keep racking my brains over who gave him that bottle of Tokaji.' Frank was rubbing his temples frantically. 'I just can't recall who it was. He had that bottle in his hand, waved the bloody thing around, spilled some of it on the floor of the landing. Kissed the bloody bottle, for fuck's sake! Shouted something like …' Frank put on Richard's broad Polish accent, which would become even thicker after a drink or two, '"*If she loves you, Frankie my boy, she'll remember your beverage of choice! Tokaji, my boy … my true love remembered … my first true love …*" Or something like that. He talked of the damned bottle, handled it, like it was a woman! And he drank from it – straight from the bottle even before he got to the table. I just can't remember who gave it to him. Which one of them rotten bastards gave it to him! How much were they paid to do the dirty deed? Which one of them was bought by the KGB? They all have a price. We all have a price.'

'It mightn't have anything to do with the KGB, Frank. Have you considered that? You know as well as I do – Richard had enemies –'

'So which one of them! Which one sold out … which one …' Frank peered at him, stubbornly sticking to his mantra.

'My neighbour has a theory.'

'Mystic Maggie? Oh yeah, she always has a theory. How does she come up with them so quick – and without any proof!'

Sam winced, but didn't show his displeasure with Frank's opinion. He had grown fond of Maggie and didn't appreciate people slagging her off behind her back. Calmly, he explained, 'I saw her this morning on her way to the market. We stopped for a chat. She said she'd come up with it in the bath last night –'

'There you go then! Need I say more!'

'It didn't strike me as entirely implausible – what she said.'

'So what's her brilliant theory then?' Frank spoke with a sneer.

'She thinks it was suicide. She thinks Richard was about to confess – clear his conscience – and drink the poison. Come to think of it, it makes sense. He told me, actually, it was to be his last birthday bash. Prophetic words, don't you think? Maybe, that was the plan: confess and die ...'

'Confess to what? Don't be stupid. Richard? Confess?' Frank's laughter resonated between the four empty walls of the room.

Sam had to agree with Frank. Richard wasn't the type. No matter how much Sam wanted Maggie to be right, he knew she was wrong.

Chapter Eleven

My conversation with Mary kept me awake at night. Mary and Dan Nolan were the two people in the whole of Bishops with the biggest axe to grind with Richard Ruta. The fact that they had gravitated towards each other and stayed in touch shouldn't have come as a surprise. Their personal tragedies, by and large caused by Richard, had almost coincided. Richard had divorced Mary and instantly married Penny – and six months later Leila Nolan had died at his wild party. Two victims of his recklessness had every reason in the world to wish him ill. Had they gone beyond wishful thinking? Had Mary given Richard the bottle of Tokaji? Had Dan spiked it with poison? Were they in cahoots?

On Monday, I decided to get on my bike and cycle to Sexton's Canning. I was planning to visit the library and the Records Office where I hoped to get my hands on everything that had ever been written about Leila Nolan's death. Richard's words about the past catching up with him were resonating in my head. I was convinced that 'past' involved Leila, and that those words were significant. They were his dying words, after all. You wouldn't waste your last breath on pointless remarks.

I wore my tight Lycra leggings, as you do for cycling. Despite their smart design aimed at lengthening my legs and narrowing my hips, the exact opposite was in evidence: the elastic waist cut into my midriff creating a double-barrel effect and my thunder thighs had nowhere to hide. I had to resign myself to flaunting my bumps and bulges in public because the only other option was driving.

That meant achieving the impossible of finding a parking space in Sexton's and, if successful, paying the hefty parking fee. At the end of the day, I am a woman nearing half a century and weight is something that comes with age; think of a tree trunk acquiring a new ring around its circumference every year it is alive. At least I am alive, unlike dozens of women I know who sustain themselves on lettuce leaves and little else. They aren't really alive – they merely exist. I live my life to the fullest, consuming Jaffa Cakes and indulging in full-fat milk at my leisure. Guess who is happier?

The cycle to Sexton's Canning took me three-quarters of an hour. I took the scenic route via Little Ogburn instead of the busy B-road with heavy lorries zooming past in fumes of diesel. I crossed the rickety bridge over the river – the one with the crumbling wall, through which a good few years ago Harry Watton's son had ploughed his quad bike while drunk. The Parish Council hasn't yet had it mended (lack of funds, I guess), though the quad bike had been fished out immediately after the accident before petrol spilled out and ravaged the fragile river ecosystem.

I pedalled merrily past barley fields on one side and the bright-yellow madness of rapeseed on the other. These days Little Ogburn is nothing more than a sleeper-hub for people who work in Sexton's Canning. The road was pretty much deserted, except for one van full of casual labourers. It had nearly mowed me down and the driver hooted just as he levelled with me. There was even a wolf-whistle, which may have had something to do with my G-string lodging itself firmly in my crack and me trying to pull it out without dismounting my bike.

I reached the end of the road, where the entrance to Whalehurst Independent School was. The school loomed in all its medieval glory behind a wrought-iron gate. I turned onto the cycle path behind it and took the shortcut via the country park. And there I emerged in Ramble Fields, a leafy little suburb of Sexton's Canning.

I went to the library and registered myself with a friendly gentleman in his late eighties, undoubtedly the last volunteer standing.

'Blinking useless piece of junk . . . What's wrong with the good old Filofax, I ask you?' He was patently struggling with the electronic registration procedure. 'A biro and a piece of paper would do the job much better, I say! But they won't take my word for it, will they?'

'Won't they?'

'Oh no! They know better up there in London how to run provincial libraries,' he sneered. 'It's all about technology nowadays, sod the books!'

The library computer beeped cantankerously over his bitter vituperations as he punched the keyboard and poked the unresponsive screen. Fifteen tortuous minutes later, I was the proud owner of a library card. I thumbed through volumes of hardcopy local newspapers and scanned a micro-film reader.

The papers dating back to the time of Leila's death were buzzing with wild speculations and brazen finger-pointing, but very few facts. Revelations of rampant sexual orgies and calls for a parliamentary inquiry into *the drug-infested Bishops Well underworld* were rife. Paparazzi snapshots of Richard in his garden, his car, in the window, and running out of the police station with his head down were endless. So were the images of Penny, Frank, Henry and Vera, and interestingly enough the famous actor whose name I had finally come to remember: Daniel McCoy, of course! He had been there too, alongside a few other semi-celebrities and non-entities captured by the intrusive lenses of the then unbridled media. Those were the days when freedom of the press reigned supreme, way before Hacked Off put an end to it.

The only decent quality photograph I found was that of Leila herself. It was a head and shoulders picture of a girl wearing school uniform, her blonde hair in two thick plaits and her smile timid under a seasoning of freckles. No wonder people could think of nothing other than child molestation when they looked at that image. Leila couldn't have been more than fifteen years old in that photograph.

From the library I pushed my bike towards the Records Office.

Along the way, I stopped at Costa for a cup of coffee (full cream latte) and one of those giant Belgian chocolate cookies. I was working hard to salvage the precious calories I had lost on my long bicycle journey from Bishops Well.

At the Records Office I requested access to the Coroner's report issued pursuant to the inquest into Leila's death. It wasn't long before the document was made available to me. I leafed through it impatiently, and I had to slow down and start from the beginning. I waded through basic information about Leila: her age, place and date of birth, her address at Bishops Well. I discovered that the person who reported her death was Frank Savage. His statement was short and to the point: he had heard Richard cry from the terrace to call an ambulance. It was approximately six a.m. He had looked out of the window and seen Richard in his dressing gown, kneeling over Leila's body. He was dripping with water. He must've gone into the pool to fish her out and had somehow managed to hoist her onto the side of the pool. It was a macabre sight as Leila had been wearing a blood-red dress. Penny had joined Richard on the terrace, screaming when she saw the body. It was then that Frank called 999.

Richard's statement confirmed Frank's version of the events. He'd woken up early, half five, because he had a terrible headache. A hangover. He went downstairs to fetch a glass of water. He dropped an Alka-Seltzer tablet into it and drank. He poured himself another glass of water and glanced out of the kitchen window facing the terrace. He saw something red in the pool and thought it was too large for a float. There were floats around the pool – he'd had a pool party the night before. He ran outside, saw it was a body, and jumped into the pool wearing his slippers and dressing gown. He turned the body around in the water and only then did he realise it was Leila Nolan, a local girl who had been employed by the catering company to wait on the guests at his party. He pulled her to the edge of the pool and tried to administer mouth-to-mouth resuscitation. She was very cold. There was no response to his chest compressions. He shouted out for someone to call an ambulance. Penny was the first person to join him on the terrace. Other guests came out slowly from the house. There was panic. Soon after, the ambulance arrived. Then the police.

There were several other witness statements, none of them contributing anything new. Nobody knew what had happened to Leila and how she had died. Nobody had heard or seen anything the night before.

According to the Coroner's report, the probable cause of death was drowning, sometime between twelve thirty and one o'clock in the morning. Leila had suffered a blow to her head which was consistent with a fall on the hard, tiled surface on the side of the pool. That however was not what had killed her. Although the scene had been trampled over by the guests and most evidence compromised, there was a puddle and a smudge of dried blood where Leila must have fallen and hit her head. It was assumed that she had temporarily lost consciousness, then recovered it, got up and tried to take a few steps, but instead slid into the pool, face down, where she drowned. Her Blood Alcohol Concentration was 11.2% and therefore was a contributory factor. Leila's death was ruled to be accidental. Case closed.

Something was bugging me as I was cycling home. Something in that report wasn't as clear-cut as it appeared. Some of it was supposition. That smudge of dried blood . . . the assumption that Leila had tripped and slid into the pool after recovering consciousness . . . the assumption that she was conscious but too drunk to pull herself out of the pool . . . And then there was the red dress. I could see why Dan Nolan poured red paint into the pool and chucked the rest at Richard – a nod to the dress Leila had been wearing on the last day of her life. But hadn't Richard stated in his testimony that Leila had been working as a waitress at the party? Would a waitress have worn a blood-red dress? That didn't make any sense. And Richard's own attire troubled me – slippers and a dressing gown. Hadn't he passed out in bed the night before? Surely he had passed out as he stood – in his party wear. So where was it?

Chapter Twelve

What drew Sam's attention to the ditch by the side of the road was a pair of Lycra-clad buttocks writhing with some gusto. A woman was trying to pull a bicycle out of the ditch and manoeuvre it back onto the road. The front wheel of the bicycle was bent. She wouldn't be able to ride that bike and this was the middle of nowhere, halfway down the busy dual carriageway between Sexton's and Bishops Well.

Sam pulled over. He turned off the engine and stepped out of his Jag.

'Are you all right there? Do you need a lift?'

Maggie Kaye peered at him from beneath her tilted helmet. Her face was sweaty and flushed with effort. She swallowed back a curse and exclaimed, 'My prayers have been answered! If that isn't my very neighbour ... God-sent!' She let the broken bicycle drop to the ground and started wiping dry grass and dirt from her bum. 'Yes, I could do with a lift! I don't know what happened. I've been stupid, really. I thought I'd be quicker going home via the ring road rather than the way I came. It may be quicker for a car, but not a cyclist! This road is full of speeding lunatics. One minute I was cycling merrily, minding my own business – I was in fact thinking. It's the case – and next minute, bang! I was picking myself up from the ditch. And then you arrived.'

'Let me get your bike.'

Sam opened the boot of his car. It was full of unpacked boxes. He realised he must have been carrying them around since he had moved to Bishops Well. That was where – he guessed – his ties were

73

hiding and, very likely, his missing coffee machine. He was chuffed with this discovery. Maggie's bike however wouldn't squeeze in there and they didn't want to leave it by the side of the road. They tried several different positions on the back seat. In the end, he put the back seat down and shoved the wounded bike on top. He opened the passenger door for Maggie, hoping that this time she wouldn't complain about the lack of space. For a split second, she looked like she was going to. She pursed her lips and stared at the seat with dismay, but then she said mysteriously, 'Well, no way am I walking home, so we'll have to put up with each other for a bit.'

'It's not a problem at all,' Sam assured her, not quite certain whether he should take offence. Perhaps his aftershave had passed its use-by date.

Seated and firmly strapped in on the passenger side, Maggie began relaying to him her findings from the Records Office. It appeared that she had embarked on a spot of private investigation. Sam wondered if the woman had a day job to go back to, but this wasn't a good time to enquire. She was in full swing.

'I think Leila Nolan was pushed into that pool. Someone – I'm guessing Richard Ruta – attacked her, she fought back ... he drowned her. He covered his tracks by the time the cops arrived, but if they'd bothered to look they'd have found incriminating evidence. Did you know they didn't even bag the clothes he had worn the night before?'

'Why would he have attacked her?'

'Why would any man past his prime attack a beautiful young girl?' Maggie gazed at him pointedly.

Sam shrugged, genuinely perplexed. If a man at fifty was *past his prime*, then what was Sam? And what reason would he have to attack beautiful young girls, assuming he was of sound mind. 'Beats me!'

'Richard Ruta, I'm afraid, liked young girls. There's no other plausible explanation.'

'What, in God's name, makes you say that?'

'Take Penny: she's half his age! As was Mary when he married her.'

'That's nonsense! They weren't children. And neither was Leila Nolan. She was nineteen at the time and, besides, she was a sexually active adult. However, at the time of the *accident*,' he stressed the word because he was enraged by Maggie's wanton accusations, 'there were no signs of recent sexual activity or any injuries suggestive of a sexual assault. Leila Nolan was heavily intoxicated. She fell, bumped her head, and ended up in the pool. Richard wasn't even there when it happened!'

'Come to think about it, neither were you. So,' Maggie snorted, 'you can't be sure of anything. You can't believe everything the press say.'

'I don't, but I saw all the reports, full disclosure, all the forensic evidence, first-hand. I read all the witness statements. I formed my own opinion based on facts. I spoke to Richard under solicitor-client privilege. And on top of everything else, he gave me his word that he didn't do it. But that bit was just between friends. As his lawyer, I was satisfied –'

'Do you mean to say you represented Richard in that case? Wow!'

'There was no case. Richard wasn't arrested or charged with anything. He simply assisted the police with their inquiries. He asked me to be there for him – purely in an advisory capacity. The media were on his back. In the end, the matter never made it to court. And it shouldn't have. Like I said, it was an accident.'

'If it was such a clear-cut case then why is Dan Nolan disputing it?'

'Because he's a grieving father. He needs someone to blame.'

Sam was glad they had arrived at the house. He was fed up with Maggie Kaye and her outrageous speculations. That was how rumours started: little nosy parkers sniffing around, coming up with saucy theories. Pure fiction. He jumped out of the car and heaved the bike out of the back seat. He was dismayed to note that the chain had left oily black marks on the leather upholstery.

Maggie was peering over his shoulder. 'Just like the smudge of blood by the pool . . .' she pronounced mysteriously, staring at the marks. He could see now why people called her Mystic Maggie.

She ran her fingers over the oily marks. 'I will clean that, I'm sorry. Your lovely seats are ruined.'

'No, don't worry. The car's going for a service. They'll valet it. Where would you like the bike?'

'In the shed, if you don't mind. The garage is too full!'

So was the garden shed, Sam soon discovered. A soon as he yanked the door open, a couple of terracotta pots fell from a shelf and, having cracked apart, joined a collection of loose screws, rugs, and rusty utensils on the floor. He pushed the bike in and shut the door. The clanking sound that followed meant another avalanche of clutter had tumbled down from the shelves.

'I can take a look at that bike, maybe tomorrow?' he offered, unsure why.

Maggie thanked him profusely and insisted – absolutely insisted – that he joined her for a cup of tea right this very minute for all his trouble. Sam was not a tea drinker and he had already endured enough trouble in Maggie's company, but he didn't have the heart to say no.

In Maggie's kitchen they sat over a cup of tea and a pack of digestives. Her kitchen was the polar opposite of Sam's. It looked the same way it must have looked in its Victorian prime: a rustic sideboard, a functional wooden table, and chairs so well used that you could detect the imprints of buttocks on them, as well as blackened pots suspended from a beam and an ancient Aga stove on bendy legs. Sam's kitchen had been created when Priest's Hole was subdivided into two independent flats. It was a collection of modern units and stainless steel appliances.

The tea tasted surprisingly agreeable, especially with the added bonus of the biscuits. 'I've been wondering – if you don't mind me asking ...'

'Fire away!' Maggie dipped her digestive in her brew.

'Well, just wondering what you do for a living.'

'Not much, as you can tell, I'm sure,' she chuckled. 'I am what you call a jack of all trades and master of none.'

'I see.'

'I have my funds – thanks to you, really.'

'Oh?'

'Well, you paid handsomely for your cottage.'

'Yes, of course! What was I thinking! So, you live off your capital gains?'

'My what? Don't be daft! It's not that much *capital*! I do work, you know! I do some supply teaching, mainly in Bishops Primary. That keeps me busy, and it's a good hourly rate when you do supply. I'm also a roving correspondent for the *Sexton's Canning Herald*.'

'Horoscopes?'

She looked at him sharply. 'Why would you say that?'

Like a frightened turtle, Sam drew his head down to hide it between his shoulders. 'Um, I don't know what made me say that.'

'Mystic Maggie, that's what! I know people call me that. Oh well,' she shrugged and sucked tea out of her digestive, 'I don't care what people call me. But no, I write – occasionally – about cultural events, locally. And quite a bit about the history of Bishops and the surrounding areas. Results of our research, through the Archaeological Association –'

'Nice tea, thank you!' Sam changed the subject promptly. He wouldn't be drawn into this or any other society. He had come to live in the country in peace and solitude, thank you very much. 'I'd better be going then.'

'I'll get you another cup!' She would have none of it. As she produced another cup of tea, she said, as unpredictably as always, 'So you see, I can't stop thinking about Leila. She didn't hit her head on the edge of the pool and go into it straight away. She fell by the pool, about half a metre away from the edge – that's where the patch of dried blood was.'

'Yes, everyone agrees on that.' Sam sipped his tea.

'But it was assumed that she tried to get up and, in an alcoholic daze, slipped into the pool where she drowned.'

'The evidenced pointed to that, yes.'

'The smudge of blood on the tiles.'

'Precisely.'

'But there was at least half a metre to the pool from where she first fell!'

'She was drunk – she got up, staggered, lost balance –'

'Or she was dragged!'

'There was no evidence of physical violence. No bruising, no cuts, no broken nails. You're making too much out of it.' Following Maggie's example, he too dipped a digestive biscuit in his tea and waited for it to soften, then sucked the soggy edge before devouring the whole thing.

'OK, but it wasn't just a puddle of blood, or a random splatter. It was a smudge, like a skid mark!'

Splitting hairs, Sam thought, but said nothing, relishing his newly discovered fondness for digestives.

'You agree that she was drunk?'

He nodded slowly.

'You agree that she fell and hit her head? She was pretty much incapacitated at this point, wasn't she?'

He nodded again and reached for another digestive.

'What if, instead of getting up – or trying to – she was lying there, unconscious? What if someone dragged her the distance of half a metre and then pushed her into the pool? She wouldn't be able to put up a fight, would she? That's why there was no evidence of it. Someone hauled her and pushed her into the pool as she was lying there, knocked out for six!'

Sam's digestive biscuit dissolved in his tea as he paused to contemplate Maggie's words with all the seriousness they deserved.

'Do you see my point? The smudge of blood was there because she was dragged to the edge of the pool by someone and then pushed in!'

'It's a possibility . . .' he conceded at last. She wouldn't relent if he resisted.

'So, it is also possible that Richard was that someone! He drowned her for . . . for whatever reason, which we're yet to find out.'

Sam wasn't sure about her use of the pronoun *we*.

'And when you think about it calmly, everything suddenly makes sense – Richard's strange words at the party –'

'What strange words?'

'Come on! Wake up! About the past catching up with him. Was it his conscience? Guilt? He was a Catholic, did you know that? Well, Catholics are big on confessions. I bet you my bottom dollar, what we saw there was Richard making his Last Confession –'

'And taking his own life? That would be irreconcilable – confess and then commit another mortal sin.' Sam frowned. He wasn't buying it, not wholesale, but he was thinking. What if someone *had* killed Leila? What if it hadn't been Richard? What if Richard *knew* who it was?

What if he had been planning to expose them?

Sam jumped to his feet with all the abruptness of a sudden Eureka dawning on him. 'I must be going. I forgot ... I've an appointment,' he stammered and left without thanking his host for the tea and biscuits.

Only in the safety of his own home did he allow himself to articulate his suspicion. *What if it was Henry ...*

Sam recalled – vividly – Richard's words at the clubhouse. Bizarre as they seemed at the time, they made sense now. *I know things ... have to keep politicians accountable ... for all their sins. He's a bastard ... I know things ...*

And then, the party.

Penny had been telling Henry something – something he didn't like very much. He was angry. Was he afraid? Had she told him that Richard was planning to reveal his secret – *his sin*? Henry had been a guest at Richard's fiftieth – he had been there in the house when Leila died. Had Richard been covering up for him all those years, and now that he had become a public figure – an MP nonetheless – decided that it was time to hold Henry to account? Sam wouldn't put it past Richard. Richard was a stickler for honour, God, and duty – all that political romanticism he had learned in his homeland ... Had he suddenly decided that Henry was unworthy of public office?

'Oh, Alice, how I wish you were here!' Sam sighed. Alice would know what to make of it. She used to be an investigative journalist – the best there was. The absolute best! Uncompromising. Persistent. Tough. How much he missed her! How much he missed talking to her. Listening to her. Being near her. He had forgiven her a long time ago for dying – for leaving him. Now, he just wanted her back, no questions asked.

He poured himself a stiff whisky and slouched in front of the TV. He didn't want to think – or to feel. He hoped for some mind-numbing gibberish to take the edge off his pain.

Fiona Bruce spoke with her usual calm poise, her left eyebrow slightly elevated. She was shaking her head in sad disbelief. 'Daniel Nolan, fifty-nine, has been arrested in connection with the murder of the film director, Richard Ruta. Eighteen years ago Mr Nolan's daughter, Leila, died in a tragic accident at the director's house. Mr Nolan, who did not accept the accidental death verdict, had been campaigning ever since to reopen the investigation into his daughter's death. His appeal against the Coroner's verdict was unsuccessful and he exhausted all other legal avenues. We have approached the Sexton's Canning Constabulary for comments but no one was available to speak to us at this stage of the investigation.'

Sam gaped at the recent passport photograph of Daniel Nolan. The impassive, unsmiling face of a middle-aged man with thinning hair and heavily hooded eyes gaped back at him. There was none of the white fury Sam had witnessed ten days earlier at the party.

'Is that the face of a premeditated killer? What do you make of him, Alice?' Sam asked the empty space next to him. He had his doubts. Alice would neither confirm nor deny them.

'The cops have their reasons. Apparently.' He poured himself another stiff drink and turned off the TV.

Chapter Thirteen

I am an active member of the Bishops Well Archaeological Association. We sometimes call it Bishops AA. Our AA meetings are every Wednesday fortnight. Primarily, we meet to discuss research and project funding, but also for a bit of socialising and a touch of gossip.

The Archaeological Association usually holds its meetings in the Community Hall. Ironically, the hall is a contemporary building designed by an architect with a penchant for the era of Anderson shelters, or possibly, a fan of *The Hobbit*. The structure is half buried in the ground; it has a dome-like roof which has been laid to lawn, and its windows are circular. Its walls are made from mud, manure, and straw – all sound eco-friendly materials. It doesn't look like much from the outside, but inside it is quite impressive in both its size and its creature comforts. The hall was built twenty years ago following vigorous fundraising by patriotic Bishopians of means. One of them was Richard Ruta, who contributed an undisclosed fortune to the project. Another one was Philip Weston-Jones, a member of our local upper crust, who also dug deep into his pockets. The rest of the money came from sales of homemade scones and muffins. Numerous local waistlines have never recovered.

Anybody and everybody in Bishops who has little else to do is a member. That includes Vera Hopps-Wood, Vanessa Scarfe, Mary Ruta, and Michael Almond, who only really works when someone dies in suspicious circumstances. Our chairperson is a real-life historian, Cherie Hornby. She has a doctorate in European military history and a particular interest in the Napoleonic Wars. Incidentally, with her small but corpulent body and rigidly sculpted short crop of hair she is a modern-day female version of Napoleon Bonaparte in his heyday. She has the personality to go with it: driven and ambitious.

Another member is Dr Edgar Flynn. He is a doctor of psychiatry with a private practice in Bath. God knows who his private patients are. They certainly have to be rich to afford his fee, irrespective of their emotional and mental deficiencies. But, like Michael Almond, he also works for the police. Unlike Michael, who is a forensic pathologist, Dr Flynn dabbles in profiling disturbed criminal minds if and when so required. He calls this service his zero-hour contract and complains about its unreliability. He lives with his mother. He often says that both his home and the disturbed minds that he studies are *very lonely places*. Our AA meetings must be his equivalent of sex, drugs, and rock 'n' roll. I am wary of him. He has a rustling voice which he probably uses to hypnotise people. He is also spidery in appearance: long bony limbs, a full head of wiry hair sprouting in all directions, and glasses that make his eyes seem very small and distant. I am afraid of spiders and hard as I try, I don't like Dr Flynn very much.

But I like James Weston-Jones. He happens to be the son and heir apparent to Philip Weston-Jones, the aforementioned Bishops Well blue-blood benefactor. James is in his mid-fifties, well-built, with a pleasant appearance and dashing manner, riotously curly black hair, and soulful brown eyes. He has those dark smouldering looks you can't resist. I can't, anyway. I look at him and think *Denzel Washington*, and I go weak in my knees. We always flirt rather shamelessly, having no regard or consideration for the wedding ring on his fourth finger. But, I hasten to add, it is all harmless. James Weston-Jones is inherently chivalrous; his remarks about my charming dimples fly off his tongue without an ulterior motive whatsoever. Routinely, I find myself drifting towards James during our meetings to bask in his charming proximity – what woman wouldn't!

However, this Wednesday I had a bigger – or rather, different – fish to fry.

This Wednesday, my plan was to grill my fellow members with connections to the police about the arrest of Dan Nolan. I was hoping that either Vanessa or Michael would have some light to shed on the case and on the available evidence. Being married to the Detective Chief Superintendent, Vanessa could be a font of all inside knowledge. If she tried. Normally, she has little interest in her husband's line of work, and thus has little information to share. However, on this occasion, I speculated, her personal involvement with the case might have inspired in her some curiosity about its outcome. And Michael was obviously seeing that detective, DI Marsh. She would be in charge of the murder investigation, I assumed.

I arrived bang on time for the seven p.m. start. I'm usually a little late – the prerogative of a lady – but that Wednesday I nearly managed to break the habit of a lifetime and get there early, such was my burning curiosity. All my early bird fellow members were already there. I didn't want to come across as too eager so I sat next to Vera and asked after Henry.

'He's back at Westminster,' she spoke with a hint of relief in her voice. 'Out of harm's way. And out of mine, frankly.'

'Best place for him,' I agreed. Lately, I had been detecting an air of animosity between those two. It was not a bed of roses in the Hopps–Wood household. It hadn't been for months. But I didn't wish to go into that. My interests lay elsewhere so I gravitated towards Michael.

'And how is the case? DI Marsh must have her hands full with Dan, and all . . .' I probed.

Michael gazed at me without comprehension. Mary, on the other hand, glared at me resentfully. She still hadn't forgiven me for suspecting her and Dan. I may have – briefly – suspected them, but I hadn't reported my suspicions to the police. The police had other grounds for Dan's arrest. Nothing to do with me! I simply wanted to know what those grounds were.

'I couldn't help noticing that DI Marsh –'

'Gillian,' he said.

'Right . . . I couldn't help noticing that Gillian moved in with

83

you a few days ago. She's handling Richard's murder case, isn't she? I don't want to pry, but I wonder if she talks about it . . . at home . . . over dinner, or . . . I can't help being nosy – we could've all died there!' OK, that was a bit overdramatic.

'No,' Michael disagreed, but I wasn't clear about what. That's the downside of asking too many questions, all at once.

'Dan's arrest was way over the top,' Mary said. 'The man has done nothing wrong.'

'The police must have found something . . . incriminating,' I countered, and peered pleadingly at Michael, 'Haven't they?'

'I wouldn't know, Maggie. Gillian isn't the SIO. Mark Webber, the new acting DI, is. He had Nolan arrested. Gillian isn't up to it. She is actually convalescing at mine. I can look after her, you see? Otherwise she would carry on with the case. She's impossible – all workaholics are.'

'Oh dear me, what's the ailment?' Dr Flynn enquired. The conversation wasn't going the way I had planned.

'Acute anaemia. Plus she's had a chest infection.'

'Those two often go hand in hand,' Dr Flynn nodded. 'When the immune system is undermined, everything goes.'

'Precisely. She needs lots of rest.'

'Please pass her my best wishes.'

'So, she has no interest in the case?' I attempted to put the derailed conversation back on track.

'Oh, she has plenty of interest in it. I have to keep Webber at bay. I even confiscated her phone.'

I made a feeble squeak, followed by, 'Poor Dan . . .' I was disappointed. My face must have looked crestfallen for, unexpectedly, Vanessa came to my rescue.

'They're going to let him go, if they haven't already,' she said. 'It turns out that poisoned wine, Hungarian Tokaji, is very rare, not commonly available in Britain. Anyway, they've tracked the purchase down. It was bought duty free, most likely at an airport in Europe. Only someone who travelled abroad could've bought it duty free –'

'And Dan hates flying. He's been nowhere near an airport in all his life,' Mary finished the sentence for Vanessa, glaring at me with the triumphant look of vindicated innocence. There went my earlier theory that Dan had followed his wife to Australia after Leila's death. I would kill to know where he *had* been for all those years.

That evening I was glued to the TV. There was nothing about Dan's release on the national news, but BBC *Points West* had a live scoop on the action as it unfolded. They had their cameras rolling as Dan emerged from the police headquarters in Sexton's, escorted by DI Webber. The latter made a curt statement in which he confirmed that Mr Nolan was no longer a person of interest due to new evidence having come to light. New lines of inquiry were being pursued. He would not elaborate on what that evidence was, but he didn't have to. I knew what it was. He withdrew inside the building, leaving the floor to Dan.

Cameras zoomed in on him. You could tell that he was seething with fury and that he wanted to have his say. 'I was illegally incarcerated! Unfounded accusations!' he foamed. 'I'll be seeking legal advice to claim compensation from the police. They haven't heard the last of me, mark my words!'

A reporter shoved a mic in Dan's face. 'Would you care to elaborate on the nature of those accusations, Mr Nolan? Were they related to the unfortunate accident involving your daughter eighteen years ago?'

'Accident?' Dan groaned under the weight of that word. His facial muscles tightened. To him, it was like waving a red flag before a bull. 'My daughter was murdered – that was no accident. And I have been persecuted ever since! Because I want justice for her.'

'Is it true that your daughter Leila had been having a sexual relationship with Mr Ruta? Do you believe –'

The overzealous reporter had no chance to finish his question. Dan's fist landed squarely between his eyes, captured by the cameraman and witnessed live by *Points West* audiences across the Shires.

'How dare you taint my daughter with this filth! You take it back or I –' Another sentence that could not be fully delivered. This time, it was DI Webber who stopped Dan. He materialised from behind the closed door, grabbed Dan in a well-executed headlock and marched him back inside. Dan was re-arrested on the spot, this time for assault.

The reporter lay for a few tense seconds on the steps of the police HQ, temporarily unresponsive. Then he sat up and looked around him bewildered. The crew filmed the arrival of an ambulance and the departure of the unfortunate reporter to the hospital. At least there was no need for a stretcher. He merely had a bloody nose.

I couldn't believe my eyes.

I sat in the dark for a while after the news. I thought of Dan Nolan. How could I have ever imagined – even for one minute – that he was capable of murder? I had known Dan since I had been a little girl. I had even fancied him for a while: he, a rugby player at county level, several years my senior, a rebel without a cause. He used to play in a band: drums. When he'd started going out with Debbie I had thought she was the luckiest girl alive. She had sung in the same band. Bishop and the Beast, they called themselves. My big brother Will had played keyboard, and there was that guy from Sexton's – brilliant on the guitar. I had forgotten his name. But it was Dan and Debbie who ran the show. They had been the golden couple of Bishops Well, and Leila their precious princess. She too wanted to perform, wanted to be an actress or a singer – they let her believe that she could, that the sky was the limit. Dan was a good dad. A good man, just broken with grief. He was not a killer.

What was I thinking? What the hell was I thinking. Dan was a bundle of raging emotions. He wore his heart on his sleeve. He didn't mince his words. Yes, it was his style to chuck paint around and punch people in the face. It wasn't his style to resort to something as underhand and dastardly as poison. Someone else killed Richard Ruta – to stop him from talking.

Chapter Fourteen

Sam had every beneficiary of Richard Ruta's Last Will and Testament gathered in his office – everyone, that was, apart from Richard's mother, who inherited the bulk of his estate. Sam had tracked the woman down in the depths of Poland and had written to invite her to the reading of the Will. She had declined the invitation politely, blaming her old age, poor health, and a recent death in the family. She informed Sam she was grateful for the money but had little use for it at her age. She asked for Richard's body – it was her wish that he be buried with his own flesh and blood. That was Richard's wish, too. He had made a stipulation in his Will that his remains were expatriated to his native Poland and buried there, in his family's tomb. As the executor of Richard's estate, Sam would have to see to all the arrangements to ensure that Richard's wishes were duly fulfilled. But did those wishes still stand? Sam had been wondering about those *tweaks* Richard had intended to make to his Will, and never got a chance to do. He had mentioned it out of the blue, at the party. It had crossed Sam's mind that perhaps those tweaks were what had got him killed.

As it was, the Will was clear and stood unrevoked: Penny inherited Forget-Me-Not (worth a small fortune) and a cash legacy of £350,000. Identical cash legacies went to Mary and Dotty – *in equal shares to my wives, past and present, so no unfavourable comparisons are made or grudges held – Be good to one another, I loved you all the same*, as Richard had quaintly put it. There was a proviso that should any of them die within thirty days of Richard's passing, her share would revert to the pot and be shared between the other two. Mary got the freehold of the cottage where she had been living rent-free since the divorce. Frank Savage received the handsome sum of a quarter of a million pounds for *his friendship and devotion beyond the line of duty.* A hefty three million pounds was to be donated to the Lodz Film School *to train a new generation of world-class film-makers.* Ever the joker, Richard bequeathed the neat sum of a hundred thousand to Sam *in full and final settlement of all those unpaid bills for services rendered, and for not judging me.* Another hundred k was given to the Bishops Well Archaeological Association on the condition that it was used in its entirety to *get to the bottom of that swamp and uncover that elusive Celtic village (or a few Tesco trolleys and broken bicycles that may lurk there instead — I will be watching your progress from above).* Fifty thousand was given to the Bishops Well Rugby Club. The residue of just over four million pounds sterling went to Richard's mother, or if she should not survive him, to all her direct progeny: Richard's surviving siblings, nephews, and nieces.

When Sam finished reading the Will, he scanned his office, scrutinising the faces of all the people present. Each of them had a motive to kill Richard Ruta, including Sam. Each of them had a good reason to celebrate, but only Cherie Hornby and Maggie Kaye of the Archaeological Association sat there unable to contain their delight and undying gratitude to their benefactor.

'Oh my, Cherie, our prayers have been answered! I don't know what we'll do with such a sum of money!' Maggie was beside herself. She clapped her hands like a child on a sugar rush.

'It's a good thing that I do, my dear. Oh, I do!' Cherie was flushed with the excitement of someone ready and well-funded to take on the world. 'I'll be looking for land surveyors — I will get my feelers out. And we need to put together a team of respectable professionals, archaeologists with credentials ... We'll need to engage an accountant. Everything must be above board. An extraordinary meeting may have to be called this week. Leave it to me, Maggie. I must go and share the good news.' She squeezed Maggie's hand, shook Sam's with profuse thanks, and headed for the exit. Maggie was welling up, unable to get to her feet to follow her friend.

Tomasz Sojka, the dean of the Lodz Film School, and Aaron Letwin, the CEO of Bishops Well Rugby Club, also expressed their gratitude and left. Sam saw them to the front door (his office was located in the reception room facing the road). They shook hands. He waved as each of them jumped into their respective Audis and rolled off the lawn. The only car left in the courtyard was Richard's Bentley, in which Dotty and Penny had arrived, driven by Frank.

When Sam returned to the office, the atmosphere appeared tense. You could cut it with a knife. Dotty peered at him down her nose, none too pleased. She was tapping her healthy foot on the floor with growing irritation. She didn't feel like she had anything to celebrate. To be treated in the same way as all Richard's other wives – a travesty! She felt belittled, trampled on, humiliated. He had told her she was his first – his true – love. So much for true, so much for only: *I loved you all the same!*

Dotty snorted. 'Oh well, if that's all there is to it, I'd better be going back home to Florida. I miss the sun. Wire the small change over to me, Samuel, will you? My PA will give you my bank account details.' She rose to her feet and leant on her walking stick, twisting her body to address Frank, 'Let's go, Frank. I've got a plane to catch. As planned.'

Frank didn't stir. He had hardly lifted his eyes to her when he muttered under his breath, 'You aren't going anywhere. We're all to stay put – we were told by the cops not to leave the area without their say-so.'

'They didn't mean *me*, Frank. Let's go! I'm tired.'

'Then go,' he growled.

Dotty should have known better than to push her luck with Frank. He sounded at the end of his tether, ready to strike out. It doesn't take much with those ex-soldiers, thought Sam, one small spark and they blow up. But she was too self-absorbed to take any notice of other people's feelings. She insisted, 'You can't expect me to walk, what with my hip! You must drive me back, and I still need to pack.'

'Get the hell out of here! Get out of my face! Just fuck off, you witch!' He jumped up, his spittle flying in Dotty's face.

She went pale as a sheet and looked close to fainting. Her lip was quivering on the edge of indignation, but she was incapable of articulating her feelings.

'Come, Dorothy,' Penny spoke calmly, 'I'll drive you. If you don't mind walking home, Frank?'

He waved his arm in dismissal, which Penny took as a concession. 'Right then, let's go, Dot. If you want to catch that plane.' The two Mrs Rutas took their time to cross the room with all the dignity they could muster. It seemed that Richard's death had somehow united them in their loss. Dotty was leaning on Penny's arm and clutching her hand, trusting and affectionate. Penny's head was inclined towards her.

'I'll be going, too.' Mary rose to her feet. She looked flustered. The scene she had witnessed had reminded her of her turbulent times with Richard and the ever-present Frank guarding him from all evil like a big bad Rottweiler. She remembered fearing Frank on occasions. There had been times when, drunk and high on his Prozac (or whatever he was on to deal with his PTSD), Frank would barge in on her and Richard and sit sulkily in the corner, watching them without a single word. The man was a nasty piece of work, in Mary's experience. She followed Penny and Dotty to the exit. She had come on foot, seeing as she only lived a stone's throw away from Priest's Hole.

Sam accompanied the ladies, saying, 'I'll be in touch with the final formalities.'

Penny opened the front door of the car for Dotty to settle into the front seat, which she did with all the theatrics of huffing, puffing, and wincing in pain.

Penny took the opportunity to talk to Sam in private on the doorstep. 'I need to see you later. The sooner the better, actually. Lunch tomorrow at Sexton's?'

'Sounds good. I'm free.'

'I will call you with the time.' She rushed back to the car. Dotty was by now well installed in her seat, looking impatient. Her door was open, awaiting closing by someone other than her. She wouldn't be seen performing such menial tasks.

Sam flashed a smile at them, 'Thank you for coming. Goodbye.'

'And good riddance,' Frank grumbled from the office, loud enough for them to hear him, bearing in mind that the office window was open to let in some warm summer air.

'The cheek of him! Why don't you just sack him and be done with the sodding bastard?' Dotty snapped back.

'He's grieving,' Penny explained.

'We all are, only in a civilised way –' Dotty continued talking, but Penny shut the car door on her diatribe, and they drove off.

Only Frank and Maggie remained in the office. Sam offered them brandy. He could do with one himself. They both accepted the drink. Sam could tell that Frank had already had one or two. His bloodshot eyes and unequivocally oaky breath testified to that.

'Bloody women – in it for the money. Circling like vultures . . . That's women for you,' Frank grimaced after downing the brandy.

'Mind the presence of the lady, Frank.'

'I don't mean Maggie. Maggie is fine. Aren't you, Maggie?'

'Um –'

'You know who I meant. Those two: the old trout and the whore –'

'Frank, that's enough!' Sam warned.

'They're in it together, you know?'

'What are you on about?'

'It wouldn't surprise me if it was them who did it, in cahoots. Just look at them: chums, hand in hand, plotting. Have you ever seen Penny try to be nice to anyone? Have you? Me neither. But look at her now. Best friend with *Dot*!' He spat out the last word with contempt. 'Did you hear that? *Dot* she calls the old trout. And who was it that brought *Dot* from the airport? Wasn't me. It was young Penny. Oh yes! Buddy-buddy, the two of them. Have been in on it from the start.'

'You aren't being fair, Frank. I know you're struggling with this, but we're all dealing with his death as well as we know how. Penny's lost her husband. Dotty too – he's been part of her life for over thirty years. They have lost Richard too.'

'But I loved him!' Frank thumped the wall with an open hand, and if that wasn't enough to alleviate his pain, he punched it with his fist, repeating with each thrust, 'I loved him! I loved him!' His knuckles began to bleed. He made bloody marks on the wall.

Maggie ran to him and grabbed his arm with both her hands. 'Stop, Frank, sit down, please.' She spoke softly and led him towards a chair. 'Let me see to this.' She peered at his battered hand. 'Samuel, have you got any bandages?'

'Yes, I should somewhere . . .' Sam hurried to the kitchen where he kept his first-aid box. He fetched the whole thing and carried it to his office, all the while considering the possibility of Frank going mad. Sam had always had vague misgivings about the nature of Frank's relationship with Richard. There was something intense about it, something that went, as Richard had put in his Will, *beyond the line of duty.*

'Here,' Sam handed the box to Maggie, who went about bandaging Frank's hand with surprising aptitude. She noticed Sam's expression of surprise, and explained, 'I *am* a teacher. I've done first-aid training, you know.' She smiled at Frank when she finished, 'Done! As good as new.'

'Thanks, Maggie,' he muttered.

'Don't mention it, it's nothing. Just calm down.' She sounded quite authoritative. Teachers have a knack for taking unruly children in hand. Frank was one big child, Sam mused. He was grateful to Maggie for sorting him out.

She took her glass and drank her brandy slowly while she jabbered, 'We all deal with loss differently, you're so right, Sam. Some of us never really get over it. Take Dan Nolan. Poor man . . . Funny you should mention it, though . . . The airport,' she clarified when both Sam and Frank looked up at her quizzically. 'When you said that Penny picked Dotty up from the airport. You see, Dan wouldn't go near an airport – fear of flying, that's why. They let him go, the police. You know that, don't you? Last night. And that was the reason.'

'What was?' Sam had been a brilliant cross-examiner in his

heyday but getting any sense out of Maggie was a tall order even for him.

'His fear of flying, of course. You see, the killer bought the bottle of Tokaji duty free – at an airport. Dan hasn't been anywhere near an airport because he doesn't fly. Too scared. Absolutely petrified of flying. He couldn't have done it. That's why they let him go.'

'Dan Nolan is out?'

'Well, not exactly. Can I have another brandy?' Maggie was only just getting started.

Sam poured her one and one for himself. He decided Frank had already had more than enough. Anyway, he hadn't asked; he was just sitting there, nursing his bandaged hand and listening to Maggie.

'It was on the telly last night. First, Dan gets released, then a journalist asks the wrong kind of question – you know, insinuating something untoward about Leila – that's all Dan needs to smash his face in.' Maggie took a swig and exhaled as if her mouth was on fire. 'Phew, it tastes stronger than the first one! Strange ... Anyway, he was arrested on the spot. Hadn't been out for more than five minutes, poor Dan. The journalist didn't look in the best of shape, either. He was taken to the hospital. Total bedlam!' She knocked back the rest of her brandy without so much as a squint.

'Another one?' Sam offered out of inherent politeness, but he was beginning to wonder if the woman hadn't had too much already.

'Are you trying to get me drunk, Mr Dee?' she slurred. The brandy must have, at last, hit home. 'I feel a bit light-headed ... I'd better go and have a lie down.'

Sam escorted Maggie to her front door, which she had left gaping open. When he looked at her alarmed, searching for an explanation, she chortled, 'I'm safe in Bishops. Everyone is. You can leave your door open. Nothing bad ever happens –' Then she hiccupped and appeared briefly confounded as the realisation dawned on her that something very bad had actually happened and not so long ago.

'I'd keep your doors locked.'

Sam returned to his office to find Frank pouring himself what was left from the brandy bottle. He was already well pickled and Sam worried that he wouldn't be in a state to walk the couple of miles back to Forget-Me-Not. Having had a couple of stiff drinks himself, Sam was unable to drive him. The last thing he wanted was having to put Frank up until they both sobered up.

'So, will you be leaving us soon now that Richard is gone?' he asked, just to say something.

'No. Why would I go and let them win?' Frank was still in a mood for a confrontation. 'I'm not going anywhere, except to the Brecon Beacons, just for a day to clear my head.'

'It's good to take a step back,' Sam agreed.

Frank twisted his lips into an angry scowl. 'I need to find something there. I know where to look. And then, when I'm back, I'll sort this damn mess out.'

'Leave the sorting to the police, that's the only advice I can offer you.'

Frank fixed Sam with an obstinate drunken glare. 'Do you really think the coppers will get Richard's killer! You're such a fool. Let me tell you – they won't. But I will. Believe you me!'

Sam nodded. He believed him. With his eyes glazed with mad fury and his raging, tragic grief, Frank reminded him of Daniel Nolan. He wouldn't be stopped.

Chapter Fifteen

A phone call woke me at the crack of dawn. It was Bishops Primary. They needed a supply teacher for the day. My head felt like an overblown balloon about to burst and skedaddle around the bedroom, bouncing off the walls with a hiss. I was not in a fit state to face a classroom full of rowdy children. I declined in a croaky voice, saying that I had food poisoning. It wasn't far from the truth: it felt like I had been poisoned. I realised it was only a hangover. I must have drunk half a bottle of brandy yesterday. I don't drink brandy. I don't know how to handle it.

I dragged myself to the kitchen and poured a glass of water down my throat. The sensation of having dust, iron filings, and sharp splinters lodged in my tongue and vocal cords subsided by a fraction. I found Alka-Seltzer tablets in my medicine cabinet and dissolved one of them in another glass of water. I drank that too and retreated to bed. I collapsed on my pillows and every conscious thought I'd ever had collapsed with me. I was out.

Four, maybe five hours later, I was forced to get up for a pee. The sun was high in the sky, the birds were singing in the garden, and I was feeling much, much better. I trotted to the bathroom and relieved myself of the two glasses of water I had drunk earlier, washed my hands, brushed my teeth, examined my tongue (no iron shavings or sharp splinters found) and splashed my face with water. I was almost ready to face the world, though I had my doubts whether the world would be that keen on facing me.

I heard noises from the other side of the wall.

Apart from the hum of water running in the shower, I heard whistling. With some difficulty I identified the tune as *Ode to Joy*. When the whistling ceased, a poor vocal rendition of *Hit Me with Your Rhythm Stick* followed. That was interspersed with a rich variety of sounds: banging, clanking, an occasional curse, the faint padding of wet feet on the floor, and a few coughs. It sounded like my neighbour was grooming himself.

Let me explain the vivid sound effects. Our respective bathrooms came about as a result of dividing the original huge one into two. Unlike the external walls of Priest's Hole, which are thick and impenetrable medieval constructions made to last, the new internal divisions are paper thin. Nowadays we don't care as much about enduring into eternity as they used to in the olden days. So, without straining my ears, I can often hear my neighbour sing, splash water, run the tap, and play with his rubber duck in the bath.

From the jolly sound effects Samuel was producing, I concluded that he was getting ready for a date. A date with Penny Ruta.

My curiosity had been aroused when I'd heard them discuss meeting for lunch in Sexton's. I would have never put Samuel and Penny together, especially because of Alice. Her presence was a clear indication that Samuel had not got over her death, that he was clinging on to her and that he definitely wasn't ready for anyone else to take her place. Only the dead who have unfinished business here in life or whose relatives can't let them go linger about. Most of them skip off merrily into the afterlife. Alice was lingering. I was convinced it was because of Samuel – he still needed her. She had no heart to abandon him. So, it did surprise me to see him go for Penny hook, line and sinker. But then again, Penny had this effect on men: she only needed to click her fingers and there they were – drooling at her feet. That applied to all men with red-hot blood cursing through their veins, including my neighbour.

It had also occurred to me that Penny and Samuel must have known each other long before Samuel had moved to Bishops Well, next door to me. What if . . . Well, I didn't want to make wanton accusations, but what if . . . I mean, how well did I know Samuel

Dee? I had only known the man for six months, and very superficially at that. Who was he really? Could *he* have been involved in murder . . . As for Penny Ruta, she was what one would refer to as a *cold fish* – she was capable of anything, I thought. Just the way she was behaving - I had not seen her shed a single tear. And when I cast my mind back to that eventful birthday bash, I recalled vividly how cool and unperturbed she had been acting. As if Richard's death had not surprised her in the least. As if she had been waiting for it.

I decided to engage in a spot of sleuthing. I would follow Mr Dee and I would listen in on their conspiracy.

I had a quick shower – I mean, really quick. I hadn't even touched the soap. When I was drying, I looked out of the window to see Mr Dee emerge from his house, wearing a very elegant shirt and a pair of suit trousers, fumes of expensive aftershave trailing behind him and rising to my nostrils. He ran his fingers through his hair and swept a speck of dust from his shoulder. He jumped into his Jag and drove off.

I threw on the first dress that peered at me from the wardrobe and grabbed the car key from the ashtray in the hallway on my way out. I skidded into the garage, jumped into my Hyundai. That's all I can afford. Well, actually that's not *entirely* true, but that's what I keep telling myself. I could of course buy a fancy four-wheel drive and, like everyone else in the West Country, bully small car owners in car parks, narrow country lanes, and on single-file bridges, but I shan't do that. Firstly, because I'm attached to my little car and I can't imagine she could survive without me in the big bad world out there – she'd probably be scrapped the moment I turned my back on her. Secondly, because although I do have money from the sale of the other half of Priest's Hole to Samuel, I have to be careful how I spend it. After all, I am one of those bottom-of-the-ladder types, with no secure income nor any reliable prospects. I reside in a small town with no industries, populated by people who look and act like millionaires but live on a shoestring, waiting patiently for some rich relative to die and remember them in the will. That even applies to the blue-bloods, which pleasing fact makes us all equal. Of course, we have new money in Bishops – celebrities such as Richard Ruta (now unfortunately no longer amongst us), or Daryl Luntz, the eminent horror writer – but they aren't really *true* Bishopians. They are passers-by, and will remain so at least until the third generation. But I might have gone off on a tangent, mightn't I?

Back to my surveillance effort. I reversed unassisted, taking off the right-wing mirror against the gate and bumping off a few daffodils that guarded the boundary of our shared driveway. I sped after my suspect, heading for Sexton's Canning where I knew the meeting was to take place.

Sexton's Canning isn't a metropolis, though it may fancy itself as such. Certainly, the introduction of traffic lights and roundabouts to replace every old, perfectly efficient crossroads, is causing metropolitan-sized traffic jams whatever the time of day or night. It may boast a disproportionately large number of restaurants, cafés, and tearooms, but the closure of three theatres and the opening of five new superstores testifies to the direction in which Sexton's is heading – an ultimate cultural demise. That's fine, because Bishops Well is waiting in the wings, ready and willing to take over the reins. Despite the ambitious *urban improvements*, Sexton's Canning remains just a town (we have built no cities in Wiltshire since the thirteenth century, and we want to keep it this way.).

That day, the town happened to be overwhelmed with people eating out. Every eatery was crawling with customers, some queuing at the doors. I found Samuel's car parked in the market square. That wasn't hard – Samuel had failed to put up the roof and a couple of urchins had climbed into the driver's seat, screeching with joy. As a teacher I contemplated approaching the hoodlums to check what they were doing out in the streets on a normal school day. But there was no time and I had more pressing matters on my mind: finding the two conspirators.

The problem was I didn't know in which of the many restaurants they would be dining. I went on a wild goose chase, going from restaurant to restaurant, peering through windows, crouching behind bars, and creeping behind other customers, using them as my invisibility shield.

It was odd, I noted in passing, how strangely people were looking at me despite my efforts to remain invisible. Critical, bemused looks with raised eyebrows and suppressed giggles flew around me. I inspected myself to discover that I was wearing my Christmas dress featuring Rudolph the red-nosed reindeer. And if that wasn't enough to attract unwanted attention, I had matched that with my house slippers. I had to hurry – any minute now someone would call an ambulance and I would be taken to the nearest mental asylum.

I doubled my efforts, and I was rewarded. In a small basement Italian restaurant I saw them. A wave of blessed relief washed over me. To their left, behind a giant Swiss cheese plant, was a small table pressed against the wall in the corner. It was empty. I nipped in and perched there, hiding behind the salt and pepper grinders and screening my face with my hand. I watched them with bated breath. Samuel, I discovered, was having a seafood risotto, and Penny, a lettuce leaf with a glass of water. That's what kept her stomach flat, I thought resentfully. She was gorgeous. Her skin was peachy and not a single strand of her long raven hair was out of place. Was she even human, I pondered further, just look at her bust! No amount of mud baths, electric shocks, and silicone would achieve that bushy-tailed pertness for me. Apart from being gorgeous, she was now also rich and famous, which in this combination was a crime against humanity. Not that I would hold it against her.

'The sixteenth of July. The dust will've settled by then. They suggested it, and I said I'd run it by you,' Samuel was telling her. I was second-guessing who *they* were. 'Are you happy with it?'

'Does that give us enough time?'

'I should think so. It's really up to –'

I could not hear the rest of the sentence. 'Madam! I am afraid this table is booked! Look, a reservation card – here!' A waiter was looming over me, waving a bit of card which he snatched from my table. He appeared deeply offended by this irregularity. Two people peered at me from behind him. They looked indignant too. I guessed my table was booked in their name.

'Fine, fine ...' I whispered under my cupped hand, trying to wriggle out of the seat without being noticed. 'I only just ... just sat here to catch my breath. I'm going, I'm going ... Take it easy, will you?'

'You must wait to be seated! Over there!' he thrust his finger towards the door.

'No, thank you. I was just leaving anyway,' I hissed. He was beginning to annoy me with his put-on Italian accent and loud manner. I could bet he'd never been to Italy.

'Maggie?! Is that you? Maggie!'

It was Samuel. He was peering at me, his face wedged between two leaves of the Swiss cheese plant.

Of course, they saw me. No thanks to the phoney waiter!

'Oh, hello! I didn't see you there!' I acted as surprised as they were.

'What is it? A mix-up with a table?'

'Um ...'

Penny regarded with suspicion Rudolph the red-nosed reindeer on my dress. I slapped the flat of my hand on his nose, trying to cover as much as possible to obscure the full picture. The people who had apparently booked *my* table, sat there glaring at us. *Us* being myself and Rudolph.

Sam said, 'Why don't you join us?' He waved to the waiter. 'Can we have another chair, please!'

'I couldn't possibly ...' I mumbled, realising it was the same waiter who had just showed me the door.

He brought the chair and pushed it under my backside, an expression of wounded dignity on his face. 'Here you are, madam. Would you like to see the menu?'

I ordered the soup of the day, whatever it was, just to get rid of him.

'I was just a .... I was meeting a friend,' I rambled, 'a friend who didn't turn up.'

'We were just discussing Richard's funeral arrangements.'

'Oh, that . . .'

'As you know, to honour Richard's and his mother's wishes, it'll be held in Poland.'

'Yes . . .'

'The sixteenth of July in the village of Katynice. That's where Richard was born.'

'Ah, how quaint!' I exclaimed, idiotically.

Penny looked me up and down, 'Are you all right, Maggie? You look rather flushed.'

'Oh yes! I'm as right as rain. I mean, just a bit peeved about my friend not turning up.'

'Who were you meeting?'

That took me aback. I couldn't think fast enough of a name. 'Who, me?'

Now they both looked seriously concerned for my mental stability. Luckily for me, my soup had arrived. It was my least favourite flavour: tomato. It didn't matter one bit that the tomatoes were supposedly sun-dried under the skies of Tuscany. Still, it was a welcome distraction. The three of us ate in silence for a few minutes.

Penny said, 'Would you believe that I've never been there?'

'Where? Tuscany?' I wasn't at my most quick-witted that day.

'To Poland, to the village where Richard was born. I never met his family. Isn't that odd?'

'Richard had a peculiar attitude to his homeland,' Samuel said. I had no idea what he meant by that, but Penny nodded in agreement.

'It will be awkward meeting his family now, under these circumstances.'

'We can travel there together. There might be quite a few of us. I'll let people know, of course. I'll be putting an obituary in the papers, with the date and the place.'

'Thank you for taking care of everything, Sam,' Penny gazed at him. 'I don't know what I'd do without you.'

'Don't mention it. I'm just doing my job.'

'Will you be going, Maggie?' Penny turned her attention to me.

'Oh, I don't think so. I didn't know him that well. But my father might. He and Richard used to sit on the parish council together. I'll tell him.'

None of us wanted to look at the dessert menu. I just wanted to go home and get out of my stupid dress. I felt like such an idiot, stalking a man's widow and his lawyer as they were busy making funeral arrangements. But then, as we were leaving, about to go our separate ways, Penny said, 'I'll see you tomorrow, Sam. At yours,' and kissed him on the cheek.

My suspicions were instantly re-ignited.

Chapter Sixteen

An extraordinary AA meeting was called for that same evening. We were going to celebrate Richard's generous bequest with cakes and champagne, and to discuss how we would spend it. I was looking forward to the meeting for two reasons.

One: I was genuinely excited at the prospect of getting to the bottom of Bishops Swamp. The swamp is a part of Sexton's Wood which is owned by Lord Weston-Jones. It lies on the south-eastern periphery of Bishops Well. It borders the vast stretch of Salisbury Plain which houses the Army. Being this close to a military target and covered in standing water for the better part of the year, the swamps are un-developable. They are also inaccessible to vehicular traffic. But they are great for rambling and for bird-watching. Wildlife flourishes there: nocturnal badgers, elusive otters, barn owls (despite the absence of barns; I suspect the species has adapted and lives in the rafters of the army barracks), rare specimens of protected bats, cute dormice, deer, and plenty – and I mean it – *plenty* of mosquitoes. Amongst all that wilderness hides an ancient Celtic village, dating back to the Bronze Age. We have found historical reports of the existence of the village in the form of Roman records referring to the village in topographical descriptions and maps. They are reliable on their own, of course, but I have further evidence to hand. Evidence which I cannot share with my fellow archaeologists, because my proof is supernatural. On my walks around the swamps, I frequently encounter a presence. It is quite feeble, perhaps because it is so ancient. I think that it is a she.

It – she – sits there, on a fallen tree trunk overgrown with moss and crawling with beetles. She just sits and looks out into the swamps. I can't imagine she is held here on earth by anybody alive (any people she knew in her lifetime must be long, long dead), so my guess is that she has some unfinished business that she needs to attend to before she finally crosses over. Fancy hanging around a mosquito-infested bog for millennia! Then again, I don't suppose the Dead view time the same way that we do.

So, that was my first reason. I wanted those swamps dried, I wanted those Celts found, I wanted that presence put to rest. That's what she wanted too.

Two: I had an ulterior motive, unrelated to the swamps. I wanted to share my suspicions about Penny Ruta with Michael Almond in the hope that he may pass them on to DI Marsh. I hoped to plant a small seed of doubt about the merry widow, and what she was getting up to.

We were all to bring cakes or beverages to the meeting. I am not what you would call *handy* in the kitchen, but I made an effort. I baked half a dozen blueberry muffins from a ready-mix pack. Then I promptly ate three of them. They were only baby muffins really, I justified my gluttony to my inner voice of conscience that was nagging at me. Truth be told, I always eat when I am nervous or excited. Some people lose their appetite altogether and others scoff everything within reach when stress descends upon them. I am in the latter category.

Feeling rather bloated and uncomfortable, I shed my Christmas outfit and squeezed into a pair of pale blue skinny jeans and a tight plain T-shirt. I checked myself in the mirror to discover to my horror that the Christmas theme was still upon me. Looking at my profile, I could swear I was seeing a fat snowman showing no intention of melting. My stomach bulging out and my protruding backside gave the impression of a perfectly round snowball, with the smaller snowballs of my breasts resting upon it. I couldn't let James Weston-Jones see me in this state. I quickly changed from the tight T-shirt to a loose blouse that mercifully spilled over my curves like a waterfall over boulders.

When I arrived at the Community Hall, I was confronted with the temptation of more cakes. I resisted. Cherie proposed a toast to our unexpected windfall and we drank to it happily. Another toast was made to the memory of Richard Ruta, our benefactor, may he rest in peace. Since James had brought a whole crate of decent French champagne, we couldn't allow it to go to waste, so we drank a few more toasts to whatever cause tickled our fancy. We were tipsy in no time and in an excellent mood all round. A loose and dis-jointed discussion followed, minuted by Dr Flynn. I truly doubt that he could make any sense of our drunkenly lisped proposals and counter-proposals about the best ways of spending our inheritance. Without Michael present, we didn't have the required quorum to make any capital-spending decisions anyway. Suffice to say, we soon decided to put off the rest of our deliberations to the day after the money was safely in the Association's bank account, and to finish what was left of the champagne. And the cakes. By this time, my inhibitions were so relaxed that I allowed myself two slices of Vanes-sa's carrot cake. It had a yoghurt-based substitute for icing and, naturally, plenty of carrot, so it wasn't hard to convince myself that I was in fact practising what one calls *healthy eating* at its healthiest.

'What was Alec thinking, sending his men over to interrogate my Henry?' I heard Vera grill Vanessa. 'He'd hardly set foot across the threshold when . . . what's his name?'

'DS Webber?' Vanessa offered meekly.

'Yes, him! He barged in like he owned the place! And he called himself a DI, come to think.'

'He is an acting DI, in charge of Richard's murder case.'

'Yes, I know, but what's that to do with Henry?'

'Well, he's looking at everybody who was at that party.'

'You were there, Maggie,' Vera turned to me sharply and rounded on me with her penetrating eyes, 'Did he interrogate you?'

I was intrigued. I said, 'No, not me. I wish, ha! What was he interrogating Henry about?'

'Everything! Just baseless – stuff!' It was an evasive answer which told me that Vera didn't know anything. They had probably shut themselves in Henry's study and kept her out of it. I felt for Vera: not knowing and having to guess can be torture.

'Why was Henry interrogated?' I addressed Vanessa directly. 'Vera needs to know. Look at the state she's in. And it's probably nothing. If only someone would tell her! If you know, Vanessa darling, just put poor Vera out of her misery and tell her –'

'For crying out loud!' Vera finished my sentence for me. She did look like a tortured soul.

Vanessa sighed, reluctant, thinking of an excuse to evade this Spanish Inquisition, but by this time everyone's eyes were on her. She was trapped. She said, 'Well, then . . . It's nothing serious, from what little I know. They're just talking to everyone who travelled abroad two weeks before the party – anyone who had the opportunity to buy that wine, duty free. That's all. They have to cover all their bases.'

'But Henry! Of all people!' Vera was appalled. 'He's an outstanding pillar of our commu –'

'He might be, but he went to Paris . . . you know, for that summit – agricultural, or something. Anyway, that was two weeks before the party. You have no idea how upset Alec is about this whole thing! Bishops is our home! Henry is his friend! But he can't be seen . . . Oh, it's just awful! Awful! I wish it was over!' This was all too much for poor Vanessa. She burst into tears.

We crowded around her to give her a gentle back rub and to hold her hand, and to be generally supportive and understanding, while Vera sat sulkily in the background, squawking something about *this simply not being on* and *people forgetting who the real injured party here was*.

I had to agree with her. Henry wasn't the only person who travelled abroad. Dotty came all the way from the States, for example. This had to be brought to the investigating officer's attention. Though I was a bit tipsy and not in the best of shape to make myself clear, I decided to pay Michael Almond, and DI Marsh, a home visit.

I staggered along the unevenly cobbled Market Street, which offers no pavement and no street lighting. I twisted my ankle twice and yelped in pain. I nearly dropped the Tupperware container holding my three freshly baked muffins with which I intended to bribe DI Marsh and make her listen to what I had to say. The fact that my balance was affected by the amount of alcohol I had consumed was not helpful to my progress. Thankfully, Michael lives on the corner of Market Street and Fields Pass (which isn't a street by any stretch of the imagination, just a rutted dirt road). I didn't have to go far.

I seized the door knocker. A deep and menacing bark, of the large-dog variety, gave me an almighty shock. I never knew Michael had a hound. I heard a commotion behind the door, someone telling the beast to *settle down and be a good boy*. There was more shuffling and finally Michael opened the door.

'Maggie? Straight from the AA meeting, I'm guessing?' He appeared underwhelmed at the sight of me. 'What brings you here?'

I pressed my Tupperware container into his hands. 'If the mountain won't go to Muhammad then Muhammad must come to the mountain.'

He looked puzzled.

'You weren't at the meeting,' I gave him a hint.

'I couldn't, I'm afraid.'

'Don't worry, I'm here now and I can fill you in.'

He let me in without much enthusiasm and led me to the lounge. DI Marsh – Gillian – was half-reclined on the sofa with the hound lying at her feet. It growled at me, suspicious of my intentions. Dogs, apparently, can read our minds. I had to explain myself.

'Here, I brought you some nourishment,' I retrieved my Tupperware container from Michael and handed it to Gillian. 'Freshly baked muffins. Blueberry. I hope you like them, blueberries are so healthy ... To be perfectly honest, I'm here to see you, DI Marsh. About Richard's murder and the wine.'

She grabbed the box and helped herself to a muffin. 'Thanks.'

Michael began to protest, 'I'm sorry, Maggie, as much as we're grateful for the cakes –'

'They aren't for you, Almond,' Gillian told him. Then she spoke to me, 'Come in, sit down.'

A large tabby cat, with half of his left ear missing, descended from the windowsill and sat in the chair, exactly where I was supposed to sit.

'I prefer to stand.' I wobbled on my feet and had to reassure myself, 'I can stand. I just need to tell you about Penny Ruta. You see, you've been interviewing people who had accessed duty free shops at airports, like Henry Hopps-Wood - you know, to buy that bottle of Hungarian wine –'

'How do you know that?'

I had no chance – thankfully – to answer that because Michael decided to interject rather forcibly, 'I am sorry, Maggie, but I must ask you to leave. Gillian isn't involved in investigating Richard Ruta's murder case. She is unwell. She needs rest. You'll have to speak to DI Webber.'

'But I don't know DI Webber!'

'You don't know Gillian either!'

'Michael, since she's already here . . . Come on, let her catch her breath. Let's be civil. I won't fall apart. Get her a cup of tea. I could do with one too. The muffins are delicious.'

'Thanks! One sugar for me,' I smiled innocently.

He left. The cat followed him, but the dog stayed put. I took a seat in the chair.

'So, what is it about the Hungarian wine that you want to tell me?' Gillian sat up, looking intrigued. I must say that as much as she was still quite tiny and skinny, she looked much healthier than the day we had sat together in Richard's library and she fainted on me. She had a hint of colour in her cheeks and her eyes were shiny.

I spoke quickly before Michael came back, 'You see, I have grave concerns about Penny. It is something that Frank said . . . Anyway, Penny went to the airport. To collect Dotty – when Dotty arrived from the States. I mean, they could've planned it together, and Dotty could've bought the wine, and Penny could've . . . I mean, there is something about Penny Ruta that is, well . . . disingenuous.

A grieving widow, but ... well, she's all over Samuel Dee. My neighbour. He was Richard's lawyer, and she's trying something with him — she wants something from him! I have a feeling about her, and I'm hardly ever wrong.' I don't know why I said that. Probably, I was just desperate for her to take me seriously. 'Don't you think it's worth checking out, because —'

'We have checked that out,' DI Marsh interrupted me. 'Do you think we would've let Dorothy leave the country if we weren't satisfied that she had nothing to do with Richard Ruta's death?'

'How can you be sure? I mean —'

'We can. We are. Dorothy arrived at Heathrow and we now know that the Tokaji was purchased at a particular duty-free shop at Charles de Gaulle Airport. She couldn't have bought it. Henry Hopps-Wood, on the other hand ... We're going through the shop's CCTV footage —'

'You promised me you'd stay away from the case!' Michael stood in the doorway with a tray full of crockery clanking in his hands. He was shaking with anger. 'You promised, Gillian! How's Webber keeping you updated? I've got your phone! How are you communicating? I've had enough —'

I stood up, feeling rather like an earthworm about to be trodden on. This wasn't my battle. 'Um, I've changed my mind. About the tea. I'd better leave you to it.' And I scuttled out sheepishly, leaving DI Marsh to fend for herself.

Chapter Seventeen

Sam paced up and down his office, waiting for Penny. She was late. He looked out of the window, but all he found was Maggie. She had been there all morning, down on her knees, rearranging dead daffodils which some reckless driver had mowed down. The tyre marks were imprinted in the flower bed. Maggie was wielding a trowel with the expertise of a seasoned gardener. Next to her stood a wheelbarrow with a bagful of compost and a tray full of seedlings. Maggie was wearing a straw hat and a pair of dungarees, both tattered and shapeless. But despite her poor dress sense – or maybe because of it – there was something endearing about the woman. She exuded warmth and familiarity, as if she had known Sam for a long time, but what she knew was only the best bits.

Penny arrived in Richard's Bentley and sounded the horn to get Maggie to remove her wheelbarrow from the driveway. Maggie jumped to her feet and clutched her chest. Her straw hat fell to the ground. She had been engrossed in her daffodils and had not seen Penny coming.

Penny waved, smiling behind her bumble-bee sunglasses, 'Sorry, darling! Did I give you a fright?'

Maggie shaded her eyes, 'You bloody well did!'

'Would you move your contraption, please?' Penny pointed to the wheelbarrow.

'It's a wheelbarrow.'

'Yes, darling, of course it is. Could you move it? I'm late.'

'Late for your appointment with Samuel?' Maggie picked up her hat and planted it on her head. She stood in front of the Bentley, hands on hips, blocking the entrance.

'Yes.'

'I see . . .' Maggie wiped her brow. 'What is it about?'

Penny lowered her sunglasses. 'The wheelbarrow? Please.'

'Oh!' Maggie pushed the thing onto her side of the driveway.

Penny drove through and parked right by Sam's doorstep. It had occurred to him that she might have been the reckless driver who had destroyed Maggie's daffodils in the first place. She emerged from her car, flexing her beautifully shaped calves. She was dressed in black – this was the first time Sam had seen her wear black since Richard's death. Her hair shone in the sunlight. She was a handsome woman – one of those you just look at and admire but have no desire to touch. On the other side of the driveway stood Maggie Kaye, not much to look at, but by golly, you would love to get your hands on her and bury yourself in her body. She was all curves and warm flesh . . .

Sam caught himself by surprise with this covetous musing. It had been a long time since he had lusted after a woman.

'Do you want to pop over for a cuppa, after you're done with Samuel?' Maggie asked Penny in a surprisingly conciliatory tone.

'I'd love to, darling, but I'm in such a rush! So much to do before I go back to London. But thanks, Maggie.'

'You're off to London, then?'

'Yes, first thing on Friday. Having supper with Edith and my new publisher. We've finally signed the contract for *Life with a Legend*.'

'Congratulations.'

Penny waved her hand dismissively, 'It wasn't a question of getting a contract – it was a question of how much. The advance has gone up in recent weeks.'

'I can imagine.' Maggie picked up the handles of her wheelbarrow and pushed it, squeaking and squealing, back to her flower bed by the gate.

Penny rang the bell.

Samuel showed her to his office, offered her a drink and she accepted a glass of water. She took off her sunglasses. Her eyes were red and swollen with heavy bags underneath. Without the shield of her black sunglasses, she appeared sad and vulnerable. Sam considered telling her that he knew how she felt, he too had lost someone he loved more than anything in this world, but Penny wasn't the kind of woman who would want to hear that. She had come to him with the sole purpose of executing her Last Will. She wanted to hear the wording of it, as per their provisional discussion yesterday.

Sam took the draft document out of his cabinet drawer. As he worked only part-time, his hours limited to whenever he felt like working, he did not employ a secretary. When he had started practising in the capacity of notary public in Bishops Well, he had never expected to have any real work to do. It was just a way of pretending that he still had a professional life.

'Right, so to recap, in the event of your death, all your savings, bonds and investments are to go to Daniel Nolan and his heirs. Any future income from your estate, royalties from your plays, and book sales will be handled by the Penny Ruta Trust with your sister and parents as joint beneficiaries and me as the Trust executor.'

Penny nodded. 'You got it, darling.'

'OK, I will read it out to you. Ask, if there's anything that doesn't make sense and I'll explain it to you.' Samuel put on his reading glasses and slowly read the Will out to her, word by word. It wasn't a long document to peruse, considering its straightforward content.

'Everything correct?'

'Yes.'

'Anything unclear.'

'No, darling. Let's sign the damn thing.'

'Your signature will need to be witnessed. I'll just pop out and see if Maggie would do it. That'd be the quickest.'

'Maggie?' Penny appeared hesitant, but then she rolled her eyes and sighed. 'She is such a nosy parker, but it's just a signature, isn't it?'

'We won't be reading it to her, no.'

'Bring her in.'

Sam hurried out to find Maggie packing up her wheelbarrow, a row of tight-budded pansies installed alongside the driveway. She gave him an unsurprised sideways glance and returned to admiring her plants. 'I must give them a chance to take root this time,' she said mysteriously.

'They're lovely. Um, would you be so kind as to take a minute to step inside my office in order to witness Penny sign a document?'

'Oh?' Maggie looked interested, but played hard to get. 'What sort of document?'

'Her Will.'

'Oh ... her Will. A bit young to be thinking of dying, but then she's a wealthy woman. I can see where she's coming from. I don't have a Will, but then I don't need one. Not much to pass on ...'

'Would you, then?'

'Yes, yes, of course.' Maggie followed him to the office. She took off her wellies in the porch and hung her straw hat on the hook. She was taking her time. She wiped her hands, checked that her hair was neatly bundled up in the bun on top of her head (which it wasn't), and rubbed her forehead, leaving a smudge of soil on it. 'Right, let's do the witnessing.'

'Thank you for doing this, Maggie.' Penny smiled at her as she initialled the first page and deposited her signature on the second. She handed the pen to Maggie, 'Your turn, darling.'

Maggie took the pen and the Will. She turned the page to catch a glimpse of the wording. Sam put his finger at the bottom corner, obscuring the paper with his arm, 'Initial here, please, Maggie.'

She did.

Then, he turned to page two, which revealed nothing of Penny's actual Will. It was just the last formal paragraph with the date and place, and space for signing. 'Sign here in full, Maggie. Print your name and add your address here.' Sam was guiding her through the process. She obliged. She also managed to leave a dirty thumbprint on the page.

113

'Sorry about that!'

'That's fine. It won't invalidate the Will. Well, thank you,' Sam smiled. 'That's all. You can return to your flowers.'

Maggie smiled back. She had a pleasant, sunny smile. 'I'm done with the flowers. Having that tea now, Penny. You're still invited.'

'Oh, yes. Thanks, Maggie. I wish I could.'

Reluctant to leave, Maggie headed for the exit. She closed the door behind her very slowly. Sam could hear her on the porch, picking up her hat and shaking the soil out of her wellies. She banged them against the step, each a couple of times. Finally, he saw her leave and cross the courtyard to her front door. He closed the window.

Penny was still sitting comfortably in the chair, showing no intention of leaving. She said, 'You're probably wondering why I'd want to give anything to Dan Nolan – the man who hated my husband with every fibre of his body?'

'No, not really. It's none of my business. I just make sure your Will meets the legal requirements,' Sam assured her, though deep down, he was curious as hell.

'Good,' Penny said. 'There's one more thing I'd like to leave with you for safekeeping.' She took a USB stick out of her pocket. She put it on the desk and pushed it towards Sam. 'It's only to be opened and made public after I'm dead. Can you hold on to it in your ... you know ... professional capacity?'

'Yes, of course. I'll prepare relevant paperwork, a type of addendum to your Will, to cover this stipulation.'

'Oh, I should've mentioned it earlier!'

'It would've made things simpler, but don't worry. I'll draw up the codicil and call you to come and sign it. Won't take long.'

'Tomorrow, if you can. Then I'm off to London.'

'I'll have it ready by tomorrow.'

'Thank you, Sam, for everything. You've been a good friend.'

Sam walked with her to her car – Richard's car. He still thought of it as *Richard's Bentley*. It would take a while to realign his thinking to reality. Penny kissed him on the cheek. She smelled exotic and spicy. She slid her bumble-bee sunglasses down her nose.

'I still can't believe he's dead,' she whispered, 'I expect him to walk in from the clubhouse, a bit tipsy, smelling of cigars and whisky. I miss him.'

'Me too.'

She started the engine and reversed carefully, not to spoil Maggie's freshly planted flower beds. Sam stood in the driveway, waving. Somehow, this moment felt final. He shook that sensation off with a shrug and turned back.

Maggie leant out of her kitchen window. 'Would you like to pop over for a cup of tea? I'm making muffins – fresh from the oven. They just need ten minutes.'

'That'd be grand, Maggie. I'll lock up and be there in a jiffy!' He realised of course that Maggie would be on a fishing expedition, grilling him for details of Penny's Will, but he was prepared to take that inconvenience. He could do with a nice cuppa.

'You don't have to lock up – not in Bishops,' Maggie informed him.

'Still, I'll feel better if I do.'

Chapter Eighteen

My muffins were magnificent, Samuel complimented me. I suggested that he had another one (or else I would end up having them all for supper – or should I say *in addition to* supper). He took the second muffin, weighed it in his hand briefly, and finally bit into it. Crumbs fluttered and settled in his lap. I could see the appreciation in his eyes. I poured more tea for both of us and nibbled on my muffin like a lady while he devoured his.

'I was going to take a look at your bike,' he said. 'Should we do it now?'

I could do with the bike being operational. I don't like driving when I could cycle.

'Are you sure now's a good time?'

'As good as any.'

We – he, actually – began to battle with the clutter in the shed to pull the bike out of it. A box with old rusty screws and nails got caught by the handlebar and tumbled to the floor. Screws rained on our feet. Samuel's feet.

He jumped up and collided with a shelf, nearly impaling himself on a pair of secateurs. He produced a traumatised look.

'Sorry . . . are you all right?' I observed that something had cut into Samuel's temple. There was blood. Well, it was only a little cut but it bled a lot.

'Fine, it's nothing.' He felt the cut and stared in horror at his bloodied finger. He wiped it on his trousers.

'I must tidy this shed . . . Um . . . I could fetch you a plaster,' I volunteered, peering gingerly in the direction of his dead wife, Alice. She got up from the garden bench and glided towards us. She halted between him and me as if she wanted to shield him from danger (the danger being me). She reached out to him, her fingers hovering over his face, unable to touch it.

'Sorry,' I repeated, directing my apology to her rather than to him.

'It's nothing. Don't worry, Maggie. And I'm allergic to plasters, I'm afraid.' He was saying that as he flipped the bike upside down and placed it on the ground with its wheels spinning aimlessly in the air. It was the front wheel that looked the worse for wear.

'Have you got a spanner?'

'Yes, loads of spanners. Somewhere in the shed ...' I realised I would be sending the man to his certain death if I let him into that shed again. 'I'll get it. I know where it is!' I jumped ahead of him. I was almost certain that I knew what a spanner looked like. There was my grandad's ancient toolbox on the floor: blackened metal, with all those compartments and drawers. A spanner of some sort was bound to live there. I grabbed the box and dragged it out, 'Here we are! There'll be a spanner there – somewhere in one of those drawers.'

There was! Alice returned to the bench and sat there, watching the bees. I remained at hand, by Samuel's side. I stood guard over him as he dismantled the chain and took out the wheel. To me, it looked irreparably knackered, but he went about hammering it and straightening the spokes until it resembled a circular shape again.

'Fingers crossed, there's no puncture. Let's pump it up,' he said and I crossed my fingers. I had no idea where the bicycle pump could be found.

Sam pulled the bicycle pump from a bracket hiding on the frame of my bicycle. So that's where it was! He pumped the tyre, felt it and declared that the thing was as good as new. He reassembled my bike and pushed it, with all due care, back into the shed. He shut the door on it. We could hear a few items plummet from the shelves. He turned to me and smiled. 'All done!'

He looked as if he had just returned from the trenches of the

Somme. His face was flushed red, his hair caked with sweat and blood; a ribbon of drying blood snaked from the cut on his temple, down towards his eye, from where it spread using the network of his wrinkles as channels.

'Oh my! You look awful,' I told him. 'I can't let you go until your face ... I need to wash this wound,' I pointed to his bleeding temple.

'Is it that bad?'

'Come in, I'll show you.'

In the bathroom, I put him in front of the mirror while I looked for a clean cloth and the antiseptic spray. I could hear him gasp.

'It's all right, it's only superficial,' I assured him. I swiped a wet cloth over the rivulet of blood on his cheek. He winced. I sprayed the antiseptic directly on the cut. He whimpered.

'OK, all done!' I was happy with my handiwork. 'I think we both deserve a stiff drink. Tea won't do.'

We sat in my lounge with a bottle of port. The conversation wasn't going anywhere as he resisted my line of questioning. I switched on the telly as the news was about to start. And there it was:

The police have now released CCTV footage of a woman they seek to interview as a person of interest in the Richard Ruta murder investigation. It is believed that the woman purchased a bottle of wine which was used to poison the famous film director at his birthday party in his home in Wiltshire. The wine was purchased from a duty-free shop at Charles de Gaulle Airport, Paris on May, 3rd. The police call for any witnesses or anyone who may have information about the identity of this woman and about her whereabouts. Please contact Sexton's Canning Constabulary or call ...

The footage – like all CCTV footage – was fuzzy and unclear. The woman appeared of average height and medium build, most likely in her late forties or early fifties judging by the style of her clothes and how she moved. She had shoulder-length wavy blonde hair, but that meant nothing as it could have been a wig. Most of the footage featured the top of her head and her back since the camera was mounted on the ceiling. She paid cash. Another camera caught her again outside the shop, but she soon blended in with the crowd and disappeared from sight.

'It could be anyone,' I said.

'But it's a start. They will find her sooner or later. They've got cameras at every street corner nowadays.'

'Let's hope they do.' I agreed.

'A top-up?' He was holding the bottle of port.

I gave him my glass to refill.

'Do you think what I think?' I said.

'And what are you thinking, Maggie?' He arched his left eyebrow in an expression of amusement.

'I think that woman is someone we know very well. She is heavily made-up, a wig, all that. She could be me, or Vera, or Mary, or Penny for that matter. I mean, take Penny. She stands to benefit the most from Richard's death. She inherited a fortune, her book will sell like hot cakes, and . . . what do you think?' I was hoping the port had loosened his tongue and he would at last start talking.

'I really don't think her appearance could've been altered beyond recognition. Don't forget, the mystery woman was at an international airport, her passport photo would've been scrutinised by an Immigration Officer.'

'She might have been travelling on false papers or she could've put on her disguise after that, in the toilet, or somewhere quiet.' I argued, pretty lucidly, if I say so myself. Then another thought occurred to me. I shared it with Samuel, 'That CCTV footage was from Paris, but she must've arrived in the UK, to give the wine to Richard. He didn't go abroad, so she came here. Would she have come via Heathrow, or Bristol, or maybe even by Eurostar? The cops need look for her in all of those places, you know.'

Samuel gazed at me, clearly inspired. He said, 'You may have something there, Maggie! I seem to remember that Richard was seeing someone in Bristol – an old friend, he said, *a blast from the past . . .*'

I endured Samuel's babbling out of politeness and because I was basking in him admitting that I was on to something.

'That was the same day that Dotty arrived from the States – two weeks before the party. Frank and I assumed that he was talking about Dotty and that he'd got the times and the airports muddled up. But what if he didn't? What if it was a different woman altogether – a different blast from a different past?'

He wasn't off on a tangent, after all, I concluded, and started listening even though I wasn't entirely happy that Penny seemed to be slipping through my net.

'I'm positive it was the third of May, which would coincide with the date that woman bought the wine in Paris. Hmm ... It could be unrelated, though. He never said he was picking someone up from the airport, but what if that was precisely the case? I need to call Alec. We may be on to something, Maggie!' He whipped out his phone and scrolled down to Alec Scarfe's private number.

'Alec, it's Sam Dee. Yes ... fine, thanks. Listen, I need to share something with you. It may be important. We've just been watching the News ...Yes, we – Maggie and I.' Samuel peered at me and nodded with a smile. As he listened to Alec's reply, his face darkened. He clearly didn't like what Alec was saying, and judging by Samuel's answer, neither did I: 'No, Alec, it isn't any of Maggie's fancies. It's hard facts, actually. It's about the third of May – Richard went to Bristol to see a lady, someone from his past. He was very tight-lipped about who it was. What if it was the woman from Paris? What if she'd arrived at Bristol? If I were you, I'd be checking all the arrivals from Paris on that day and all the cameras at Bristol Airport.Yes, yes ...'

Samuel was nodding with his mobile glued to his ear. Unfortunately, I couldn't hear what Alec was saying. 'That's good, glad we could help,' Samuel concluded. I was glad he included me.

'They're going to look into it.'

'Good.'

'There's a good chance that it wasn't someone at the party.'

'Not one of us?'

'Yes. Then the matter can be put to rest, and we can have proper closure.'

I nodded, but I wasn't convinced and I certainly wasn't finished with Penny. Deep down in my gut, I knew that she was involved, that there was something – some dark secret she was harbouring, and that it had everything to do with Richard's death.

'I'm sorry to be going back to Penny,' I started, 'but she doesn't seem to me like a grieving widow –'

'We show grief in different ways, I think.'

'But! But Richard . . . Take Richard – he's never by her side. I never saw him once around her. That's not normal. People hover around their loved ones after death, even if only for a short while . . . saying goodbye before they move on –'

I bit my tongue. It was the damned port. I shouldn't have said any of that.

Samuel was looking at me, baffled. 'Whatever do you mean, Maggie?'

There was no turning back. I had to tell him the truth. Only my mother knew it – if you can't tell your mother, who can you tell? Telling anyone else was risking it. I would be branded a raving lunatic. But I had put my foot in it with Samuel: I had said too much to back out of it now. I had to press on. 'I can see them,' I mumbled. 'I can see the dead. When people die . . . well, dying doesn't mean disappearing, does it?'

Slowly, Samuel shook his head. He looked wary.

'Well then, I don't know what to call them . . . Ghosts? They don't feel like ghosts. They don't wear white sheets and howl. It's just their presence that I can see – I can sense it. They stay around for a little bit, like they're trying to understand what the hell is going on, and when they do, they move on. Sometimes, they don't. Sometimes, they linger. Like Alice.'

'Alice?' He looked at me sharply and resentfully, as if I had just mocked him or punched him or done something equally awful.

I was wading deeper and deeper into troubled waters of my own making. The port circulating in my veins wasn't doing me any favours. My brain wasn't working very well and was lagging behind my stupid, big gob. I had to put all my cards on the table. 'Yes, Alice.

She's here, you know? She's always around you. When you moved in next door, Alice moved in with you. I think she's finding it hard to move out and . . . to move on. You're not letting her, is my guess –'

Sam rose to his feet. His face was coloured with anger. 'Are you taking the piss?! How dare you? How dare you toy with my emotions? With my dead wife's memories! You callous . . . you stupid, stupid –' He stopped himself from calling me a name which – in all honesty – I fully deserved to be called. *A cow? A bitch? A witch?* Probably just *an arsehole*.

I was all of the above. But I had to prove it to him that, at least, I wasn't a fantasist and a liar. I glanced at Alice (she was in the room, as I said, standing by the window, looking out). I searched for something that was uniquely her, something that only he would know. 'She's five foot four, slim, has brown hair with blonde highlights, a fringe – a long and heavy fringe that covers her eyebrows . . . like a pony . . .'

Sam collapsed back into the armchair. He was gaping at me with his mouth open, then his eyes shifted towards the window, following my gaze.

I approached her. She didn't budge – didn't seem to notice my proximity. I went on, 'Her eyes are hazel with the sort of . . . golden specks around the irises. She has a small scar on her left cheek –'

'She fell from a tree when she was ten, cut her face open on a root. She was such a tomboy, even as a grown woman.' Samuel's voice sounded distant, like it had travelled in time, all the way from Alice's childhood.

'I see,' I said. 'She is wearing a dress though – very feminine . . . It's a mini-dress, off her right shoulder – the sort of asymmetric look. It has a white, floral pattern. I think it's sort of . . . wild flowers, meadow flowers. Pretty . . .'

'She wore that dress when we first met, on a platform at London Paddington, waiting for the Plymouth express. She was going home – her parents live in Plymouth. I was going on my hols to Cornwall with a bunch of friends. I couldn't take my eyes off her . . . In that dress . . .'

'She has another scar – scars – on her wrists ...'

'She tried to –' An outpouring of sobs drowned his words. Poor Samuel was weeping, and it was my fault.

'I'm so sorry ...' It was a basic human instinct for me to reach to him and put my arms around him. He clung on to me, and cried and cried like a baby.

Alice turned away from the window. She gazed at the two of us: me bent over her husband, hugging him, and he with his arms wrapped around my waist, his sobs muffled by my stomach. I could swear that a shadow of a smile crossed her lips. It felt like a blessing. She was all right with me offering comfort to the man she loved and couldn't part from.

At last, Sam let go of me. He fell back into the armchair and ran his hands down his face, wiping away his tears. His expression was hopeful, almost elated. 'Can you please tell her something from me? That I love her. I forgive her ... Can you ask her –'

'I can't talk to them, I'm sorry. They don't talk to me. It's like a silent movie, I'm afraid.'

He looked crestfallen, so I added, 'But I'm sure she can hear you. She's smiling at you.'

'OK ... OK ... She's smiling ... that's good ...' He muttered. The man was in a state of shock. 'Where is she, you said?'

'By the window.'

'By the window ...' He gazed intently at the window. 'Alice?'

I really didn't want to tell him that she hardly stirred. She was facing away from him, her face inscrutably calm.

'Why did you do it, Alice? Why did you leave me?' He approached the window. Her presence shifted, but only slightly. He placed his hands on the windowsill. 'Where are you!' he cried.

I was sure that the next day he would come to his senses and regard me as a total fraud. Or a madwoman at best. For now, however, I had to tear him away from that window and send him home to bed. Coffee would do the trick, I hoped. I left him with Alice in my lounge and went to the kitchen to put the kettle on. Strong black coffee. I needed it too.

Chapter Nineteen

On Thursday, while scouring the market for a nice cake to take with me to Mum and Dad's, I bumped into Vanessa and Cherie at the cake stall. Armed with our newly acquired *homemade* Victoria sponges, we retreated to the Old Stables Café due to rain. Within seconds we were joined by Vera who burst in with her dog Rumpole at the heel, both streaming with rivers of rainwater. Rumpole, being an old Irish wolfhound, dribbled all over the floor and, if that wasn't enough, shook himself energetically, covering us in mud and what smelled like cow shit. No one had the heart to dispatch Rumpole outside in this weather, though, plus the damage was already done. We ordered tea, English Breakfast unanimously, and a selection of cream cakes.

Having exhausted the topic of the bloody English weather, we fell into an uncomfortable silence. I usually know how to defeat silence with plenty of conversation, or at least an engaging monologue, but I was feeling flat. I had a lot of half-baked suspicions about the people I had called friends all my life. Someone had killed Richard Ruta and it could've been one of us. It had to be one of us! Who else? A mysterious stranger from Paris? Wishful thinking, I say! But I didn't want to know who it was anymore. I wanted this whole bizarre experience to be behind us all so that we could sit down in the cosy and friendly ambience of the Old Stables and eat our cakes in peace.

Mary and Dan entered the tearooms and started shaking off rainwater, laughing. Mary had her hair in a ponytail and looked like a girl. They scanned the tables with dismay – the place was chock-a-block. Cherie waved to them, 'Over here! Grab a chair and join us!'

Mary beamed, even Dan smiled.

'We'll just order a cup of tea, and we'll be with you!'

We shuffled our chairs around our table when they arrived with their tea and scones.

'Did you see the news last night?'

'That woman at the airport?' Vera asked.

'Never seen her in my life. Definitely not local,' Cherie commented.

Mary nodded. 'At least, we now know it wasn't any of us – anyone from Bishops.'

'And it wasn't a man, hallelujah!' Dan added.

'That's exactly what Henry said!' Vera concurred.

I don't know what possessed me, but I guess, I am simply unable to keep my mouth shut. I just had to voice my misgivings, 'That's just the thing – it wasn't a bloke, so you're off the hook, Dan, but any one of us,' I swept my female companions with an ominous glare, 'could've put on a disguise: a wig, some makeup. Come to think about it, you are a makeup artist, Mary. And you didn't come to Richard's party. You could've given him the –'

A mortified silence interrupted me.

Everyone stared at me dumbfounded, forkfuls of cake suspended on the way to my friends' gaping mouths.

Mary exclaimed, 'I never!'

'You can't possibly be serious, Maggie Kaye,' Dan let it rip, 'I always knew you had a screw loose, but this ... this is beyond the pale!'

'I ... I ...' Well, I stammered, unable to make any coherent reply.

'You should take it all back and apologise to Mary.' If anyone could produce a positively scolding look, it was Vera. She pursed her lips into a tiny slit and looked at me down her longish nose.

I found myself suitably and justifiably chastised. I must admit I could hardly hold back tears. Memories of being a naughty little girl in the headmistress' office about to receive three strokes of the cane flooded back. 'I am so sorry, Mary. Please forgive me,' I whimpered.

'That you'd think that I could m-m-m . . .' Mary was distraught. The very idea of being considered capable of murder would not pass through her throat.

Vera gave her a hug. 'Now, now, Mary . . . You know Maggie – she doesn't think before she opens her mouth. Of course, she didn't think it. She didn't think at all, did you, Maggie?'

I nodded. Then I shook my head. I wasn't sure which was the appropriate gesture to confirm that yes/no, I hadn't thought it through. I was learning things about myself and I didn't like them. At this very moment, I didn't like myself. Vera was right: I was a blabbering idiot. That was the second time in the last twenty-four hours that I had said something I shouldn't.

Mum is an expert curry maker. She learned how to make it on a trip to India. She prepares it from scratch: all manner of ground spices, ginger, and other secret ingredients are thrown into the pot with a few tender lamb pieces, and what comes out a couple of hours later is divine. But that day, I hardly touched my curry. I sat at the table, poking at my plate with the fork and wallowing in self-pity. Mum had picked up on my mood and asked me what on earth the matter was – she'd made that curry especially for me. So, I told them about my earlier faux pas with Mary and about everyone's reaction, and about how I just wanted to die of shame.

'You lack in people skills, Maggie, my love,' Dad informed me, as if that was supposed to be a revelation, 'but lucky for you, everyone knows that. We're all on tenterhooks with everything that goes on right now, but when the dust settles, trust me, Mary'll forgive you.'

'You've known each other since you were children,' Mum added. 'She knows not to take you seriously.'

'She knows you didn't mean it.'

I wasn't sure if I should be thanking them, but I suppose, it was some sort of wisdom they had imparted to me, as parents should do. It hurt my ego, but apparently truth hurts. Oh, it did! I sniffled.

'Cheer up, girl! Let's have some of that Victoria sponge.'

Mum cleared away the dinner plates and I fetched the dessert ones from the dresser. Dad started cutting the cake; the largest slice, I knew, was for me. A consolation prize. I was beginning to feel fractionally better.

Mum gave a burst of coughs.

'Have you had those tests?' I asked.

'Oh, yes. Last week. They were very quick, weren't they, Eugene?' Mum put on a brave face. I could tell it was fake.

'They were,' Dad mumbled. He looked down, concern crossing his face like the shadow of a big black bird.

I felt a little niggle of anxiety prickling in my stomach. 'And? What's the outcome? Is it all good?'

'Well,' Mum pretended to be busy, pointlessly wiping clean forks with a dishcloth. 'The X-ray showed, perhaps – the doctor thinks – traces of tuberculosis. But that's nothing these days,' she added rapidly, 'because they can treat that with antibiotics. At an early stage . . .'

'But we're still waiting for the biopsy results,' Dad said gravely.

'Biopsy?' Something heavy sank in my stomach. It felt like a stone. The word *biopsy*.

'It's not what you think,' Mum read my mind. 'It's just to be on the safe side. To eliminate all the other – remote – possibilities. It's common . . . a routine practice. That's all.'

'It's better to be overcautious than . . . not! So, yes–' Dad bit his lip. 'Let's check out that cake of yours!'

'When will you have the results of the biopsy?'

'Next week. Mum's seeing the doctor Friday next week.'

I got home on autopilot – I didn't know how I found myself on my own doorstep. My head was buzzing with worries about Mum. I hoped she was right. I hoped it was nothing, just a routine check-up to be on the safe side. I hoped we would all breathe a sigh of relief next week, Friday. But, for the time being, the stone weighed heavily at the bottom of my stomach and wouldn't shift.

I called Will. I needed him to assure me that there was nothing to it. He is not a doctor, only an engineer, and lives far away in London, but he is my older brother. Much older and much wiser. Stable and sensible by nature, he is the voice of reason in our family.

He listened, silent and pensive, at the other end of the phone. He didn't know anything about Mum, about her cough or her lung X-rays. When I finished my chaotic monologue, he said, 'I'll find out what's going on and call you back in a mo.'

I sat on the edge of the chair with the phone in my hand, staring at the blank screen, willing it to light up.

Half an hour later, my nerves were frayed. When I began to imagine unimaginable horrors the phone startled me with its loud ding-dong.

'Will?'

'Yes. So, this is how it goes: it's true about the X-ray – they found small shadows in the lungs that need to be investigated. The preliminary diagnosis is TB, but because TB is so rare these days, the doctors want to double check. What's important is that it can be treated.'

I heard myself exhale loudly.

'I've got the telephone number of Mum's GP, and I'll call him tomorrow to confirm everything. With Mum's blessing – she has to consent to them sharing information with me, that's how it's done. But she said she'd do it, so I'm confident she's not hiding anything.'

'You'll let me know?'

'Course, I will, sis.'

It was late, but I felt claustrophobic in the house. I needed air. I needed to clear my head now that Will had injected some common sense into it to settle my irrational fears. It had stopped raining so I stepped out into the garden. The air was crystal clear and crisp like it always is after a downpour. I inhaled and set my eyes on the black silhouettes of the gravestones in the church cemetery over the fence.

I stood quiet as a mouse for a few minutes. I was surrounded by perfect stillness.

As I turned to go back inside, I was surprised to find Samuel sitting on his patio in semi-darkness, with only a feeble yellow smudge of light coming from inside his sitting room through the French doors. Alice was conspicuous by her absence.

I was even more surprised to discover that Penny was there, standing next to him, in the same red dress she had worn to Richard's birthday bash. The colour was indistinct, blending with the greys of the night, but I recognised the elegantly tailored lines of the dress.

The most puzzling thing was that the two of them sat in complete silence.

'Good evening! Samuel, Penny,' I nodded to them out of politeness.

'Good evening, Maggie. I didn't see you there,' he responded, but she said nothing. I thought that rather rude. She didn't even look in my direction. She was gazing vacantly into space.

'What brings you here at this time of night?' I asked.

Again, she did not answer.

Samuel got to his feet. 'Who are you talking to, Maggie?'

It was a bizarre question.

'Why, Penny, of course!'

'Penny? But ... Penny isn't here ...'

We stared at each other in horror. I can't remember which one of us said it first, but we both realised it at the same time:

'She's dead!'

Chapter Twenty

They could be wrong. In fact, the possibility of them being right based on the night shadows and Maggie's vivid imagination was very remote. Sam wouldn't take the risk of making a fool of himself and calling the police, but it didn't hurt to check.

It was ten forty-five at night – not your customary socialising hour in Bishops Well.

In the car, Maggie sat quietly, white as a sheet. She was in no doubt that she was driving to Forget-Me-Not to find Penny Ruta's dead body.

They parked on the road outside the estate as the electric gate was locked and no one was answering the intercom.

'What now? Should we call the police?'

Sam still wasn't convinced. They peered through the gate and, in the distance, could detect feeble yellow lights on the ground floor of the mansion. Someone was in, dead or alive.

'We'll have to climb the wall.'

The dry-stone wall was just under six foot, give or take. There wasn't a ladder in sight, but the wall was old, its surface uneven and full of protruding slates which could be used as footholds. Being a gentleman, Sam gave Maggie a hand-up. She climbed gingerly onto his shoulders, as he'd instructed her, wobbled precariously, her bottom gravitating towards the ground, but managed to grip the top of the wall to hoist herself over it. No sooner did she disappear over the ledge that Sam heard a thud and a whimper.

'Are you all right, Maggie?'

'Couldn't be better, but I think I broke my ankle.'

There would be more emergency – and pain – in her voice if she had, Sam concluded.

'Stand clear! I'm coming,' he announced in a stage whisper. It wasn't as easy as jumping over. He had a couple of false starts, but finally found his footing and landed on the other side of the wall. Maggie was limping.

'Should we check your ankle?'

'No time! Let's go.' She led the way. Her limping receded as she went. By the time they reached the steps, she was leaping like a gazelle, two at a time.

The lights were on in the sitting room. They found the door ajar at the front entrance to the house. They called out, but nobody answered. They headed for the sitting room, guided by the lights.

Maggie and Sam gasped in unison. There was no doubt: Penny was dead. Her body was twisted awkwardly, part-suspended on the sofa with her feet dug stiffly into the floor. It seemed that she had suffered some sort of a seizure and the stiffness was the result of a nerve paralysis. Her eyes were wide open and her chin and chest were covered with what appeared to be her vomit. All of her symptoms were reminiscent of Richard's.

'Should we call the police now?' Maggie whispered.

Sam took out his phone and hesitated. It would take some explaining. The first question the police would ask would be what Sam and Maggie were doing here, how they got here and what had brought them here in the first place. Samuel dialled Alec Scarfe's number. It would be easier to have his sympathetic ear first, before the cavalry arrived.

'Say again? You found a body? Penny Ruta … Where are you exactly?' Alec Scarfe didn't seem at his brightest at this time of night. Sam had to repeat himself several times.

'Stay there. I'm on my way.' At last, Alec got the message. 'Don't touch anything. You know the drill.'

Sam and Maggie relocated to the kitchen and sat at the kitchen table. The study and the library doors were locked, and the dining room as well as the sitting room were both crime scenes. This was surreal.

Maggie suggested they have a cup of tea to calm their nerves. Sam's jaw dropped: the woman was irrepressible.

'Alec said not to touch anything. That includes things in the kitchen, I think.'

'Ah ...' she sighed. She examined the kitchen. There was lots of junk on the table: glasses and cups, all unwashed, a few empty wine bottles and beer cans, and stale chocolate biscuits in an open pack. She reached for one of those, but quickly withdrew.

'How are we going to explain ourselves?' she asked.

Sam had no time to answer, and frankly, he didn't have an answer anyway. The intercom buzzed. He picked up the receiver and gazed at the small screen. Alec was standing at the gate, wearing a dressing gown.

'Alec, thanks for coming.'

'Open the gate for us, will you.'

Even as the gate was slowly sliding open, the flashing lights of the police cars appeared behind Alec. They were all here, in the full force of the law.

Within seconds, Forensics took over the sitting room. Alec was confined with Sam and Maggie in the kitchen, asking them the dreaded question, 'What brought you here in the middle of the night?'

'I had a feeling, you see,' Maggie explained.

Alec didn't see. He raised a questioning eyebrow and directed it silently at Sam. He nodded. 'Yes, Maggie had this nagging ... feeling, so we came to have a look.'

Acting Detective Inspector Webber stood in the doorway, gazing at the two of them with suspicion. With his sleek black hair, focused gaze, and a smart suit concealing the hint of a beer paunch, he reminded Sam of John Travolta in *Pulp Fiction*. Webber peered at Sam and Maggie (mainly Maggie) with sheer, unconcealed disbelief. To him, they were either a pair of extravagant, inbred country bumpkins, or dangerous criminals. Possibly both. It appeared that he couldn't make up his mind. 'You had a feeling?'

'Yes.'

'And what made you feel ... um, like there *could* be a corpse here waiting to be found?'

'It's not that simple ... I ... Well ...'

Sam charged to the rescue. He could not afford to be discovered to have relied on his next door neighbour's supernatural powers. 'The fact is that I was expecting to see Mrs Ruta today. We had an appointment in the afternoon. She didn't turn up. I ... I was telling my neighbour about it – Maggie is my next-door neighbour, see? So, she said ... Well, she said it wasn't like Penny not to turn up without a word. In fact, it was an important meeting that Mrs Ruta had insisted on before she'd go to London tomorrow. We thought – we, Maggie and I, we both agreed – that perhaps we should check on Mrs Ruta.'

'I see. Wouldn't phoning her have been a simpler way?'

Sam and Maggie looked sheepishly at the detective. It would've been simpler – of course – if they'd had the expectation of Penny being alive and capable of answering her phone. That wasn't the case, but they could not tell him that.

'Boss.' A plain-clothed policewoman appeared behind Webber.

'Yes,' both Scarfe and his acting detective inspector answered.

'We found Mr Savage upstairs.'

'Frank? Is he dead too?' barked Alec.

'Frank Savage, yes. I mean no! I mean, he is alive. He's in his bedroom, quite confused. He'd slept through everything, he says. It took us some effort to wake him. He said he'd taken his meds. They make him drowsy. Would you like me to take his statement?'

'No. I'll talk to him.' Webber turned on his heel and followed the policewoman upstairs, leaving Alec Scarfe to watch his two main suspects in the kitchen.

'You shouldn't be here, that's all I have to say to you, Gillian.' The words, hissed by Michael Almond conspiratorially in the hall, just outside the kitchen door, made Alec Scarfe prick up his ears.

'Just tell me, and I'll go home! Was she killed with the same poison? Aconite, yeah?'

'You're not in charge of this investigation and you shouldn't have followed me,' Almond was preaching. 'Anyway, I don't have the toxicology report to hand to discuss it with you, or anyone else for that matter. Can I go back to my crime scene, please?'

'But the symptoms are the same, aren't they? She threw up and she looks –'

'It's likely, yes, but I refuse to discuss it with you. No!'

'We need to know if it's the same modus operandi, the same perpetrator! Surely, you –'

'DI Marsh!' the superintendent hollered loudly even though he stood right behind the woman.

'Sir! I was just –'

'I'm ordering you to go home! You are on sick leave. You're not in charge of this investigation. Go home!'

'Could it be the same person? Who benefits from her death? If the same poison was used –'

'PC Miller, escort DI Marsh off the premises!'

Despite her protestations, Ms Marsh was shown the door, empty-handed.

If anyone asked Sam, he would be able to tell them exactly who would benefit from Penny's death – financially, that is. And they would be surprised beyond measure, just as Sam had been. But no one asked, and as a lawyer, he wasn't in the habit of volunteering information about his clients to the police.

Alec returned to the kitchen, accompanied by a middle-aged man with a bulbous nose and bushy brows. 'DC Whittaker will take your statements,' he said, 'and then you're free to go home.'

Sam glanced at his watch. It was two minutes past midnight. Whittaker decided to interview Maggie first. Sam prayed to God Almighty that she wouldn't break into any of her paranormal elucidations but stick to the version of events he had offered earlier. He waited outside the kitchen with Alec Scarfe.

'I hope I did the right thing by calling you first?'

'Yes and no, but don't worry about it. What's done is done. I brought the troops with me straight away – all above board.' Alec rubbed his chin. 'We didn't see this coming ... We should've. We should've offered her protection.'

'You couldn't have known.'

'That's precisely why we should've anticipated every eventuality. We don't know shit at this point. All we've got is a grainy image of a woman no one's seen before. We're going through tons of CCTV footage from all over the place to get a better picture. We're scouring passenger lists for flights out of Paris, heading for Bristol on the third of May. But because we can't assume it was definitely Bristol until we find our mystery woman on video there, we are also looking at other UK airports as well as Eurostar.'

'Like looking for a needle in a haystack.'

'Exactly. And my best detective is out of action. It's bloody impossible.'

Webber descended the stairs and joined them.

'What did you find out from Frank?'

'Very little. He's on medication for PTSD. When he takes it at night it knocks him for six. He went to bed early, at ten, he says, and took a dose. He slept through everything, he says.'

'And before that? What does he remember?'

'He and Mrs Ruta had been having a few drinks in the sitting room. He left her there and went to bed, feeling tired. At ten, like I said.'

The fact that Frank and Penny had a companionable drink together before bed struck Sam as unlikely. Only yesterday, Frank was cursing the woman and accusing her of all sorts of wrongdoing in cahoots with Dorothy. Perhaps though they had talked it over and made up. Grief put people in an unpredictable state of mind. Sometimes it drew them together, sometimes it pulled them apart.

'What state of mind was she in?' Sam asked, attracting a cursory squint from the detective inspector. He looked to the superintendent for permission to answer Sam's question.

Alec rephrased the query. 'What did she seem like to him?'

'He made an interesting observation – said she acted "like she didn't care to live". His words. He said maybe it was guilt that was playing on her mind. His words again. Apparently, she drank two bottles all by herself. They'd been drinking since just before six o'clock. When he went off to bed, she was passed out on the sofa, but alive, so he says.'

'What was she drinking?'

'Wine. Mr Savage had beer. He said he wouldn't be surprised if she killed herself.'

'Anything is possible. We're back to square one,' Alec sighed and rounded his shoulders in a gesture of defeat.

Sam begged to disagree – but only internally. Why would Penny have made an appointment to see him, fail to turn up and then kill herself? Wouldn't she have first tied up the loose ends with her Will? Still, it wasn't his place to teach the police how and what to think. They would get there under their own steam.

'Is that all, Webber?'

'One more thing, sir,' the detective responded, 'I asked Mr Savage about the security – do they normally leave the doors open at night? It seems strange, considering all the other safety precautions on the estate.'

'And? What did he say?'

'As I suspected: the door would – should – have been locked. He remembered locking it before going to bed. So, I asked him to check around the house to see if anything was missing. It could've been a burglary gone wrong –'

'And the thieves would make her drink poisoned wine!' Alec snorted with understandable sarcasm.

'Well, yes, there is that,' Webber conceded the point sheepishly. 'But there's something missing. Mrs Ruta's laptop. And her study has been turned out. More items may be missing.'

'Just her study?'

'Yes, sir.'

'They knew what they were looking for. So, the laptop, you say?'

Webber nodded, and added quickly before the Chief Super thought of it first, 'We're going through the CCTV footage.'

Maggie emerged from the kitchen, looking bewildered and exhausted. 'DC Whittaker wants to chat to you,' she said to Sam.

As soon as DC Whittaker thanked Sam for his co-operation, confirmed that he would be seeing him tomorrow at the station to sign his statement, and left the kitchen, Maggie returned in the company of Frank Savage. Frank looked awful: bloodshot, puffy eyes, broken veins on his cheeks, and wispy facial hair growth. He smelled like he hadn't washed in days. All he was wearing was a pair of boxers. As opposed to his knackered face, his toned torso rippled with pure muscle. The man knew how to stay fit even though years had passed since he was in the military.

'Sam,' he nodded absently and went straight for the tap to pour himself a glass of water. He drank it noisily and immediately filled the glass again.

'How are you keeping?' Sam asked.

'Me? Fine. Absolutely fine,' he offered him a broad grin to back up his words. 'But knackered. I'm going back to bed. You can show yourselves out.'

As Sam and Maggie were showing themselves out, Scarfe was hollering orders to his men, 'I want every single bottle of wine in this house bagged for testing. Every last one of them!' He had clearly decided not to take any more chances by leaving even a drop of wine in the house.

'The cellar is full of wine, sir. There must be hundreds of bottles,' the voice sounded like it belonged to DI Webber: deep and strongly accented with a West Country flavour.

'Bag them all! You've been fixated on that one damn bottle of Tokaji, but have you thought – just for one minute – that it isn't the bottle?'

'Sir?'

'It's not the bottle, it's the poison, Webber! It could've been injected into the other wine bottles in the house and here we are on a wild goose chase, looking for some hapless woman from the airport! Do I have to do your job for you?'

Chapter Twenty-one

'She didn't kill herself,' Maggie said in the car. She sounded like she knew what she was talking about: assertive and in full-combat mood. Her eyes were shining.

'Frank said –' Sam started to contradict her, but even he wasn't buying Penny's suicide.

'I don't care what Frank said. Penny did not kill herself. She wouldn't be hanging around if she'd killed herself. She's here right now, breathing down my neck. She's been with us all along. She wants us – you and me – to unmask her killer. She won't move on until the truth is out.'

'Why doesn't she just tell you who killed her? That'd save us a lot of grief!' Sam snapped. He was tired and confused. He regretted it straight away. Maggie had a deeply hurt look on her face. She went silent and stared ahead at the road lit by the headlights. An owl crossed their path; it flapped its white wings twice and then went into gliding mode. It vanished beyond the frame of the black roadside hedge.

'Sorry,' Sam muttered.

'It's all right. You don't have to believe me. Sometimes I don't believe myself.'

He really didn't know what to make of her supernatural revelations. He was, after all, a rational man. But Maggie had brought Alice back from the dead. Virtually at least. She knew things no one could have told her but he himself, and he had never spoken to her about Alice.

Still, there was no excuse for being rude to her. To show

goodwill, Sam said, 'You may be right, Maggie, but you see, Frank mentioned guilt.'

'So you think she poisoned Richard – for the money, I presume – and then, within a month, before she even got her hands on the money, in thrall to her guilt she decides to kill herself. That's quite a radical change of heart, if I ever knew –'

'No, not quite. It's Penny's Will I'm talking about. It'll become a matter of public record soon enough – I guess the police will be knocking on my door tomorrow to officially inquire about it – so, I suppose, I can tell you now.'

'Tell me what?' Maggie took her eyes off the road and fixed them firmly on Sam. 'Don't stop, do tell.'

'Give or take small legacies here and there, Penny Ruta left her entire estate to Dan Nolan.'

'You don't say! Do you think what I'm thinking?'

'I don't know what you're thinking, Maggie.' Sam was busy turning into their shared driveway. The security lights came on. A fox popped out from the bushes. Stunned briefly by the flood of lights, it froze and gawped straight at the approaching car. Its eyes were as green as the brightest of emeralds. Sam slammed on the brakes and the creature scampered. It had a lucky escape.

'I'll park on the driveway, that's what I'm thinking,' Sam spoke grumpily. 'I don't want to be scraping a carcass from my tyres in the morning. I'm dog tired.'

'Me too,' Maggie agreed, but then took the matter to an entirely unexpected level, 'I could do with that cup of tea you never let me make at Richard's. My mouth feels like an ashtray ... Except that I've run out of milk. I can't have tea without milk.'

Reluctantly, Sam invited Maggie in for a cup of tea. At one o'clock in the morning! It was ridiculous, but for her it seemed like a perfectly natural courtesy. She headed for the sitting room while Sam pottered in the kitchen. Just as the kettle whistled, he opened the fridge to realise that he too had run out of milk.

'How about a glass of something stronger? I've brandy. I could do with a proper drink myself.'

Maggie accepted, but not without wrinkling her nose with disappointment. She had already made herself comfortable on the sofa, cuddling a cushion and blabbering about her suspicions. Sam listened half-heartedly, registering snippets of the most bizarre and disjointed speculations: '. . . so Penny has served her purpose, and he disposes of her. She is an inconvenient witness, or an accessory . . . She was close to Richard – she would've asked him about that Tokaji . . . Remember, he was trying to tell all of us something about – what was it about?' Maggie puckered her forehead. 'Well, something about,' she put on Richard's accent and attempted to authenticate it by lowering her voice to a manly bass tone, '*Tuppence and I, we have no secrets – we have a –*'

Maggie pointed her finger at Sam, 'What? What did they have? No secrets between them – that means there were secrets they kept from the rest of the world. Did he change his mind and decide to share those secrets with us? She didn't like it. Just looking at her, I could tell – she was mortified of what he would say next. But if she killed him to keep a secret, then why would she then kill herself? Unless she discovered that the secret wasn't safe. That's where Dan comes in. She leaves him her money. Is that some form of hush money? But then again,' she scowled, 'if it is only on her death that he can get his hands on it, he won't wait and decides to act swiftly. He kills her. I suspected him the moment I found out he was here in Bishops, living with Mary. Don't get me wrong – I love Mary, but I can't argue with facts, can I? But, you see, there's more to life than facts. You've got to agree . . .'

Sam nodded absent-mindedly and poured their drinks. Maggie downed hers in one go, screwed up her face, exhaled theatrically, and said, 'God, that was lethal! What did you put in there?'

'Brandy.'

'Can I have another one, please?'

This time, Sam gave her a double so he wouldn't have to get up again before he finished his own drink.

Maggie went on, 'And I've been having these suspicions about Dan and Mary ever since! There was a time when I felt really, really

140

silly about it. I mean, come on, Mary's been my friend since we were in junior school. And Dan, honestly, Dan's been in a band with my own brother. So, I parked it. I thought: no! No, Maggie! Leave these two good people alone. They've been through a lot without you rubbing more salt into their wounds.' She gulped the double brandy with the same ease that she had done the single one. 'But now ... gosh! Where do we start? Do you think that Dan knows about Penny's Will?'

'I've no idea.'

'But she must've felt one hell of a lot of guilt to give him all she had! My God, that explains everything: she killed Leila ... Of course, it was Penny who killed Leila Nolan!'

'And last night she killed herself.' Sam said that without conviction though he wished he could believe it. He sipped his brandy slowly. Something wasn't right. He echoed his reservations, 'Something isn't right, Maggie.'

'What? Do you mean the woman at the airport? Don't worry about that woman. There was no woman. I have a perfectly good explanation. Mary! It was Mary. She's a makeup artist, did you know? She worked in films – won endless awards. She could've transformed herself beyond recognition.'

'No, that's not what I meant. It's the codicil. Penny was coming today to sign the codicil to her Will. Why didn't she? She gave me a USB stick for safe keeping. Whatever is on it was to be made public after her death. We had to write this stipulation into her Will. She was going to sign it in the afternoon. Why didn't she come? She was insistent that the thing was published on her death and I said it had to be formalised as part of her Will ... Otherwise, you see, the benefactor of her Will could choose not to release any of its contents into the public domain.'

'Maybe she didn't care anymore? She was about to kill herself so, who cares? Hang on!' Despite the copious amount of alcohol in her bloodstream, Maggie rounded on Sam with a sharp eye, 'What USB stick? What's on it?'

Chapter Twenty-two

Samuel went to fetch the USB stick from his office. Penny was sitting on the window seat, looking on. For a brief moment, our eyes met. She seemed to be looking through me, but I knew she was keen for me to understand that she had unfinished business she needed me to finalise – me and Samuel, in partnership. She would hang around until then. I said to her, even though I had no guarantee that she could hear me, 'We'll get to the bottom of it, Penny. Trust me . . . And for pity's sake, what have you done to Alice? You elbowed her out . . . God knows how she must be feeling right now, cowering somewhere in the shadows! You can be such an inconsiderate cow, you know that, don't you.'

'Who are you talking to?' Samuel was back with a laptop and a memory stick. It looked disappointingly tiny and I wondered how much information could be downloaded to such a midget of a storage device. Perhaps we were putting too much faith in this little thing and the secrets it might harbour.

Samuel looked at me questioningly and I had to ask him what the matter was.

'You were talking to someone as I walked in. Talking to yourself?'

'No, of course not. I'm not insane. No, I was just having a word with Penny. You really don't need to know what about.'

He pulled a face that told a thousand words, most of them to the effect that it was widely accepted that insane people usually claimed to be perfectly compos mentis. And that one should not attempt to correct that misconception with them. They could turn violent.

I ignored his facial contortions. 'So, let's have a look at it!' I pointed to the tiny device.

Samuel switched on the laptop and pushed the USB stick into a slot. Fortunately for us the device was not password protected. Within seconds, we learned that it contained audio files. We were up for some listening. Samuel poured two more brandies for us and we sat back to hear what Penny Ruta had to say from beyond the grave.

This is my transcript, retrieved from memory the following day and committed to paper. Paraphrasing dialogue and dramatisation were inescapable in order to vividly evoke the events Penny described, but what follows reflects faithfully the essence of her account:

You'd think Leila Nolan was all blue-eyed innocence. You would be wrong.

She was part of the catering crew: a sweet little waitress with a ponytail. They all packed up and left at ten, after the dinner. The night was to be an exclusive event, only VIPs, my darling husband and me, and a touch of harmless debauchery.

Leila gatecrashed the party.

I didn't recognise her. The little bitch must've hidden in the house and changed her clothes in the toilet. At first, I thought she was one of the strippers. I'd organised them for Richard as his birthday treat.

But Leila hadn't been planned into any of it. She took me by surprise. Caught unawares, I had a knee-jerk reaction to her. It happened so quickly.

The strippers were a high-class act. Three lithe brunettes in high heels and little else. We were all drunk and in the spirit for some fun. We clapped as the girls curled their supple bodies around my darling husband, and touched themselves — and him — shamelessly, and took turns in his lap. We were all aroused by the spectacle. Even that poor, emotionally retarded Vera Hopps-Wood sported flushed cheeks and eyes glazed with lust.

I swear I wasn't insecure. At no time! I had paid them to be there. I was controlling them. If I felt anything towards them at all, it was superiority. What wife would have the guts to pay other women to please her husband? I was so bloody avant-garde! I wanted to show my darling husband how secure I was in our marriage – how high I could rise above all that pathetic domestic monogamy he so despised. Of course, I knew about his philandering past. I wanted him to believe that I'd embraced it.

I loved him so, so unconditionally. I still do.

Richard was having a whale of a time. I could see it in his blissful smile, in his half-closed eyes, and in his hands weighing the girls' boobs, wandering in and out of their skimpy G-strings. All the other guys watched and salivated with their cocks erect, no doubt, craving a wife like me.

It was my moment of glory. It was a success.

After the show – it was close to midnight, by then – the strippers were packed back into the limousine that had brought them to the party, at my expense, and sent on their merry way. The next day, they would be just a bleary, drunken memory for Richard. He kissed me hard on the lips and told me it was the best birthday present anyone had ever given him. I told him, 'That remains to be seen,' and left him with the promise of more to come soon. We were both sozzled and horny. Everyone was.

I left Richard by the pool to tend to the guests who were staying with us overnight, those too intoxicated to drive home, which frankly was most of them. Frank helped me distribute them to different rooms. We had to drag some of them up the stairs and throw them on their beds. They were legless. The house was full of inebriated intellectuals with their trousers wrapped around their ankles and their faces down the toilet. Frank and a couple of other single men – I can't remember who they were - would sleep downstairs in the sitting room. There was even one fat slob passed out under the dining table – we couldn't drag him out of there or wake him. I recall thinking that he might be dead, but I'd deal with that the next day because all I wanted was to be back in my darling husband's arms, and the rest of it, of course.

My hostess' duty done, and with the house fast asleep, I squeezed myself into the hot leather lingerie Richard so liked and hurried out to my darling husband waiting for me by the pool.

And there she was.

Like I said, Leila Nolan wasn't the sweet innocent she was portrayed to be. She wasn't the same person I saw later in newspapers – a girl with plaits and freckles. She was a sexy vamp in a short silk dress, backless, with narrow straps holding it together over her bra-less breasts. I could see there was no bra as she was leaning over Richard and her dress hung low revealing her heavy boobs - all the way.

I hadn't planned for that.

I wasn't thinking. I just reacted.

I charged at her like a wild animal.

I wasn't thinking.

It wasn't murder – it was not premeditated. It was an impulse. I smashed into her and she bounced out of my way.

She fell. Hit her head.

She was light like a feather, couldn't have fallen very hard ... But we saw blood trickle slowly from the side of her head and from her nose.

Blood.

'What have you done?' Richard was sitting up in his chair, staring at Leila Nolan – at the way she fell: awkwardly, her legs wide apart, her silky dress rolled up, showing her naked pubic area.

Why wasn't she wearing any underwear? That only confirmed my suspicions – proved me right! I was still furious with her.

The way she lay there sprawled for the world to see looked so indecent. Richard bent over and pulled down her dress, pushed her legs together.

'Why did you ...' he started but didn't finish once he looked at me and saw my face.

'Is she dead? Did I kill her?'

'It looks like it ... In God's name, what-' Once again, he halted halfway through a sentence. He clutched his mouth to hold back vomit. He walked around her, squatted, slapped her on the cheek, and again. He listened, waiting for her to make a sound, but didn't check if she was alive. I don't think he knew how to. The whole pulse-taking thing – whoever knows how to do that! It's even harder when your own heart is racing madly.

I did nothing. I was paralysed. My anger had evaporated as my head sobered up, hit by the shock.

He said, 'I'll fetch Frank. He'll know what to do. I'll tell him I did it – I won't get you mixed up in it ... I'll tell him it was an accident.'

'It was! I didn't mean to ... You have to believe me!'

He was staggering away, towards the house. For a split second I thought he would betray me. I thought he would call the cops and tell them what I did. I would've done the same. But he was back with Frank in tow.

Frank stared at the girl, at me and finally at Richard.

'Don't ask,' Richard said to him. 'I don't know how it happened. I was asleep, I woke - she came from nowhere ... She startled me ... I must've pushed her away, or she just lost her balance ... She was drunk – I think ... She hit her head ...'

'It has to look like an accident.'

'It was an accident,' I repeated, desperate to make the point.

Only now did Frank notice I was there. 'Did you see what happened?'

'No,' I said truthfully because I didn't see anything. I didn't see – I just did it. It was an impulse.

Frank didn't ask any more questions as if he was afraid of knowing. We didn't say anything else. No explanations. He decided he and Richard would push the body into the pool – it would look like she had hit her head as she had fallen, lost consciousness and drowned. It would look like an accident.

It had been an accident.

Upstairs in our bedroom, we did all the ordinary things we would have done normally before going to bed, except sex. We each had a shower, brushed our teeth, kissed goodnight.

'Thank you,' I said when we kissed. 'Sorry ...'

He said it was OK. He sounded weak and tired when he spoke. 'We'll have to leave her for now and pretend to find her in the morning,' he was telling me. 'We must be the first ones on the scene. That way, if our DNA is to be found anywhere on the body, we'll be able to explain it away. We are each other's alibi, but that's not enough. Frank will vouch for us ... Nothing else we can do now. Go to sleep.'

I wasn't convinced we could trust Frank. I was scared. I didn't believe I would get away with it. That's when Richard told me ...

'Frank is in love with me.' My darling – philandering - husband took off his Rolex and put it neatly on his bedside table. 'Frank will do anything to prove it.'

And he went on, matter-of-factly, about how they had made love: he and

146

Frank. Several times over the course of one week. Richard had been exploring the ins and outs of gay sex for his film The Other Side of the Moon.

You see, Richard liked to know everything first hand. He'd sell his soul to the Devil to ensure authenticity in his films. He wanted them to be as close to the skin as possible, he always said. Sleeping with Frank had been an experiment, but Frank thought . . . Well, for him it was real. Richard had no heart to tell him the truth. He let Frank believe he was – kind of – confused about his sexuality. So the illusion continued. Delusion, actually . . . Frank lived in hope. I think he still does.

To be honest, I didn't feel betrayed. It was research, I told myself, purely academic research. Bizarrely, having just killed a woman in a jealous rage, I couldn't care less about my husband sleeping with another man. It sounded like a prank – a silly, childish thing to do, like prodding a broken electric socket with a fork. Something my darling husband was famous for.

I shook my head, smiled – rather ruefully – but I forgave him. In fact, I'm not sure he was after my forgiveness. He had simply told me how things stood with Frank – the depth of his loyalty.

But I wasn't finished with Leila Nolan.

'What were the two of you doing?' I demanded to know. I would never be able to forgive him if . . .

'You're such a silly thing, aren't you?' my darling husband chuckled. 'I've no idea what the poor child was trying to do . . . I can only guess she was after a part in my next movie. They all are! An aspiring actress . . . God, the world is full of them! You have to get used to it, Tuppence. It's part of the scene, but it means fuck all.' And he turned off the lights, and in no time, I could hear his soft snoring.

Looking back, I bet he thought of all that had happened in terms of acts and scenes – pulp fiction. That's why he was able to sleep.

I wasn't. I tossed and turned, going in my mind through the events at the pool. I kept telling myself I didn't deserve to go to prison. I didn't mean to kill that girl! It had been an accident.

It took a while before a nasty, alien voice in my head began telling me that the girl didn't deserve her fate, either. That she deserved to live. That I had killed her.

I took a life. I took a person's life.

147

The audio recording had stopped. Samuel and I gaped at each other, dumbstruck.

'A confession then?'

'It explains the guilt Frank was talking about.'

'But Frank doesn't know it was Penny,' Samuel threw a curly one at me. 'Richard told him it was an accident. Why would Frank think Penny felt guilty all of a sudden?'

'Maybe he put two and two together – just came to realise that it had to be her ... Maybe she made a few careless remarks? Remember he said she was soused after going through two bottles of wine. Might've let it slip?'

'So, she gets drunk – Dutch courage – makes her peace, and tops herself. After killing Richard first. But why kill Richard?'

'And she says she still loves *her darling husband* ...'

'Not to mention that she was nowhere near Paris to buy that damn wine.'

'Though, think of what Alec said: it's more about who put the poison in that bottle of wine, not so much about when the wine was bought, or by whom.'

'I'd better call Alec and let him take it from here.'

I wasn't so sure about bringing the police into this so early. The cops were bound to come anyway, just like Samuel had predicted, in the morning. Meantime, we had another few audio files to listen to. I was burning with curiosity and I would be damned if the police confiscated the USB stick before I had heard it all.

But the most convincing argument came from Penny herself, who was still lingering about, sitting idly on the windowsill, without the slightest intention of sailing into the afterlife. She wasn't going anywhere. The case was not solved. It couldn't be closed because she was still here, trying to tell us something. Was it that she had not killed herself? Then we would have a whole new dilemma on our hands. Because if Penny Ruta hadn't killed herself and she had not killed Richard, then the killer was still out there.

I shared my misgivings with Samuel – as well as I could because my speech was slightly impaired due to my brandy intake. Thankfully, his thought processing capacities weren't as badly affected as my speech. To my surprise he nodded slowly and said, 'You might be right, Maggie, you might be spot on.'

'Might I? That's ... um ... yeah ... I might be right, huh?' I was flattered. I gulped down the rest of my brandy to celebrate.

'Yes, very much so. You see, assuming the same person killed both Richard and Penny – and the same method in both cases seems to imply that, then well ... Don't forget Penny's laptop is missing. Someone stole it, probably last night. Tomorrow – today, actually,' Samuel looked at the clock that showed a few minutes past three, 'Penny was planning to take her manuscript to London. She sold the rights to her memoirs to some publisher. They were due to be meeting with Edith Brenmar and her new publisher to finalise the deal. What if there's something in her memoirs that someone desperately wants to keep hidden? Things that could destroy him ... or her. He – or she - killed Penny and took her laptop. They went to the trouble of searching Penny's study so they may still be looking for this little fellow,' Samuel pointed to the tip of the memory stick protruding from its slot.

'We'd better find out what it is, then.' I wholeheartedly embraced his argument.

Chapter Twenty-three

I promised Henry this would not see the light of day . . .

When we heard that preamble to the second audio file on the USB stick, we paused for breath. This had to be about Henry Hopps-Wood, the right honourable Member of Parliament, an upstanding pillar of our local community, a man beyond reproach. And Vera's husband.

'Should we have another brandy?' I suggested. Even I wasn't sure I wanted to hear it – warts and all – without anaesthetic.

Samuel didn't object though he had to open a new bottle; the old one had been drained. He poured us two expertly measured drinks. We raised our glasses and drank silently, feeling like two cat burglars helping ourselves to beverages in somebody else's home. After all, we were about to dive into the whole truth, and nothing but the truth, about Henry Hopps-Wood. Without his knowledge or consent.

We played the audio from the beginning.

I promised Henry this would not see the light of day, but I won't keep my promise beyond the grave. Henry and his feelings can go to hell, frankly. This isn't about him. This is my story with Richard and the reason for our parting.

Just like Frank, I spent my best years by Richard's side, proving myself to him – trying to be like him, trying to live up to his standards. But with time, it had become as plain as day that it was an unattainable goal: Richard had no standards. He was a rebel without a cause, and he pulled it off

*without breaking sweat with that impertinent grin on his face. That's prob-
ably why I was so madly in love with the bastard.*

*Richard was free from standards. Free from conventions, free from his
own past, free from regrets, free from scruples. He did as he pleased. He did
not see why he should have to explain himself. He didn't dwell on conse-
quences. And he didn't apologise. He just bounced from one insane idea to
another, and somehow he managed to turn them to gold. People bought into
his insanity. They worshipped him for it. They hung on to his every word. I
can't figure out why, which is bizarre because I was one of those people. If I
wasn't in love with the man, I'd envy him. And I'd despise him. And I'd
want to kill him to weed him out of my mind.*

*I assumed, right from the beginning, that Richard wouldn't practise
monogamy. That it was beyond him to comprehend it. I had him down as
the Nietzschean man – a man who would not tolerate sentimentality, conventions, or prudishness. I'd almost lost him after Leila's . . . um . . . incident.
He didn't say it, but I knew. My jealousy was a turn-off. The more I clung
on to him, the further he'd push me. So, I worked it out: if I were to earn
his respect, I had to become like him. I would be careless, promiscuous, I
wouldn't conform - and he'd love me back.*

I craved his love. I strived for his approval.

*Henry and I started quite unexpectedly. I didn't set out to seduce him. Who
would! But he was handy and it just happened. Henry needed a good but
discreet speech writer, someone to put his point across elegantly. He had
learned somewhere I was a playwright. I guess Richard must have told
him – he was so proud of me, not just of my long legs and big brown eyes,
but also of my intellect. We had met at the Film School, Richard and I. I
had attended his lectures: all of them. He liked that. He once said, he was
through with bombshells and airheads – he wanted someone to talk to after
sex. He chose me.*

And I made the greatest mistake of my life and chose Henry.

*Henry and I would meet in our house. He was shit-scared to take our
filthy liaison to his own doorstep – what if Vera found out! He is an
arsehole – an opportunistic arsehole.*

It wasn't a regular affair but an ebb and flow of trembling encounters (guilt and fear of being found out were never far away from Henry's mind) followed by quiet stretches when he wasn't campaigning or engaged in large public events. Henry didn't need a ghostwriter between those massive engagements. He is good at everyday fussing, ankle-biting and small-time gossip mongering – but he struggles with the widescreen, panoramic-type orations where he has to hold people's attention for more than five minutes. That was when he would come to me.

I enjoyed the challenge. I was the pen for hire - a paid mercenary saying convincingly what he wanted me to say, without believing in it (Henry's politics is just cheap drivel; my job was to dress it in respectability). I was proving myself to Richard – I could do anything I put my mind to. An uber-woman. And I could seduce simple Henry just like that – I'd have him to heel at the click of my fingers.

I gave it a go.

That monumentally tragic day, we were working on a speech, sleeves rolled up, sweaty arm in sweaty arm, breaths crossing on the paper. I realised that Henry was aroused – like a puberty-afflicted teenager, breathing heavily and dying to peer deeper down my bra. I went with the punch. I said I was hot, unclipped my bra and pulled it off in front of him.

'I hope you don't mind, darling . . . It's awfully hot in here . . .' I purred like a high-class whore. I guessed he liked whores – what man doesn't – but for Henry, even the whores had to be high-class. He is such a sad snob.

Poor Henry got hopelessly tongue-tied. Blushed like a virgin. I asked him if he cared to help me with my panties. And that was it – hook, line and sinker! Henry Hopps-Wood MP needed no more encouragement. He pounced on me, his average-size manhood (I'm being kind here) bumbling between my legs, his round spectacles steamed up. I could hardly contain my amusement –

If I enjoyed the experience, it was only for its entertainment value. Henry isn't a tiger in bed, not even a meerkat. He is a heavy breather and a profuse sweater. He makes lots of guttural noises and has the strangest ideas about sex, which he must be sourcing from some untested version of the Kama Sutra.

I fucked him because I was proving myself to Richard. If he could sleep around with men and women alike, so could I. And I did. I slept with a

randy old bastard who claimed his wife was from prime breeding stock, but
breeding with her was tiresome and possible only with the lights out – his
words, not mine.

I pressed the pause button and drew a prolonged breath. 'Can we
please delete this? Think of Vera. I can't imagine what it'd do to her
if she ever … My God, Penny, that is so cruel! How could you!' I
glared at her faint silhouette that was fuzzily reflected in the win-
dowpane like a moved photograph. I wanted to throw something
at her to make her repent, but I knew that all I would achieve
would be a broken window and the considerable inconvenience of
having it mended for my neighbour. I gazed at him pleadingly, 'Let's
delete it, please.'

'We can't. That'd be tampering with evidence. And I wouldn't
know how, anyway. We can't possibly erase the whole file and I
really don't know how to edit bits out of it. Do you?'

No, I didn't know. I wanted to cry.

'I'm sure Alec will be very discreet. He won't want a scandal on
his watch. It won't hit the public domain, I'm sure of it.'

'Are you? What about Penny's dying wish?'

'Um … It wasn't formalised.'

'*Formalised*, my arse!' I despaired. 'It'll be leaked to the press.
Everything gets leaked these days, and poor Vera – it'll kill her. And
why can't we delete the whole file? It's only short –'

'Short but important. This recording gives Henry a compelling
motive. I watched him and Penny at the party. I saw them argue.'

'I saw it too. It looked more like she was taunting him.'

'Laughing at him. She could've been telling him that their secret
affair was about to become public – she'd sold her memoirs to a
publisher. She was going to break her promise to keep it under
wraps. Henry'd be finished, his political career over, his marriage in
tatters … He could not stand by and let her do it. It's a motive,
Maggie! A motive to kill Penny.'

'You think what I'm thinking, aren't you? You're thinking that
Henry stole her laptop to destroy her manuscript. But he can't be

sure he destroyed every last copy of it. What if he's still looking? What if he's after us now?'

'I don't think he knows about the recordings. Anyway, let's not get carried away. We're only guessing. Do you want to listen to the rest of it or have you had enough?'

I am ashamed to confess that my curiosity was slightly more pressing than my respect for Vera's dignity and incomparably greater than my respect for Henry's privacy. Of course, I wanted to continue. And I wanted another drink – for shock.

We had another double brandy each and, thus fortified, waded deeper into the seedy world of decadence and depravity.

I was wrong. Richard didn't appreciate my infidelity. He didn't take it well at all. He didn't think it was amusing, or wickedly decadent, or adorable . . . He felt betrayed – full stop.

I found that out a couple of days before his birthday party – before the great big bash, two days before he died.

We were having dinner. Usually Frank would dine with us – we were like one big, sick family – but that day Richard asked Frank whether he'd mind awfully if we ate alone. Richard and I had private matters to discuss. Frank looked shocked and hurt – he was the man whose business it was to know everything, but he left without a word of protest. Military obedience: obey orders, don't ask any questions.

There were no introductions. No nice way of saying it. Richard simply said, 'I think our marriage has run its course. I want a divorce.'

Is that how he had ended it with Mary? And with Dotty before her? Was that all it took – a straightforward statement of intent? I stared, speechless.

'If you fight it we will have to go the less pleasant route of marital infidelity.'

'Yours or mine?' I tried to be brave, and clever, and Nietzschean.

'Mine? I don't know what you're referring to, Tuppence.' He looked me straight in the eye and at that moment I knew he had remained faithful to me throughout our marriage.

It was me – only me.

'Yours, of course. I've known about you and Henry for a while. Frank told me. You were making a terrible racket, the two of you lovebirds. You should've been more discreet.'

I wanted to correct him – it wasn't me making the racket. It was Henry – his moronic grunts and squeals. But I realised how pathetic that would sound. Instead of defending myself, I said, 'I thought we had an understanding.'

'So did I. We got married – that surely should mean something. Something like marital fidelity, I daresay?'

I burst into tears. In a puff of smoke, the illusion was gone and all I had left was shame and regret. I loved him. I made a mistake!

He let me cry. Tears are therapeutic. I had to stop at some point. Richard sat there, his elbows on the table, his fingers elegantly entwined in front of him. He looked cold. He looked as if he was just a mildly intrigued bystander in all of this. It was striking how unmoved he was by my affair with Henry. And yet, he was leaving me. Why?

My tears had no effect on him. I stopped crying.

I said, 'If you knew for a while, why now?'

'Things have changed, rather radically, at my end.'

'All because of a stupid affair? It didn't mean anything. I was doing it for . . .' I was dying to tell him the truth: I was doing it for him. But it was a nonsensical notion, an illusion . . . I bit my tongue.

'It's not your pathetic little affair, Tuppence. What do you take me for? It's . . . it's life. Like I said – things have changed at my end. I'm an old man. I've an unresolved past which I would like to revisit. You're not part of it. I don't want to hurt your feelings, so let's leave it at that.'

'I shan't! I love you, Richard.'

'If you don't let go, I'll make your affair public and we'll part in anger. But we will part, either way. You don't want that. I don't want that. Henry, certainly, doesn't. Let's call it quits on an amicable basis. I will see that you're provided for. Don't fret – I am a happy man. I've been given a second chance to make up for . . . It doesn't matter – it doesn't concern you. I have no problem with you, Penny. I'm OK with whatever you do, whoever you see. I'm just getting out of our, um . . . arrangement. Do we have a deal? Say, yes, and give us a smile. That's my girl!'

Sniffling, I nodded and I smiled. What was I supposed to do? I was all over the place! And he said he was a happy man. He was being incongruous! I couldn't argue with him because I couldn't understand what was going through his mind. There was clearly something he wasn't telling me — something that would help me make sense of his words, and his inexplicable calm, and his dogged determination to end our marriage even though, apparently, my affair didn't play a part in it.

Like a good girl, I smiled.

Until the last minute, I didn't know Richard was planning to announce our 'amicable' separation at the party. He told me in the morning. I warned Henry, just in case. I assured him Richard wouldn't drag him into it if I went along with the divorce. But Henry, being Henry, was panicking. How can you be sure, how can you be sure, he kept asking me. As if I knew. As if I could be sure of anything when it came to Richard.

I told Henry to hold his nerve. I told him to stop wetting his pants. He made me promise that our unfortunate liaison, as he put it eloquently, would not see the light of day. I swore it wouldn't.

But now I wonder: does Henry trust me to keep quiet? Could he afford to take his chances with Richard, or did he decide to play it safe and kill him?

Chapter Twenty-four

Having emptied a whole bottle of brandy between the two of them, it was inevitable that they would be drunk and their deportment impaired. Sam had to admit that to himself. But at least, he stayed awake. Maggie, on the other hand, bombed out at the first hurdle. She had muttered a few expletives aimed at Henry Hopps-Wood and addressed a few commiserations to 'poor, poor Vera', and promptly passed out on Sam's sofa. Her mouth gaped at Sam blankly as he attempted to wake her and send her to convalesce in her own house. When he shook her gently by her shoulder, her mouth came briefly to life to tell him to bugger off in a slurring fashion. Maggie wasn't budging and there was no way he could carry next door the bulk of her unwilling and uncooperative body. Resigned, Sam fetched a pillow and a duvet from the spare bedroom. He pushed the pillow under Maggie's head and tucked her up inside the duvet. He peered at the sleeping woman thoughtfully, something akin to longing or regret churning in his stomach. An irrational desire bubbled to the surface, a desire to lie down next to her and feel the warmth and softness of her body. He was missing that simple act of sharing a bed with a woman, with her scent and her breath fluttering somewhere between his shoulder and his cheek. He surprised himself. For the first time, he was thinking of a woman – any woman – not only and exclusively of Alice.

'Sorry, my love,' he said to the four empty walls of his sitting room.

He unplugged his laptop and carried it to his study. There, he copied and saved all of the audio files from Penny's USB stick into his cloud. *For backup*, he justified it to himself, but his true reason was to listen to them again alone and in peace, after he had handed the memory stick over to the police.

He left his laptop to continue with its saving activities. It was taking its sweet time. Sam took that time to go to the kitchen and brew a strong cup of black coffee. He added several teaspoons of sugar to it and drank. Thus fortified, he telephoned Alec Scarfe, apologised for the early call (it wasn't yet five o'clock in the morning) and explained that he had in his possession evidence of a rather sensitive nature. He ventured to suggest that Alec, and his men, ought to see it – hear it – as a matter of priority. Alec replied grudgingly, the huskiness of disturbed sleep grating in his voice, that he was on his way. He also uttered a few disgruntled mutterings about Sam's *crap timing*.

When they arrived half an hour later, Sam ushered the two officers directly to his study and left them there to listen to Penny's recordings behind the closed door. The last thing he wanted was to show them to the sitting room where they would be obliged to find Maggie Kaye sprawled on the sofa and to start asking questions about her involvement in all of this. He would be hard pressed to explain to the police how and why she had come to hear the evidence before they did. He was hoping that they would take the USB stick off his hands and depart without ever setting eyes on Maggie blissfully asleep in the other room.

It had taken more than an hour for Alec and Mark Webber to listen to Penny's audio recordings. Sam paced outside, praying that they hurried up and that Maggie didn't wake up. He made himself another cup of coffee but didn't offer anything to the policemen. Inhospitably, he didn't want them to get too comfortable and extend their stay beyond the bounds of what one would call a *flying* visit.

At last, his patience was rewarded. The detectives emerged from the office. Webber was wielding the memory stick. Alec slumped on the kitchen stool, next to Sam. He looked defeated. His only commentary was, 'Blimey . . .'

Webber was more professional. He remained standing.

'How did you come into the possession of this USB device?' he addressed Sam.

'Penny came to see me on Wednesday. She gave it to me for safe keeping. Her verbal instructions were to hold on to this and to release it into the public domain on her death. She also executed her Last Will and Testament with me. I should inform you that – understandably – she bequeathed her estate to Daniel Nolan.'

Alec groaned and tousled his hair ferociously. 'This is a bloody mess. Bloody mess! Our local MP! Blimey!' He fixed Webber with bloodshot eyes. 'This has to be handled sensitively.'

'Sir!'

'One good thing is that Marsh isn't leading this case. No people skills, that woman. Keep her out of it, understood?'

'Yes . . .' There was a note of hesitation in Webber's answer.

'Henry, of all people! Would you believe that?' Alec was scratching his head. His hair was a tangle of bewilderment.

'Unfortunately, yes. I should've thought of it earlier,' Sam confessed.

'How do you mean?'

'A couple of weeks before Richard's party, we were having a drink at the clubhouse. Richard and Henry had a bit of an eyeball-to-eyeball. Actually, it was more Richard taking umbrage to Henry coming to his party. He was quite offensive towards Henry – even threatening . . . He said something to the effect that – well – that he had something compromising on Henry. He said something about holding politicians to account, if I remember correctly.'

'Now, that's that then! What more do you need!'

Maggie materialised out of nowhere, or more precisely from the sofa in the sitting room, making the two police officers jump. They gaped at her, befuddled, as she broke into a slurred diatribe (she was still quite visibly – and audibly – inebriated), 'Henry had a motive! He's your man! Killed Richard . . . as you can tell – I don't have to

159

tell you. There is your motive! Killed Penny ... My God, does that make him a serial killer? Poor, poor Vera! Married to an adulterer ... And a mass murderer! My, my ... But yes, you've got it – we solved it!' She hiccupped and collapsed on a stool next to the shocked Chief Superintendent. From there she continued with her exposé in an increasingly disorderly and unintelligible fashion.

'And we've got evidence, straight from the horse's mouth!' she concluded.

Sam shut his eyes tight and buried his face in his hands.

Penny's confessions had opened the floodgates of hell and unleashed torrents of speculation. By the time Sam emerged from his house to organise supplies for lunch for himself and Maggie (who was back on his sofa, having succumbed to a debilitating hangover), Bishops Well was awash with gossip exchanged in suppressed whispers and with nervous glances shooting in all directions. Angela Cornish, the bakery owner and source of oven-fresh news, had it on good authority that Henry Hopps-Wood had been arrested in the early hours of the morning.

'So much for the blue blood,' she told the audience of four of her customers who were waiting for the new batch of steak and ale pies baking in the oven, 'he be having more skeletons in his cupboard than you can count in the whole of St John's graveyard! I never trusted that weaselly face of his. Always knew he was up to no good ...'

She suspended her voice on that ominous note, letting her listeners draw their own chilling conclusions while she transferred the pies from the oven onto a tray. The aroma drifted out of the shop and into the street. In no time, Angela's audience had doubled in size.

'And I hear from someone in the know that the weasel had something to do with young Leila Nolan's death. In the end, he'll get his comeuppance, but the harm he's done so far is ... done, and mark my words – it can't be undone. Shame on him! Calls himself our MP! *Our MP*, I'll be damned!' she huffed, dishing out pies with her allegations. 'A plain and simple criminal – that's what he is!'

That allegation was supported by the appearance of a helicopter with BBC markings flying low and incessantly over the Hopps-Wood estate. Something newsworthy was going on there, big time! The press was all over Bishops Well like a bad case of chickenpox. Vans bearing logos of every conceivable TV station, local and international, were parked illegally on every double yellow line alongside the main road. The traffic warden, Ron Worsley, was having a field day dishing out parking tickets. A TV crew from Richard's homeland had decamped on the green next to a group of French reporters (nothing like the French to sniff out a juicy story with a scandalous finish); they were exchanging intelligence in broken English. A German-sounding journalist was scouring local shops for inside information. A six-person-strong Japanese crew had booked the last available bedrooms at Parson's Combe Inn, and even a Dutchman flew in by night. The eyes of the whole world were on Bishops Well!

By the time the *Six O'Clock News* was over, Bishops Well was a household name around the globe. Maggie was still sofa-surfing at Sam's because of a crushing headache and an alleged loss of navigational skills necessary to guide her home, so they watched the news together. The sombre Huw Edwards revealed to the world at large that the Right Honourable Henry Hopps-Wood, Member of Parliament for Sexton's Canning, was being interviewed by the police in connection with the murders of the Polish-born director, Richard Ruta and his playwright wife, Penny. 'This morning the police swooped on Mr Hopps-Wood's home with a search warrant to look for and secure evidence in this case.' Huw Edwards gave the floor to a reporter in situ who provided a running commentary of the bird's eye view close-ups of the roof of the house, followed by a few peeks through the second-floor windows and down to the commotion on the ground. Uniformed policemen were carrying out computer equipment and boxed-up items. With a loud gasp, Maggie identified the top of Vera's head as the poor woman ran after the officers, flailing her arms. The reporter interviewed

Detective Chief Superintendent, Alec Scarfe, who reluctantly confirmed that the police had grounds for the search but denied that Mr Hopps-Wood was under arrest and clarified that he was simply being interviewed in connection with the murders. *Interviewed under caution?* the reporter asked. *Correct*, replied Alec.

Maggie stared at Sam. Her cheeks flushed and ploughed with the imprint of the sofa upholstery, her hair entangled, her eyelids swollen, and her breath atrocious, she didn't look her best but more like a squirrel who had just about, by the skin of its teeth, escaped from the clutches of a deadly predator.

'Does it mean that Henry's going to be kicked out of Westminster?' she croaked. 'Poor, poor Vera!'

'No, far from it. He hasn't been arrested, never mind convicted.'

'But they might force him to resign his seat, mightn't they?'

'It depends, I guess.'

While the rest of the news hummed in the background telling them nothing new, followed by the weather forecast, Sam shot off to the kitchen to fetch two glasses of tap water. He sat down and both he and Maggie drank greedily while David Garmston peered at them grimly from the newsroom of *BBC Points West*. The whole drama about the invasion of Henry and Vera's home started all over again. Sam was about to turn off the TV when a brand-new revelation in the Ruta double-murder case was made. This time about the arrest of Frank Savage.

A mugshot of Frank in his younger days, wearing an army uniform and an inscrutable face, appeared on the screen. 'Francis Savage, fifty-three, an ex-military officer employed by Mr Ruta as his personal security consultant –'

'Does he mean *bodyguard?*'

'Shush!'

'. . . was detained by the police in connection with the death of Leila Nolan eighteen years ago at a party held at Forget-Me-Not, Richard Ruta's country estate. At the time, the death was declared an accidental drowning by the County Coroner. Earlier today, *Points West* was briefed by the spokesperson for Sexton's Canning

162

Constabulary that the investigation into Miss Nolan's death had been reopened thanks to two vigilant members of the local community who came forward with vital information that sheds doubt on the Coroner's ruling of accidental death. Mr Savage was arrested following an interview under caution. The charges are related to the death of Miss Nolan, and extend further to withholding information and obstructing the police in their original investigation.'

Sam and Maggie exchanged panicked looks, half-expecting to hear their names being mentioned alongside the badge of *vigilant members of the local community*. They breathed a sigh of relief when Garmston moved to the next news item, leaving their names out of the limelight.

'My God,' Maggie exclaimed, 'half of Bishops Well is dead or under arrest! And I can't begin to imagine what's going through Vera's head!'

'Yes, it's all rather unfortunate,' Sam nodded dolefully.

Maggie presented a wide, chubby-cheeked smile with two dimples. 'But just think what we achieved, Samuel – we solved two, no, wait – three murders! Single-handedly!'

Chapter Twenty-five

I was in my garden, pruning. The sun was high in the sky, its warmth slowing the wildlife from a busy buzz to a lazy lull. I too was feeling a little slow and sleepy. My headache was pulsing faintly, suppressed by two paracetamol tablets, but not entirely defeated. I couldn't convince my poor head to engage in any meaningful thinking, so I just pruned mindlessly. Until I heard voices over the wall, coming from the cemetery. I was instantly jolted into full alertness.

Not all voices coming from the cemetery belong to the dead. There are also living people visiting the tombs of their loved ones, and sometimes they talk to them. I don't eavesdrop. I respect their privacy. However, on this occasion, the conversation over the wall didn't involve the dead. Both parties were very much alive. As soon as I recognised the female voice as that belonging to DI Marsh, I just had to steal a little peep to establish who the owner of the second voice was. I crawled towards the wall and slowly elevated myself from a squat to a semi-erect position. On the other side, seated on the bench Mrs Rowling had built by her late husband's grave, were Gillian Marsh and DS Webber.

'You must be loving this,' Webber reflected, 'I wish sometimes I could pack it all in and –'

'Yes, Mark, I'm sure you do, but trust me, this is like watching paint dry,' Marsh declared in the brusque manner I recognised from our previous encounters. 'Forget the lap of nature. You're fed up because the case isn't going anywhere – that's your problem.'

'Actually, we've got a strong suspect in custody.'

'Hopps-Wood?'

'Yeah. He had a motive to kill both Richard and Penny Ruta. He had been having an affair with the wife and, as always happens, the husband found out – and was going to get a divorce, and threatened to make the affair public. Imagine what it'd do to Hopps-Wood if the affair hit the front pages . . . You don't need a stronger motive than that. And he had the opportunity – he was at the party, and before that he travelled to Paris when that bottle of wine was bought –'

'But you don't have him on CCTV buying the wine?'

'Nope.'

'You have that mysterious woman instead.'

'Yep. But you see, Scarface thinks the damned Tokaji doesn't matter. Hopps-Wood could've spiked the bottle at the party, minutes before Ruta drank it. He had an opportunity.'

'So it doesn't really matter that he was at the airport when the wine was bought . . . It sounds like you have a patchwork of ideas rather than a cut and dried case. You don't buy Hopps-Wood as the perpetrator, do you?'

'It's all circumstantial. We looked for Penny Ruta's laptop at his house – scoured the whole place top to bottom, and nothing. Not a shred of evidence to link him to either murder. He could've bought the wine, but there's no proof. He could've spiked the wine, but there's no proof. He denies everything. His wife swears blind that he was at home all day and night when Penny Ruta was being poisoned. We found nothing incriminating at his house. We were hoping to find Penny's missing laptop at the very least, but like I said, no luck.'

'Blimey, I saw the coverage on TV. You went in all guns blazing!' Gillian gave a short laugh.

'Scarface wanted to be seen as acting with integrity and insisted everything we did had to be above board. He's friends with Hopps-Wood, so he had to, I suppose.'

I guessed that the unflattering nickname *Scarface* belonged to poor Alec. I am so used to his cleft lip that I hardly notice it, but not everyone is as gracious as me. As much as I wanted to give those two a piece of my mind about common decency, I had to bite my lip and remain silent. I was hoping to acquire more valuable inside knowledge.

Webber went on, 'He wants to hand the case to the CPS and let them evaluate the evidence and see if they're happy to run with it.'

'You don't think they will? And more to the point, are you happy with what you have? What concrete evidence is actually there?'

'Not much. And there is this: the aconite used to kill Richard was not exactly the same as the aconite used in Penny's poisoning. Didn't Michael tell you?'

Gillian Marsh sounded seriously disgruntled when she answered, 'Obviously, he didn't. You'll need to enlighten me.'

'Well, the composition of the poison in Richard's murder indicates that a synthesised product was used. Traces of other chemicals are present, as you would find in medicines for PTSD for example. The aconite in the wife's murder was pure root extract, no contamination from other agents.'

'So potentially, we have two killers ...'

'It's a great probability.'

'That could mean Hopps-Wood is innocent of at least one murder.'

'Or both. He had the motive to kill both Richard and his wife. Both of them posed a threat to him and it looks like both of them were about to talk.'

'So, to kill one and not the other would be only half the job done.'

'It wouldn't solve the problem for Hopps-Wood, not really.'

'You're right, Webber. You got there in the end. There's no hard case against Hopps-Wood. What you need is evidence. I'm proud of you – I taught you well!'

'Well ... I mean – if you say so,' Webber stammered. Like him, I also couldn't detect any connection between his lack of progress and his supposed success.

'But don't get carried away, because now you've no suspects and you don't know where to go next? That's why you need me, Webber, you'll always need me.'

'Oh, buzz off, Marsh! So what if I do?'

I was listening to DI Marsh laughing: a hearty, wholesome chortle. I was surprised. I didn't know the woman could laugh.

'Get off it! What are you thinking?' Webber, like me, didn't find her comment amusing.

'Here's what I'm thinking, Watson,' she was serious again, 'follow the trail. You must find the woman from the airport. She's the key. She bought the wine that only Richard would drink – that was no coincidence. It was to avoid other, unintended poisonings. She must've known it was his birthday – why else would she have gifted him the wine? And if she knew him at all, she would've known a big bash was on the cards, but that Richard would keep his favourite drink to himself . . . The alternative of someone sneaking into the house to poison the entire reserve of liquor is highly improbable. I don't believe for one second that someone'd spike several wine bottles on the off-chance of killing one man at a party with twenty-odd guests in attendance. Unless he or she is a psycho . . . No, Richard Ruta was targeted. Find that woman.'

'Easier said than done. Scarfe has parked that line of inquiry.'

'Re-open it, behind his back if need be. Go through all the passenger lists of all flights from Paris to the UK that day. And look for Richard Ruta! If our mystery woman gave him that wine, they had to meet somewhere. Look for him – he's more recognisable. People will remember him and that may lead you to her.'

'It's like looking for a needle in a haystack! There were seven flights from Paris to five different airports in the UK. And what if she didn't travel to the UK? What if she met with Hopps-Wood in Paris, gave him the wine, and simply walked away? We don't have the resources to wade through all of the possible footage!'

I couldn't bear this any longer. I had to stick my head over the parapet – literally on this occasion – and give them a nudge in the right direction. I stood up.

'I'm sorry to barge in, but I couldn't help overhearing you. I was just pruning my roses, and –'

'Maggie Kaye? What the hell are you doing here?' DI Marsh gaped at me with disbelief – or rather, dismay – and so did Webber.

'Well, yes, that'd be me. I live here,' I informed them. 'Anyway, going back to your needle in a haystack. If I were you I'd ignore all other airports and train stations, and concentrate on Bristol. Richard was meeting a lady in Bristol. I have it on good authority . . . Well, Richard told Samuel and Samuel told me. He also told Alec. Maybe Alec forgot to pass it on. Maybe he thought it wasn't important. Anyway, I thought you should know.'

'Thank you, ma'am,' Webber managed to mouth, but Ms Marsh remained speechless.

'No problem. Any time.' I was just about to return to my pruning when I remembered one more thing, 'And incidentally, it's very unkind to call your superintendent nasty names behind his back. How would you feel, DI Marsh, if someone called you . . .' I assessed her head to toe, looking for a suitable descriptor. 'A scrawny little pixie.'

Chapter Twenty-six

Henry Hopps-Wood MP had been released from police custody without charge and wanted to meet. His stipulation was that they would meet on *neutral ground*, as he had put it. He was insistent that Vera should know nothing about this; she had been through enough heartbreak as it were. She didn't need to be reminded of the police raid and the humiliation of her husband being arrested without ceremony or any regard for his community standing. Or for his innocence. But Henry wasn't prepared to forgive and forget. He wanted to have a word with Samuel Dee QC about *his options*.

Sam had tried to explain he was no longer practising law and that his specialty had never lain in privacy or defamation laws. He had offered to recommend to Henry a good lawyer with a proven track record, but Henry wouldn't hear of it. He didn't wish for strangers to stick their noses into his personal affairs. Samuel was a trusted friend. Did friendship stand for nothing these days?

Sam was taken aback by the assertion of friendship: he had known Henry for less than a year and the casual nature of their random encounters and passing greetings did not in his view warrant a word stronger than *acquaintance* to describe it. But he succumbed. He didn't want to appear a supercilious prig snubbing a man who was already on his knees. They agreed to meet for lunch at the clubhouse.

Sam arrived early and sat in the bar to wait. He ordered a pint of lager from Rhys and was just about to peacefully drown his sorrows in it when he spotted Frank nursing a glass of whisky – his third one, Rhys whispered – and looking positively unkempt. Sam approached him.

'They let you go?'

Frank peered at Sam with bloodshot eyes, and said, 'Yeah, on bail. I ain't going anywhere – they didn't think me a flight risk. Mainly though, they had nothing on me to keep me locked up. I told them what I did, which was bugger all – just helped Richard push the body into the pool, as I was asked, and kept quiet about it. All I'll get is a suspended sentence or community service for tampering with the crime scene and obstructing police in their investigation, my brief tells me. I'll live.' He raised his glass to Sam and downed his whisky.

'I don't imagine you knew it was Penny who'd attacked Leila?' Sam had to be careful how to word his questions. Nobody even suspected that he had heard Penny's confession on tape.

'Ha! No, I didn't know that, did I. I bloody didn't. I thought I was helping Richard. I wouldn't raise my little finger to help *her*. She killed that damned girl and then she killed Richard, that's what I know. For a fact!' Frank sounded like a stubborn old mule, his alcohol-drenched voice devoid of sober reason. He waved his empty glass to Rhys, who rolled his eyes signalling that he should refuse to serve Frank: the man was already well sozzled. But, on reflection, Rhys decided to avoid confrontation with the mulish drunk. He nodded and approached with a bottle of Jameson's to refill Frank's tumbler.

'How can you possibly know that for a fact? You didn't see her do it – you didn't see Penny poison the wine ... or did you?' Sam enquired after Rhys departed.

'I didn't have to. Richard told me – simple as that.' Frank lowered his voice and leaned towards Sam, his breath flammable and his forefinger wobbling unsteadily in Sam's face. 'Richard told me who gave him the bloody Tokaji, didn't he!'

'Did he?'

'Oh yeah! He says, *Nothing gets past you, Frank, old man*. And I say, *No,* and I grin, but I'm curious because I didn't see who brought that wine to the party, do you get me?'

Sam nodded.

'So Richard taps his nose and is acting like he ain't gonna tell me, but he says, *The love of my life, old man, the love of my life! You go and figure that!* So I did. It was that bitch of his wife. She killed him.'

Henry marched in briskly and tapped Sam on the back just as Sam was about to ask Frank for further clarification.

'Sorry, I'm late, I had to go into a long explanation to Vera where I was off to. She's become paranoid. Anyway, the table is waiting. Frank,' Henry offered Frank a curt nod.

Frank turned away and focused his attention on his drink. He had nothing else to say.

Reluctantly Sam followed Henry to their table in the restaurant. Henry sat facing the window. Only now, in broad daylight, had it become brutally evident what a day in a police cell could do to a man. Henry's complexion was pallid, heavy bags sagging under his eyes, and he looked even thinner than his usual thin-as-a-rake self.

'You must be glad the whole ordeal is behind you.'

'Well, it isn't, is it?' Henry blinked rapidly behind his spectacles. 'I've been wrongly accused. They had nothing on me.'

Sam had heard the same expression earlier from Frank. An eerie sense of déjà vu, he thought: two men protesting their innocence by pointing to the lack of evidence against them. The last thing Sam would do was debate Henry's conscience and his definition of wrongdoing with him. He buried his face in the menu.

Henry planted his hand on Sam's menu. He was agitated. It clearly didn't occur to him that he was being rude. He went on, 'Nothing! They were looking for some sodding laptop – turned my office upside down, took away confidential documents, letters from my constituents – private, sensitive documents! They frightened Vera! They frightened the bloody dog! My house ... my whole house was on display on the national News. Do you know how that felt? Can you even imagine? I felt like I was being gutted in public!'

'Are you ready to order?' A pretty young waitress with liquid, chocolate-brown eyes and a touch of a Jamaican accent stood by their table, holding a pad and a pen at the ready.

Henry glowered at the poor girl. He yelled, 'No, no, no! We do not want to be disturbed! Not now! Are you blind? We haven't looked at the menu! Not yet! Give us time! What is this – a fast food joint?'

The waitress winced and almost ducked under the barrage of Henry's vituperations. She hid her pad and pen behind her back and scampered.

'That was uncalled for,' Sam lowered his voice, 'you must apologise, Henry. Now.'

Henry rubbed his temples. His face was contorted in deep discomfort. 'I don't know what possessed me. It's this whole bloody ... the false arrest. I'm sorry, Sam.'

'Apologise to her, not to me.'

'You aren't serious?'

'Yes, I am. Or I'll leave.'

'Do you see what this is doing to me!' Henry jumped to his feet and slammed his napkin on the table. 'My whole life's in tatters! My nerves–'

Sam just glared, determined to compel Henry to deliver his apology to the waitress. Henry pushed back his chair, groaned, thrust his chin up and marched towards the door marked STAFF ONLY. Before he crossed the threshold, he threw a fatalistic glance back at Sam. His eyes shouted, *I'm about to cross my Rubicon!* and then he dived in. He stayed there, behind the closed door for less than thirty seconds and was back, looking like someone who had been to a leper colony and survived the experience.

He sat at the table and said, 'I ordered a bottle of Shiraz. They've a decent year.'

'Did you apologise to that girl?' Sam would have nothing to do with even the most vintage Shiraz or any other wine until he was satisfied.

'Of course! What do you take me for?'

Over starters, which consisted of a duck pâté for Sam and grilled goat's cheese for Henry, the subjects of privacy infringement and false imprisonment came back like a boomerang.

'I have investigated all the remedial avenues, Sam, and I want to run it by you. I need your legal – you know . . . seal of approval, so to speak. Take the Cliff Richard case. Similar – I'd even say identical – circumstances: police leaks, BBC reporters having a field day, helicopters bursting into his home, and not a shred of evidence. Not a shred of evidence! I should receive millions in compensation!'

'Are you sure, Henry?' Sam was beginning to experience bouts of mild irritation. First of all, a few droplets of Henry's spittle had splashed into his pâté, rendering it inedible. Secondly, he knew Henry was lying. There was the circumstantial evidence of Henry's presence in Paris on the day the wine was bought. And there was more: Penny's confession of their affair, which gave Henry the motive to kill both Richard and Penny. He also had the opportunity. The only missing link was the means and the precise sequence of events: had that unfortunate bottle of Tokaji passed through Henry's hands between being purchased in Paris and drunk by Richard at his party?

'Of course I'm sure! They interrogated me as if I were a murder suspect, for God's sake! And they had nothing on me! Nothing!'

'Not even a motive?' Sam pinned raging Henry with a narrow, knowing gaze. 'Be careful, my friend. If you sue the police, or BBC, secrets will crawl out to see the light of day. You won't be able to suppress any details – say, written confessions or testimonies the police have on file. On your file . . . Do you understand what I'm saying?'

Henry blinked. Several times. He swallowed what seemed like a huge chunk of goat cheese.

'I see that you do. I'm glad. You wouldn't want all that dirty laundry to be done in public view. You have your reputation to protect. Trust me – you accuse the police of fabricating evidence in this double murder case, their lawyers will pull out everything they have to discredit you, whether it directly relates to the case or not. Your character will go on trial, and everything you get up to in your spare time. Nothing will be sacred, certainly not your privacy. You sure you have nothing you'd rather keep to yourself? The nature of your past relationship with one of the murder victims, for example?'

Henry mumbled something under his breath. The last few sparks of his righteous fury seemed to go out in a puff.

'If I were you, frankly, I'd park this idea of damages and make a short, friendly statement to the press about how you were happy to be able to assist the police with their inquiries into the deaths of your dear friend and his wife. Your civic duty duly discharged ... You were only too happy to oblige, etc, etc, etc ...'

Sam pushed his plate aside and aligned his knife and fork neatly to signal to the pretty young waitress with chocolate-brown eyes that he was finished with his starter and ready for the main. Henry was still busy swallowing.

Chapter Twenty-seven

It was Wednesday. I had the meeting of the Bishops Well AA to attend and to face Vera. Knowing what I knew about Henry and Penny, and what he thought of his wife, I couldn't bring myself to look her in the eye. Two weeks ago I had called in sick – the discovery of Henry's affair and his motive for murder had been all too fresh in my mind. Two weeks later, I was still struggling with my conscience. Although it was irrational, I had been feeling responsible for Henry's arrest and wouldn't be able to face Vera without breaking into profuse apologies and making a full confession for something I didn't do. As it turned out, it had been a waste of a sickie as the meeting had been called off. Understandably, nobody had been in the mood for cutting into Vera's fresh wounds with the scalpels of pointless commiseration. We had put it off until later.

But life had to go on and sooner or later the meetings had to be resumed. We could not bury our heads in the sand for ever. This week's meeting was happening.

I mounted my bicycle and hit the road, heading for the Community Hall. I realise it is only a few hundred yards away, but I was late. I dropped the bike at the door, inhaled, and braved the adversity. Everyone was there but Vera. I exhaled.

James Weston-Jones was taking the minutes. He noted my late arrival, which would go against my record. I was disappointed. I had thought we were friends.

The atmosphere was stiff with discomfort. It felt like we were at a wake: stale biscuits, cold tea and one of us sadly missing.

'She didn't call to say she wasn't coming,' Cherie said. 'We'll wait a bit longer, another five minutes and then we'll have to start without her.'

I squinted glumly and squeezed into an empty chair between Michael Almond and Dr Flynn. In the fervour of their conversation, they hardly even noticed me. My ears pricked when I realised that they were exchanging notes about the properties of aconite, the poison used in the two murders. Of course, I had to act as if I hadn't overheard DI Marsh's conversation in the graveyard.

'So, two different forms of aconite?'

'One was a natural extract and the other a composite.'

I wasn't sure what a composite was but I knew it wasn't the same thing as a natural extract.

'They couldn't have come from the same source,' Dr Flynn shook his head.

'Definitely not. The one that killed Penny was just a root extract of *Aconitum* –'

'Common wolfsbane?'

'Wolfsbane?' I echoed Dr Flynn's words. I knew what wolfsbane was. I call it monkshood, but it is one and the same plant: it has lovely bluish flowers shaped like bells, or if you look closely, you will find that they resemble medieval monks' hoods. Thus its name. I quite like it. It shocked me that such a pretty little thing was actually lethal.

'Yes, common wolfsbane.' Michael gave me a passing glance, but his attention returned to Dr Flynn, whom he considered a more worthy interlocutor than me by virtue of, I'm guessing, his medical background. 'Now, Richard was killed by an aconite composite in large concentration, probably several pills crushed and dissolved in the wine.'

'That's so very interesting,' Flynn's voice squeaked with unhealthy enthusiasm.

'Yes, indeed. It sheds new light on the case – new possibilities.'

'So that's why they let Henry go?'

'He isn't quite off the hook yet, but yes. We could be looking at two different killers. He could still be one of them.'

'I bet Gillian is itching to get back to work.'

'So much so that she's moved out.' Michael's lip twitched. Keeping a stiff upper lip was proving too much of a challenge for him. He looked upset. Poor Michael doesn't have much luck with women – I'd be hard pressed to remember the name of his girlfriend before Ms Marsh, if indeed there had ever been one.

'Moved out? Have you, two ... separated? How do you feel about it?' There was a glint of excitement in Dr Flynn's eyes. Was he eyeing up his next patient in need of psychiatric therapy? Maybe it was just a trick of light in the room. I could never tell with Dr Flynn, but he gave me the creeps.

'Not separated. At least I hope not. We're still seeing each other, in theory. She's just moved back to her own place in Sexton's.'

'Finding country life too boring?'

'That too. But we had a small misunderstanding about how she should go about her recovery.'

'So she *was* itching to get back to work.' Flynn was triumphant, his original diagnosis proving correct.

'Am I late?'

Vera had arrived. We didn't know for how long she had stood there in the doorway, and how much she had heard. She looked awful: grey and drawn, skin and bone. She was also dishevelled and wild-eyed.

If our meeting resembled a wake, then this appearance was nothing short of a resurrection.

'Vera!' We all flocked to her. We led her to the table and sat her down.

Nobody really knew what to say. We just gawped at her idiotically, waiting for her to say something – anything!

She smiled.

It was a ghastly smile – it bore a resemblance to Jack Nicholson's crazed grin in *The Shining*. But she had made the effort to come to the meeting and she was smiling, so there was hope that things were slowly returning to normal.

'How are you, darling?' I went to hug her. She took it awkwardly, stiffening in my embrace like – no, I won't make any more comparisons. She was just rigid. But still smiling.

'How's Henry? You must be relieved they let him go –'

'Without being charged, it's worth noting,' Dr Flynn chirped in.

'You two have been through so, so much –'

'Not at all,' Vera interrupted me, and still as rigid as an ironing board, put her chin up and said through her teeth, 'Henry and I, but Henry, in the main – he was actually very happy to assist the police with their inquiries. That's the least he could do, even though there was very little he could contribute. Every one of you would've done the same – help the police, I mean ... with their inquiries.' She sounded like a schoolgirl reciting a poem from memory, a poem she didn't like or even understand.

Vanessa was staring at Vera, struck with disbelief. She probably knew more about Henry's dalliances than she was letting on – Alec must've let something slip at the dinner table. I, too, knew more. I knew Henry was teetering on the brink of what one would call *full disclosure* – not the best place to be for a high-profile politician. And once dodgy links between Penny and Henry were established in the public eye, no self-respecting journo would stop at that. Speculations would start flying about Henry's involvement in Leila's death. Even if untrue, such rumours could lethally wound Henry's standing in the community. Sordid secrets had a way of coming out.

But how much did Vera know? She was being a brave girl and a loyal wife to her scoundrel husband. My heart bled for her, truly.

Chapter Twenty-eight

I was weeding the flower beds, trying to relax in my garden after a day full of tension and unpleasantness. Firstly, there was that whole debacle with Vera at the meeting. If that wasn't enough, on my way home, I had stopped at R. Kane & Sons, the local butchers. For some reason, Robert Kane (five-times removed from the first Robert Kane, the butchery founder) had taken umbrage to me innocently enquiring if he had fresh chops. Apparently, an entire busload of them lay before my very eyes, still twitching their muscles. He wouldn't accept my explanation that I had not seen them as I hadn't been looking because I preferred to ask the expert. But all he wanted me to do was to answer this apparently *simple question:* had he ever sold me anything that wasn't fresh? He was unrecognisable in his righteous indignation. Robert, affectionately known as Bobby, is a gentle giant of a man and although he can wield an axe better than a medieval executioner, he would not use it to harm a fly. Yet he was in a state of uncontrollable rage and there was a moment when I feared for my life when he pointed his bloody butcher's knife in my face. It was all due to growing unease. Bishops Well was shaken to its core. Two murders and no sign of a murderer. The pressure was beginning to get to us all.

So, later in the afternoon I decided to relax in the garden, tending to my flowers. Even that was easier said than done with Penny hovering over my head, refusing to move on into the afterlife or at least somewhere where her loved ones would appreciate her company. I didn't like her that much in life and didn't intend to revise that sentiment now just because she was dead.

I said to her, 'Why don't you get on with your life, Penny? You're wasting your time here.'

'Is she still about?' It was Samuel. He had popped out on to his overgrown patio, carrying his customary mug of coffee.

'I'm afraid so,' I sighed.

'And Alice?' He gave me that semi-nonchalant look self-conscious people do, as if his question was just a joke, but I could tell he was anxious.

'She's not here. The dead – they never get in each other's way. Obviously, Penny's business is more pressing, so Alice has stepped aside to give her the floor, figuratively speaking.' It sounded outlandish, I know, but that's the beauty of all things out of this world: they sound daft.

Samuel took an abrupt and ill-judged sip of his coffee and burned his lips. He cursed, thus spilling more coffee on his fingers. 'Damn it! Damn her!'

'I've a feeling she'll hang around until we've got her killer.'

'Now that Henry is out, we may be running out of suspects.'

'I have heard – through the grapevine – that there could be two different killers.'

Samuel looked intrigued so I proceeded to explain for his benefit the differences between extracts and composites. 'So, as much as Henry could've killed Richard, someone else might've killed Penny.'

Samuel was frowning and mumbling something under his breath. He was thinking, I deduced, and I was curious to know what it was that he was churning in his head.

'A penny for your thoughts, Samuel,' I prompted him.

He was now looking inspired. 'Yes! I should've seen it earlier. Of course, it's been staring me in the face. I mean, he as much as told me that he killed her!'

'Who?'

'Frank! Frank bloody Savage! He was raving about a woman – *the love of Richard's life* – she, according to Richard, gave him the poisoned Tokaji ... and Frank said he'd worked it out and that it

180

was Penny. Who else! Richard chose her over Frank, over every other woman in his life – she had to be *the love of his life!* And Frank hated her – openly hated the very notion of her. It was Frank.'

'Frank killed Penny?'

'I've no doubt. He told me.'

'In so many words? I don't think so. If he had, you'd be calling the cops.' I leaned over the low wall separating our respective gardens. 'Did he confess to killing Penny?'

'No, he didn't confess, but – I mean –'

'We need a confession. He's probably dying to tell someone anyway. We need to go and see him. You'll sit down with him, put him at ease and get him to talk. You can record the whole conversation – his confession – on your phone. I will be on standby in case . . . in case something happens.'

He gazed at me, befuddled. 'We can't possibly . . . What are you – It's only a wild guess, Maggie. We can take this to the police, report Frank, and see what they can do.'

'What can they do? Like you said, it's only a wild guess. Do you want to get rid of Penny, or not? Do you want Alice to come back?' I hated resorting to supernatural blackmail, but I had no other methods of persuasion at my disposal. I was convinced Samuel was right about Frank. But we needed hard proof, and what better proof than a confession.

As any self-respecting, rational man would, Samuel offered resistance, 'I really don't want to hurt your feelings, Maggie, but I don't think you realise how . . . how ridiculous you sound?'

'Oh, yes, I do,' I conceded, confident that although I might have lost that particular point, he would forfeit the whole argument. People like to put on appearances of cold logic, but deep down we are all superstitious pagans. We all jump up in our beds when we hear strange noises in the night. We all cross our fingers behind our back when we lie. Most of us feel aversion towards bats and a mistrust of black cats. And some of us wouldn't dream of walking under a ladder. 'But I've no time to chat about it right now. Shall we go?'

And, rolling his eyes and swearing he was only coming along to protect me, he joined me.

The conversation was going nowhere fast. I was crouching under the sitting-room window on the outside, and inside Frank was venting his spleen. I was getting pins and needles in my legs but didn't dare to move or make any noise that could attract unwanted attention to myself. I was holding my mobile slightly above the window parapet, so my arm, too, was beginning to ache. Meantime, Samuel was sitting comfortably in a nice chair with a high back, listening to Frank saying all sorts of things – anything but a direct and unequivocal confession.

'Since she came into our lives everything started going tits up. On every level. We had that Nolan girl dying on us, and that was the mad cow's fault, it turns out – she told me. Richard hadn't made a single film since he married the harlot. He started a couple of projects, but never finished anything. It's like she pulled the rug from under his feet. Sucked the creative juices out of him . . . He put money into her so-called play scripts – the plays bombed, all of them,' Frank chuckled. 'Bombed big time – bang, bang!' He blew the imaginary smoke off the two fingers representing his imaginary pistols. He scowled, 'She changed him. He used to love life, take risks, you know? She put a stop to it. He aged around her, became an old man. And then, if that wasn't enough, she goes and fucking kills him!'

Samuel jumped on this opportunity. 'How could you let her get away with it?'

'How could I . . .' Frank turned all pensive. It was no good.

'It was your job to watch Richard's back.'

'And I failed him. I failed the man I –' Frank was weeping. He swiped his wide thumbs over his eyes and pressed the bridge of his nose.

'It's almost poetic justice that Penny is dead, don't you think?' Samuel kept probing. His every word was like another juicy worm on the hook at the end of his fishing line, but Frank wasn't taking the bait.

'Oh yeah! You bet! She brought it on herself –'

'You mean she provoked you?'

Frank paused. I heaved myself a fraction over the windowsill to assess if Samuel hadn't taken it too far and wasn't in danger. Frank got up and approached Samuel, looking intimidating.

My finger hovered over the screen of my phone, ready to tap 999. But there was no need. Frank took Samuel's glass away from him and said, 'No, she didn't. She killed herself, out of guilt.'

Samuel nodded eagerly, reminding me of that nodding toy bulldog some people have in the back of their cars.

He rose to his feet. 'I'd better be going.'

'You had better, yes. I've got a couple of things to take care of. Thanks for the ... visit.' Frank's suspicious eyes followed Samuel all the way to the driveway.

Samuel waited for me on the road outside the estate. I traversed the lawns on low haunches and climbed over the wall in the same place that we had trespassed into Forget-Me-Not on the day we found Penny's body.

'Shit!' I muttered as soon as I eased myself into the passenger seat. (For once, Penny had the decency to be content with the back seat.) 'We can't leave now.'

'We tried, we failed. Let's go.'

'No! He's clocked you, can't you see? He's now going to get rid of all the incriminating evidence. Everything will be lost!'

'So what do you propose we do?'

'We go back and place him under surveillance. We wait for him to go to bed and then search the house for evidence – there's that missing laptop ...'

'And when we do that, we will compromise any evidence that may still be there,' Samuel warned me, but seeing that I had already turned on my heel and headed back over the wall, he had no option but to follow.

We clambered over the wall which was beginning to show signs of wear and tear at the point of our frequent crossings. The lawn was also well trodden. I would lie if I said I wasn't enjoying myself. It felt liberating to climb walls, sneak up on unsuspecting suspects, and squat amidst thorny bushes, listening to people's private conversations. I could make a living out of this, I thought as I navigated the maze of box hedges, and I would love it. Maybe, I mused further, Samuel Dee could join forces with me as my business partner; he knew the law and it was clear from living next door to him that the man had nothing to do all day but wallow in his grief.

I found myself brutally pulled down by my sleeve and all my ponderings scattered on the ground like bruised apples. From the corner of my eye, I saw a beetle beating a hasty retreat from under my cheek. Samuel was lying next to me, hushing me before I even opened my mouth to demand an explanation. He pointed to the terrace.

At first, I saw nothing but orange light streaming from the house through the French doors and onto the top terrace. Then a flicker of brighter light ignited as Frank lit a cigarette. He was leaning against one of the plinths at the bottom of the steps, the one holding a stag. His silhouette blended into the twilight greys. He was gazing down the driveway where, minutes earlier, Samuel's car had disappeared round the bend.

'Is he making sure you're gone?' I hissed into Samuel's ear.

'Let's hope he doesn't take the trouble of going down to the road to find my damned car parked by the wall,' Samuel hissed back into my ear.

'While he's out here, we could enter from the back and search the house.'

I knew Samuel was going to counter my suggestion as unwise, so without waiting for his reply, I pounced up and dived into the hedge maze, my plan to circumvent the garden to the rear entrance – the *tradesman's door*, as it was known.

There was a line of wheelie bins and a compost heap with a spade and a rake propped against the wall next to it, just outside the kitchen at the back of the house. I treaded carefully so as not to bump into anything and cause a clamour.

'And what are you hoping to find here?' Samuel was hot on my heels, still hissing into my ear.

'I'll know when I find it. How about Penny's laptop, or its hardware matrix, or something like that?' I really didn't know what I was looking for but I relied on the well-established fact that any suspect's rubbish bins were a valuable source of information (and of course, rubbish). I plunged in.

It appeared that recycling was practised religiously at Forget-Me-Not, as it was in all the other households around Bishops that employed Cathy Hicks. Cathy is very particular about the environment and recycling is high on her priorities list. Her cleaning services are sought after and she will not take on a house that doesn't have its recycling well sorted. From the arrangement of bins, I could tell that Forget-Me-Not was one of Cathy's hunting grounds. I started with the black box containing plastic – a laptop could be lying camouflaged amongst the milk bottles. It could be but it wasn't. I moved to the wheelie with general waste. The search would be harder in there as everything was bundled up inside black bin liners.

'Do you want to give me a hand with this?'

Samuel peered rather fastidiously at the bag I had pulled out of the wheelie. 'Um, if I must engage in any of these ... illegal activities, I'd rather examine the glass bin.'

I shrugged with contempt, but only internally. His heart wasn't in it, but at least he was here in person to assist. The man needed to be trained in the art of obedience, but this wasn't the right time. I tore a hole in my first black bag to have my nostrils assaulted by the vile stink of rotting leftovers being slowly overcome by a colony of wriggly maggots. Retching, I decided that a better way would be to feel the bags for any hard or sharp objects in the shape of a laptop, and only then to sink my teeth into them (metaphorically, of course). As I was feeling the bags, it occurred to me that since the party nobody had bothered to wheel the rubbish bins to the road for collection. Nobody seemed to be responsible for housekeeping and Cathy Hicks' services had not been requisitioned by Frank, who had no head for anything but his grief. In fact, when I visited the corner shop to get milk this morning, I'd heard Cathy lamenting loudly about the ingratitude of the stuck-up Rutas, 'both him and her swimming in dosh but counting every penny', and paying her 'less than peanuts for her hard work'. She had sworn blind that her foot would not cross the threshold of Forget-Me-Not until her outstanding wages were paid in full – 'plus the blinking interest!'

This could be our lucky strike, I thought! Our evidence could still be there, in the bins, rotting away, undisturbed. Meantime, Samuel – half-heartedly – approached the glass recycling bin.

'Funny, that,' he whispered, 'that someone'd put weeds with glass bottles while there's a perfectly good compost heap just there.'

'Yeah, everything else looks sorted out meticulously in these bins.'

Then his comment truly caught up with me. I abandoned the general waste and went over to the glass to examine the weeds. It was some sixth sense that made me do it. I shone the light from my phone on the *weeds*, and squealed with delight. Distinctive bell-shaped, violet-blue flowers, though wilted, could belong to only one plant.

'It's monkshood, Samuel! You found the murder weapon!'

It was at that precise moment that the lights came on in the kitchen. We fell to a squat. I was sure Frank must have heard my squeals, and he was coming for us. I felt a sensation of dizziness wash over me and was ready to faint in a controlled manner. But I was wrong. Frank pottered around the kitchen and embarked on the process of collecting dirty pots and dishes for washing up. Now, that was entirely out of character! He was emptying their contents into the sink, under running water, washing everything down the drains, and then transferring them into the dishwasher.

'He's cleaning up,' I whispered. 'He must've extracted aconite from the plant in one of those pots. We must stop him!'

'I'm going to call Alec Scarfe. Don't do anything stupid.' Samuel gave me a hard look and I knew he meant business so I stayed put.

'Alec, it's me, Sam Dee, yes . . . Yes, I know it's late . . . We are at Forget-Me-Not . . . Maggie and I. Um, we found monkshood concealed in Frank's rubbish bins . . . The plant you get aconite from, you know? . . . Yes, yes . . . And Frank's inside, cleaning away the evidence . . . The pots, Alec!'

I pushed my face closer to Samuel's phone and made a helpful suggestion in a stage whisper, 'Shall we go in and effect a citizen's arrest before it's too late?'

Even from a distance I could hear Alec shout and holler for us to do no such thing. I could see where he was coming from – Frank was a big man, trained in hand-to-hand combat – but there was no need to shout.

Samuel terminated the phone call. 'He said to wait.'

We waited, watching haplessly as Frank busied himself in the kitchen, erasing evidence.

The cops arrived fifteen minutes later, led by Detective Chief Superintendent Scarfe wearing a sombre expression. They acted swiftly, seizing the pots and dishes in the dishwasher before Frank had a chance to press the START button. They bagged the shrivelled bouquet of monkshood from the glass recycling box, and then began a search of the house, starting with Frank's quarters. At which point, Alec Scarfe thanked us grudgingly and told us to hit the road, someone would come to take our statements tomorrow.

I patted myself on the back – job well done. I was exhausted, mainly emotionally, and I stunk of rotten eggs and fermented cheese, but I was proud of us. We had solved this murder - all over again, and this time I was sure we had got the right man.

When we reached Samuel's car on the road, I flopped onto the back seat.

'Why are you sitting there?' he gazed at me as perplexed as he had the first time I had done it, on our way to Richard's birthday bash. 'What's wrong with the passenger side?'

This time I could tell him the truth: 'One reason is that I smell like shit – I wouldn't like to put you through the experience of inhaling my aroma. But primarily it's because of Alice – she's back and she's not shifting.'

He turned his head to peer at the space next to him, even though he obviously knew he wouldn't be able to see her. Only I could see Alice and only I could see the little tear that rolled down his cheek. Penny, on the other hand, was nowhere to be seen. She had moved on at last.

Chapter Twenty-nine

Detective Chief Superintendent Alec Scarfe called DI Gillian Marsh to his office the moment she arrived.

'Close the door behind you and listen up. No funny business, Marsh,' he said unceremoniously. 'We've got a suspect in custody, and we're ready to forward the case to the CPS. DS Webber is the acting SIO, bear that in mind.'

'Yes, sir, I'm aware of that.'

'He's doing a damn good job, so don't charge in, raining on his parade.'

'No, sir. Can I sit in on the interview?'

'No.'

Marsh narrowed her eyes, contemplating her options. Clearly, she had some and she wouldn't be easily defeated. At last she said, 'Sir, I don't want you to take it the wrong way, and it pains me to point out this lapse to you —'

'What bloody lapse are you talking about, Marsh?'

'Your lapse of judgement, sir. You knew Richard Ruta had met with a lady — *a blast from the past* — at Bristol. Yet you failed to pass that information on to the investigating team. It could've saved us lots of precious time scouring different airports if we'd concentrated our attention on Bristol.'

Scarfe's eyes bulged. There was a mixture of genuine, innocent puzzlement and haughty indignation in them. 'I still don't know what the bloody hell you're on about!'

'Samuel Dee told you about that meeting. Didn't you find that

189

nugget of information vital to the investigation? I would've if I were you. The woman Ruta was meeting could well be our mystery woman. She could've flown in from Paris. The dates coincide. You knew about it and you said nothing.'

'I … It didn't … It didn't occur to me … I mean, you're not suggesting I withheld information?' The superintendent's eyes blazed with panic.

'I wouldn't dream of it. I'm sure it was an innocent oversight. I just want to help with the investigation.'

'OK, OK, you can help – it's your job anyway.' Scarfe straightened his posture and raised his chin. 'By the way, how do you know about it? I can't imagine Sam would've gone to you, stirring shit. Was it Maggie Kaye?'

Marsh nodded. 'It was. She was trying to be helpful.'

'Can't fault her for trying, but by golly, sometimes I could throttle that busybody!'

Marsh stopped him before he incriminated himself any further. 'I'd better get on with the interview, sir. I take it I can sit in on it?'

Scarfe scowled, and that wasn't a pretty picture. 'You can sit in, but Webber leads. Are we clear?'

Marsh managed a barely perceptible nod.

'You can read the file, if you like – that should keep you out of trouble,' the superintendent quickly re-asserted his authority, 'and you'll be leaving at noon. If I see you around here a minute after noon, you're back on full-time sick leave. Are we clear?'

Another reluctant nod.

'Oh, and welcome back, DI Marsh. If there's anything you need, you know where to come.'

'Sir.'

Sitting in on the interview with Francis Savage, as a mere observer and without the right to ask questions, was the cruellest and most sinister torture that Gillian Marsh had ever been subjected to. Webber was doing a mildly decent job, but she was aching to butt in.

'You travelled to the Brecon Beacons two days before Penny

Ruta's death.' Webber changed the subject swiftly from his previous line of enquiry about Savage's – hostile - feelings towards Mrs Ruta, feelings Savage was only too happy to admit. In his own words, he hated the *sodding harlot*. Having established the motive, DS Webber moved on to the means, 'It was quite sudden – the trip to the Brecon Beacons?'

'What of it?'

'Wolfsbane, also known as monkshood, can be found up in high altitudes in the Welsh mountains. Is that why you went there? To collect the plant?'

'I was taking time off, I needed air.' Savage gave Webber an insolent look, which said something to the effect that he was a man at peace and didn't give a shit whether Webber could prove him guilty or not.

'We found discarded wolfsbane in the recycling bin outside the kitchen at the Forget-Me-Not estate.'

'Penny could've put it there. Anyone could.'

'But your fingerprints were the only prints on the pot where we found traces of Aconitum root extract – the same extract that was used to poison Mrs Ruta.'

'That doesn't surprise me – I was about to wash up just before you people turned up, sirens blazing,' Frank snorted with contempt. 'I handled all the pots. You might find my prints on all the other dishes, too. Will you accuse me of making scrambled eggs as well as poisoning Penny? She killed herself. Out of guilt.'

DS Webber reached for Penny's laptop, bagged in a transparent evidence sleeve, marked EXHIBIT 234/1RUT.T and placed it on the table in front of Savage. 'Do you recognise this?'

'Penny's laptop, I'm guessing. Only because it was missing. You found it, I take it?'

Gillian fidgeted in great discomfort. She felt like wiping the smirk from the man's face by taking over the interrogation from Webber's gentle hands, but refrained.

'We found it in your possession – attached by heavy-duty industrial tape to the bottom of a wardrobe in your bedroom.'

Savage looked bored. He gave his lawyer a quick glance as if asking if he really had to answer this. The brief said, 'It wasn't a question, DS Webber. My client can't answer that.'

'I'll rephrase –'

'Don't bother. What if I said I didn't put it there. Someone's trying to frame me. Maybe Penny herself, from beyond the grave. She never liked me either. The feeling was mutual.'

'But we found your fingerprints on the tape – only your fingerprints.'

'OK . . . Was that a question?'

'We have also found that you've been deleting files from the laptop – your fingerprints are all over the keyboard and the touchscreen, sir. Can you explain how they got there?'

'Do I need to? Isn't it obvious? I must've used her laptop at some point.' Savage leaned back in his chair and stretched ostentatiously.

'Yes, you did. You used her laptop to delete sections of her memoirs before you discovered that we already had the audio files from a different source. We knew more than you did: about Mrs Ruta's role in the death of Leila Nolan, for example. You must've been so angry when you found out it was Mrs Ruta's crime you had helped to cover up all those years ago. You wanted to punish her. We have concrete evidence, Mr Savage: the wolfsbane plant could have only been collected by you no more than two days before it was used. You were the only person with an opportunity to obtain the fresh wolfsbane plant when you travelled to the Brecon Beacons at exactly that time. You left your fingerprints on the pot where the poison was extracted from the roots, Penny Ruta's laptop is covered with your fingerprints, and do I even have to mention your irrational hatred of Mrs Ruta –'

'Irrational?!' Savage stiffened in his chair and leaned forward to fix Webber with a furious glare. 'Irrational? She killed Richard! I told you over and over again, but you did nothing about it!'

'So you did something about it?'

'Someone had to.' He relaxed in his chair, his expression returning to smug and self-congratulatory. 'Someone had to put the bitch in her place.'

'So you confess to killing her?'

'Yes, yes, yes! Guilty as charged!' He was grinning, looking like a madman. But a happy madman at last.

'OK.' DS Webber shot DI Marsh a triumphant glance. 'Let's now move to the killing of Richard Ruta – why would you –'

'I told you!' Savage jumped to his feet, forcing PC Miller to step forward to restrain him. 'I told you, Penny killed Richard! She gave him the fucking Tokaji – he told me so! And I told you! Remember, DS Webber? I told you personally when you were banging on about Leila Nolan and all that ancient history, I told you it was Penny that poisoned Richard! I told you to arrest her – told you to do something!' He banged his fist on the table. '*The love of my life*, Richard said … She gave him the bloody wine. It wasn't me, I'm not delusional. He didn't give a shit about me. But I didn't kill him. I loved him.'

He sat back in his chair – slumped into it without the need for PC Miller's intervention. He hung his chin to his chest and added in the most tender tone, 'I loved him.'

Chapter Thirty

When it was over and I looked back, it seemed as if I had been hit on the head and twelve days had been stolen from me. I was left with a blurry smudge on my memory, and nothing else.

On Thursday, after buying a cake at the market, I went for lunch at my parents' — it is our longstanding tradition. I didn't expect to see Will there. Just seeing him standing silently in the lounge, without a greeting, sent a chill down my spine.

Will is a high-flying if otherwise unimaginative civil engineer, married to his perfect match in the shape of Tracey, his lab technician wife. In his younger days, my big brother used to dream of being a professional musician. He self-taught himself to play keyboards, sported long hair and a Bjorn Borg bandana, wore bell-bottom trousers, and did lots of head-banging to the heavy metal music he played loudly in his room. But he had left it all behind him when he met Tracey and moved away. The big city had sucked all his dreams out of him, leaving him as dry and bitter as black pepper. He was a professional, no-nonsense man now. And he was also very busy, so seeing him out of the blue in my parents' lounge on a Thursday afternoon was an ominous sign.

If that wasn't enough to scare me witless, more was to come. For the first time since I could remember, Mum had not cooked anything that day but ordered a takeaway. If Will appeared sombre and anxious, Dad looked devastated and Mum seemed to have shrunk overnight. They sat arm in arm on the sofa while Will loomed over them, standing. He must have come directly from his office for he was wearing a tie and an expensive work suit.

'What is it? Have they found Andrea?' That was the first thing that sprang to my mind. For our family to be gathered together in the middle of the week outside of Christmas and Easter, it had to be something huge.

'No, no, nothing to do with Andrea,' Will told me. 'Sit down.'

'Why should I sit down – you're standing.' I had always been quite obstinate in my relationship with Will. His naturally dominant personality never failed to provoke the inner rebel in me.

'Sit down with us, darling,' Mum asked me nicely.

I perched on the sofa next to her, and she reached for my hand and squeezed it. She smiled at me, but it was a doleful smile.

'OK, so what happened? Is everything fine at home, Will? Is Tracey all right, the kids?'

'It's about Mum.'

That was the point when blood drained from my brain and went down the gutters of my veins.

'Is it cancer?' I only mimed the word.

Tears welled up and poured out of my brother's eyes. I think he tried to say something like yes, but couldn't speak. He gazed at me pleadingly as if I had the power to unsay what I had just uttered.

Mum's hand that I was holding felt like a fragile, warm chick, and as much as I wanted to squeeze it hard and never let it go, I was conscious not to crush it.

Dad spoke in the unfamiliar trembling voice of an elderly and feeble man. 'Luckily for us,' his words clashed with his tone and his emotion-ravaged face, 'it was discovered at an early stage, still localised in the lungs, and it's operable.'

'How long have you known?'

'Only a week. Maybe a bit longer – a couple of weeks.'

'And you kept it away from us?'

'We didn't want to worry you, darling. We knew how you'd react. You always take everything so . . . so much out of context.' My

195

mum's warm hand was soothingly stroking my frozen back but didn't have enough energy to thaw it.

'What matters now is that Irene is going to have an operation, Tuesday week, so they can take it out, all being well.' Dad's voice trailed off, but he summoned it back, and finished telling us what mattered now, 'and then there'll be some chemo and, the doctor tells us, around thirty radiotherapy sessions, daily, to finish the bugger off. And then, we can go back to normal.'

We didn't have any of that takeaway my parents bought for lunch, but we had the cake I'd brought, with tea, and more tea. It gave us comfort. Will struggled with keeping a dry eye, but I didn't cry. I couldn't. My frozen brain was incapable of accessing and processing information, so I couldn't react. I felt numb. I felt like I had missed something important – something that would have made the news more palatable, if only I had listened carefully enough. I guess it was a symptom of pure and simple denial. I was grasping at straws; there was nothing that I had missed. The truth lay bare before me in all its macabre glory. Mum had cancer.

The twelve days that followed between the revelation of Mum's cancer and the surgery was a slowly unfolding nightmare of waiting, sleepless nights and tortuous internet surfing in search of answers and reassurance. All I got was more uncertainty, more doubts and growing panic.

Everybody tried to act normally. Will returned to London and was due to come back on Tuesday to stay a few nights at mine – for as long as it took. Mum and Dad carried on watching their favourite programmes on TV, rambling in the fields and having early nights. I must have turned my whole garden inside out and weeded several perfectly healthy species of decorative flowers – I just couldn't see what I was doing. A blur.

On Tuesday, Mum went into the operating theatre and Dad, Will and I sat outside, waiting.

And waiting.

Afterwards the surgeon, Dr Devlin, came out and smiled warmly at us. He invited us into his office. He told us the operation went well and that he was able to remove all the cancer-affected tissue that he had identified prior to the procedure. There had been no surprises and no complications, thank God. Mum was a trooper and we would be able to see her when she woke up. He also told us about the long recovery process and all the chemo and radio-therapy that would follow, and then called upon us to cross our fingers and pray that Mum would go into remission. Dr Devlin struck me as a very saintly man and a little voice at the back of my mind whispered hopefully that a saintly man was bound to be a miracle maker.

It was good, then, wasn't it, Dad kept asking. It was good news, wasn't it?

As good as it could be, under the circumstances. There was hope – plenty of it.

Good news, Dad wept and laughed, and wept again. He went mad with relief. And I joined him in a spectacular meltdown from my freezing state. The two of us – the emotionally unhinged half of the family – wept and laughed in turns while Will watched with an indulgent twinkle in his eye.

By the time we were allowed to go in and see Mum, we had wiped away all the tears, but kept the smiles. She peered at us from under her heavy, anaesthetic-swollen eyelids, and a faint smile played on her lips too. She looked so frail and tiny, and so very drained of life force that my tears burned their way back to the front of my eyes and I had to turn away to hide them because there was no stopping them.

Dad was giving Mum the good news and Will was repeatedly asking if he could get her anything. Will likes to be useful and prac-tical. I was crying, but then I tend to be impractical and wasteful on principle. Finally Mum confessed she was very, very tired and we were sent packing by a watchful nurse.

Yesterday, Mum came back home. We had a small impromptu party, listening to my parents' original sixties vinyls, some of which were scratched badly and kept jumping to the same spot and getting stuck there. But it was fun. Dad sang along to some tunes, which was painful. Dad is tone-deaf. Then it was Will's turn. Dad had kept a few tapes of demos by Will's old band. We listened to that, and it was fractionally less painful.

Will left after a hearty lunch of a Chinese takeaway. He had a long drive ahead of him and wanted to beat the peak-hour traffic on the M3. Mum told him to call as soon as he got home.

I stayed behind for another couple of hours, blabbering about my sleuthing triumphs. Mum was dozing on and off and wasn't really listening, but that was fine because she needed rest.

Reluctantly, I rose to my feet. 'I'll be off now. I'll leave you in peace till tomorrow.'

'Make it after lunch. We've got a radiotherapy session in the morning,' Dad informed me.

'Do you want me to drive you?'

'I can drive, thank you very much. I'm not taking chances with you behind the wheel.' He winked at Mum; she shook her head pretending – with little conviction – that she wasn't laughing. He always pokes fun at me and my driving abilities, or lack thereof. I am used to it.

'I'll bring cake.' I insisted on making myself useful in some way.

'You do that. Your cake doesn't sound half as dangerous as your driving.'

Dad saw me off to the front door.

'Mum and I – we were planning to go to Richard's funeral in Poland,' he started, 'but, as things are . . . we'll be in and out of hospital in the next six weeks. Are you going by any chance?'

'I haven't thought about it.'

'He was a good friend of mine from our parish council days – we fought a good few battles together, and won! I'd like to be there, but . . . you could go on my behalf, so that he knows I didn't forget.' It was important to Dad, I could tell. My view is that funerals are a pointless exercise in emotional self-harm for those who are left behind. I don't like funerals, maybe because for me the line between the living and the dead is rather fluid. But Dad seemed upset that he would be letting his old friend down.

'OK, I'll go. I'll check with Mary, she may be going – I'll tag along with her.'

He kissed me on the forehead – he had started doing that lately, since Mum's illness. 'Thanks, Maggie.'

I was cycling home, carrying with me this new, eerie sense of impending doom. I was seeing everything in a new light. Every day seemed like a victory, but only a passing one. Every moment tasted like the forbidden fruit – snatched from the jaws of some invisible, hungry monster looming in the shadows. I told myself it was normal and to be expected: we couldn't take anything for granted – not yet, maybe not ever.

Chapter Thirty-one

Only two mourners would represent Bishops Well, Richard Ruta's adopted home in his adopted country, at his funeral: Sam Dee and Maggie Kaye. Other Bishopians, who were once upon a time close to the deceased, refused to attend for reasons of their own: Henry because he was still under suspicion for Richard's murder and felt that, frankly, this was beyond the pale and all Richard's fault. Mary boycotted the funeral in solidarity with Dan Nolan, with whom, according to the local gossipmongers, she was now involved romantically. Frank was in custody for Penny's murder and, taking into account his SAS past, the magistrate refused to release him on bail on the grounds that he was a flight risk.

The journey to Poland was uneventful. Both the travellers and their luggage arrived on the correct flight, un-tampered with by the Customs and Border Control officials. The gentleman at Immigration in the Arrivals hall hardly looked at them. This was propitious for Maggie, seeing as she declared unwisely when still within the man's earshot that her passport photograph was nine years old and featured her as a redhead with a single chin.

'I'm totally unrecognisable from that photo!' she bumbled, shaking her blondish tresses and the extra chins.

'Next!' the man called out, and Maggie was spared a full body search.

Sam and Maggie picked up their suitcases and wheeled them along, following the flow of passengers through a maze of corridors. They emerged on the hot and dusty pavement outside Arrivals and haplessly watched as other travellers were picked up one by one by their relatives and friends amid kisses, bear hugs and exclamations of unspeakable delight. In the end, Sam and Maggie were hanging out on the pavement like two lemons in an apple tree.

'So, what now?' Maggie asked. 'What's the plan, Samuel?'

'Well, tomorrow we take a train to Lublin,' he replied helpfully.

'That still leaves us with the question of tonight,' she pointed out, appearing fearful that there was a gaping hole in his itinerary, rendering them homeless for one night.

'Tonight we're booked into a hotel, hang on.' He fumbled in the countless, intrepid traveller's pockets of his cargo trousers. He retrieved a crumpled sheet of paper. 'Oh yes! Hampton by Hilton Hotel!'

'I always knew I could rely on you, Samuel.' Maggie squinted against the sun, looking rather charming. 'So, how do we get there?'

They scanned the street. It looked like an Olympic running track of many lanes, each with its important purpose and a mysterious final destination. Beyond the distant layers and spirals of the motorway the tall buildings and towers of Warsaw shone in the bright July sun. There was no sign of a bus stop and no directions to the Underground, or if there were, Sam and Maggie were unable to identify, read, and follow them.

A corpulent man wearing a winter jacket in the height of summer and an impressively competent expression on his face, materialised before them, relieved them of their suitcases, and bellowed, '*Willkommen im Warschau! Folge mir, bitte!*' He was pointing to a black passenger car with wide open doors, parked just a few steps away from them. Sam was astounded to discover that Polish sounded remarkably like German.

'Is he speaking German?'

'Maybe he thinks we're Germans?'

'Well, tell him we aren't!'

Sam smiled at the friendly cabbie. 'We are not German,' he said very slowly, in English. 'We are from England.'

'*Tak, tak!*' the Pole agreed with him eagerly, and started walking, pulling both their suitcases behind him. '*Ja, ja! Willkommen! Wohin gehen Sie? Ich fahre!'* He pointed towards his car, and looking at their blank faces, added some universally understood sound effects, 'Vroom, vroom, vroom! Hotel?'

'I think he's offering to take us to our hotel,' Maggie translated for Sam's benefit.

Despite his slight irritation, he didn't tell her he had gathered as much himself. Instead, he handed his crumpled piece of paper to the happy cabbie, and again, spoke very slowly in the Queen's English, 'This is the address we want to go to. Do you know this place? Hotel – it is a hotel.'

'Ooo, tak, tak!' the cabbie read the paper, grinned and bowed for some inexplicable reason. He then loaded their suitcases into the boot of his car. 'Hampton by Hilton Hotel, *ulica Wspolna, ja, ja!* No problem! You English? I think you German first – you look German. You say you English – I speak English, no problem! You just tell me!'

'Good man!' Sam jumped into the car. Now that the man was speaking his language, he would trust him with his life.

'We go now!' the cabbie announced. He took off with screeching tyres and bulldozed his way through what seemed like peak-hour traffic in Warsaw. The man was clearly a homicidal maniac.

The Hampton by Hilton Hotel was a very colourful place. It was reminiscent of a Cubist painting, the impression that Picasso had been engaged as its interior designer inescapable. It was a very tall building, sitting in the very heart of Warsaw and looking down on all its quirky landmarks, like the spikes of the Palace of Culture or the red tramways rattling about. The central train station from where Sam and Maggie were to travel to Lublin was just a stone's throw away. Sam felt a sense of accomplishment. They could now put their feet up and relax.

They had a lovely dinner in a psychedelically bright restaurant. The waiters were obliging and friendly, the waitresses aloof and unsmiling, all part of their natural allure. At least they spoke English, which endeared them to Maggie who ventured into telling them all she had learned about Poland and its history from a travel guide on the plane. It wasn't much but she remembered to mention Solidarity and Lech Walesa, and the fall of the Berlin Wall, which the waiter informed her haughtily wasn't actually in Poland, madam — it was in Germany. Maggie attempted to argue that it was all the same, all part of the Eastern Bloc, but that for some reason didn't go down well with the waiter, who became tight-lipped and demanded to know if they were ready to order, please.

Flustered, poor Maggie ordered whatever was on special and a glass of chardonnay. Samuel was less adventurous and asked for tomato soup followed by pork chops with apple sauce and mash, accompanied by a home brew.

'Samuel, you need to let your hair down,' Maggie instructed him. 'Try something unusual — traditional local cuisine. That's what I always do.'

Judging by her twisted lips, she regretted it when her special arrived. It was a dish called bigos. It consisted of cabbage — it was cabbage through and through, plus a few scraps of meat and perfumed sausage. That would no doubt leave her suffering from wind and stomach cramps. Sam was glad he didn't have to share a room with her. He found the scent of cabbage and associated wind most disagreeable.

After coffee, Sam said goodnight to a very pale Maggie who was already holding her stomach and screwing up her face in agony. He went to his room, had a shower — sang in it — then put on a white fluffy dressing gown and reached for his laptop. He started listening to Penny's audio files from the beginning and nearly dozed off until he came to the section about Richard's defection and his secretive past. Of course, it wasn't such a secret to Sam — he was aware of Richard's spying for the communist government in return for his freedom of movement around the West. Naturally, it wasn't something Richard would have been proud of and willing to share with his young, impressionable wife. Naturally, he had preferred the past to stay in the past. And naturally, Penny had grown increasingly insecure and suspicious. But even Sam knew nothing about the other woman from Richard's past – the woman whom Penny feared so much.

Sam replayed that bit of the recording a few times:

Richard didn't talk about his past. I knew he came here in 1981, just months before Poland relapsed into the grip of the Cold War. I studied the subject thoroughly – I wanted to understand who my darling husband really was. I knew there was more to him than his carefree, bohemian flamboyance. By the time he defected to the West, communism was already on its knees following the rise of Solidarity, but it could still bite. That's what happened when they introduced martial law and began the big purge across the whole country. Richard once referred to it as the last nasty frostbite of the Cold War.

Days before martial law was declared, Richard had arrived in London. He had been allowed by the regime to travel to the West for a film festival where he was to collect an award in the short film category. He was already a celebrated director in Poland – the nation's proud son. He duly collected his prize and then strolled to the nearest police station to ask for political asylum. He stayed in England, listening to the News about the arrests in intelligentsia circles back home and watching the situation unfold on the other side of the Iron Curtain. He was waiting for the big thaw. When it came, he would go home – I think that was his original intention – but for some reason, things didn't go according to plan and he stayed here for good. He gave me the impression that he was scared to go back, that if he went back he would be a dead man. He never explained that to me. He said, laughing, that it was top secret and that if he told me he would have to kill me. Daft nonsense!

He tried to get in touch with his family and friends, but all his letters were intercepted and telephone calls blocked. Even after the state of emergency was lifted, he still had to reckon with the overt censure of his correspondence. In the end, he stopped writing. It was pointless.

Once he told me a funny story about how he sent money to his mother in Katynice. He had a good chuckle about it. It was a few years after his defection and the Cold War was getting warmer, so he gave it a go. He had put five hundred pounds-worth of banknotes in an envelope, together with a short note, and sent it on its way. The letter and the money had miraculously reached their destination. He knew that for a fact because within two weeks the whole amount was back with him, accompanied by an even shorter note from his mother, reading:

'Dear Son, Keep the money, you need it more than I do. They tell me England is very expensive. God bless! Yours, etc'. *We both laughed about it. I told him how much I wanted to meet his mother – his whole family. And he said, 'One day. Maybe.'*

He had a mother and a younger sister in Poland, this I knew. I kept insisting that he take me there and he kept promising that he would, but it never happened. It was as if he wanted to keep me away from them, to keep them and his past in Poland to himself – top secret. I hated his secrets. But he went on about how the past must stay in the past and how he would have to kill me if, blah, blah, blah . . .

But then one day, when he'd had way too much to drink and given to a bout of nostalgia, he started speaking about his past. The more I found out, the more I wished I had not asked. He wept when he told me about the love of his life. *He didn't mean me, of course. It was someone else – the woman he had left behind or been separated from when he'd defected. He told me he had gone to Poland,* in search of the lost time, *as he'd put it. It had been ten years after he'd defected – when it was safe for him to go back. He had gone to look for her. He had looked for her high and low. He had left no stone unturned. He had asked everyone, hired private detectives. But she – whoever she was – she was gone. Vanished.*

People told him that she had disappeared soon after he'd left the country. No one had heard from her, not a single word. His mother told him that he was ten years too late, that he was a fool. She didn't mince her words. I think I'll like her when I finally meet her at Richard's funeral.

She also told him that he didn't deserve to find that woman. He would only disrupt her life and bring chaos. She called him a scoundrel and a waster. Shame on him, she said, he'd had a decent girl, she had been in love with him – it was in her eyes – and he abandoned her.

In the end, Richard concluded that she was dead – that they, the Special

Security henchmen, had killed her for his sins. That's what he said: For my sins. He had stopped looking for her.

Still weeping into my shoulder, he took his wallet from his bedside table. There, in an inside pocket, he kept a photograph. Of that woman. He showed it to me. It was a crumpled old Polaroid taken in a photo booth: two smiling faces, cheek-to-cheek — Richard and her. She was statuesquely beautiful. She had a mid-parting with her straight long hair falling onto her shoulders. I recognised her. I had seen her in a short film directed by Richard in the late seventies. It was called Death Becomes Her *and it was about a woman killing herself by drowning in a lake. He had received many awards for that film.*

I was mortified and felt helpless against her. I sensed that if he ever found her she could easily take him away from me. He would run to her in a heartbeat. So, I crossed my fingers and willed her dead, like he feared she was. I have never been jealous of his two previous wives or any other seasonal attractions that passed through our house, but I was petrified of that nameless woman. I always looked over my shoulder, expecting her to turn up and steal him away from me.

Sam stopped the recording. He threw his head back in his chair, stretched his legs and pressed his fist to his lips. He had a lot of thinking to do. He was fairly positive that this was the mystery woman from the airport. Who was she and why had Richard never mentioned her name? And more to the point: did she kill Richard? And if she had, then why?

At breakfast time, Sam shared his thoughts with Maggie. She looked distracted. The fact that she hardly touched her food could mean that she was still tender after last night's cabbage extravaganza, but there was something else. She didn't seem to care. That wasn't like her.

'What is the matter, Maggie? You're not listening.'

'Oh, sorry, Samuel. It's nothing. I've been . . .' She looked as if she was racking her brain for an adequate excuse, but then flicked her hand and confessed, 'Ah, I'd better tell you! I try not to worry, not to think about it, and I keep telling myself that it's all behind us, but,' she bit her lip, 'something is niggling at the back of my mind, and I can't help worrying.'

'About what?'

'My mum,' she sniffled and then told Sam about her mother's cancer and her surgery, the series of therapies, and about the saintly Dr Devlin who seemed to believe that her mother was on the road to recovery. The more she spoke, the higher her spirits seemed to lift. Talking about one's troubles makes it easier to deal with them, Sam reflected, and wished he could talk about Alice as freely. But he couldn't, not yet, and maybe he would never speak a word about how he felt because he wasn't one to wear his heart on his sleeve.

Instead of bringing Alice into the conversation, he stuck to the subject of Maggie and her mother. It was much easier. 'So the prognosis is good? It's amazing what medicine can do these days. People can live with cancer for years.'

'That's true, Samuel. You're right – I'm blowing it out of proportion. That's what Mum says I always do. I must stop fretting and be thankful. She is back at home recuperating, the operation was a success. I must focus on the positives and count my blessings.' Maggie perked up. A bright smile danced on her lips. She began to butter her toast.

Sam was appalled to realise that he was filled with resentment. He envied Maggie even if her mother were to get worse and die. Because, unlike him, Maggie had been forewarned. She knew what could come. At least, she would have a chance to say goodbye. He had never got that chance with Alice.

Chapter Thirty-two

Katynice was a village buried in the middle of thick forest dominated by birches and conifers on the easternmost outskirts of Poland. Given a pair of binoculars one would probably see the outline of Russian tanks on the horizon – that was what a chatty posh lady told Sam and Maggie when they were waiting for their luggage in the hotel foyer. She said, in a conspiratorial tone, that the Russians were never quite far enough away for her liking.

Firstly, they took a train to the city of Lublin from where they would be catching a suburban train to Katynice. As they had a couple of hours to spare, they explored Lublin, which was ten times better than sitting in the stuffy waiting room at the station.

Leaving Lublin felt like leaving the Western world and venturing into the unknown. Even Lublin seemed surreal – it was a jigsaw puzzle of old historical edifices interspersed with distinctly communist architecture and a few strong accents of contemporary EU influence. But it was a city with streets, houses, and modes of motorised transport. From that last bastion of civilisation, Sam and Maggie tumbled away in a clattering old train. Not only did it clatter, it also grated, screeched, whined, and shook them like a baby's rattle as it pulled in and out of remote country stations. Maggie clung firmly to Samuel's sleeve, nervously mumbling irrational warnings that their lives might be in danger.

'I have a bad feeling about this train, Samuel . . . Something's not right . . .'

'Maggie, be reasonable. No terrorist would ever bother to come all the way here to the middle of bloody nowhere to blow up a train carrying a few local peasants and the two of us,' Sam assured her. The passengers also looked like they wouldn't be having any of that terrorism malarkey on their watch. Sam gestured towards a thickset man with a tattoo of a dragon on his arm bulging with muscles, and added, 'Besides, no terrorist would get away with murder on this train.'

This was aimed to bring comfort to Maggie, but she countered his words with, 'I'm not talking about terrorists! It's the train – it's going to go off the rails of its own accord!'

'It won't, Maggie. I bet it's been covering this route for forty years, if not longer, and it's still in one piece.'

'You call this one piece!' She groaned, dug her nails deep into his arm, and hid her face behind his shoulder. 'Oh, how I miss my trusty Hyundai!'

Sam raised his eyebrows. 'Your car and this train have more in common than you care to admit.'

'My car stands head and shoulders above this . . . this . . . wreck! It has a history of regular service.'

'So does this train, I imagine – a *long* history.'

'Yeah, it's been around, but not being serviced!'

Another judder dislodged Maggie from behind Sam's shoulder. She was whipped forward, her face momentarily pushed between her knees, and then, just as suddenly, jerked upwards, her head bouncing off the metal handle on the back of her seat. She yelped and invoked God's intervention.

'You all right, Maggie?' Sam peered into her eyes, looking for symptoms of concussion.

'Even my bicycle would do a better job getting me there. I'd be there in a jiffy and without bruises all over my body,' she said. She wasn't making much sense but, in Maggie's case, that didn't necessarily mean that she was concussed.

Everyone knew everyone else in their carriage. Maggie and Sam were openly scrutinised by every new passenger boarding the train. Adorned with two wreaths, they looked like a couple of clown fish out of water. But as time went on and the journey proceeded unimpaired by their presence, they began to receive friendly grins and even an offer of a punnet of fresh blueberries from a woman carrying a bucketful of them. She instructed them to eat by gesticulating wildly, saying *Dobre, dobre,* and rubbing her tummy with a blessed expression in her eyes. Sam did as he was told (she didn't look like someone who'd take no for an answer) but Maggie took her chances with the woman and politely refused. Her *bigos* experience was clearly still hanging over her like her worst nightmare. The woman pulled a disappointed face at Maggie but offered Sam a warm smile, and more blueberries.

They arrived at Katynice station, which boasted nothing but a broken sign stating *Kat--.c-* and a few impressive weeds on the platform. Sam and Maggie had to be pushed out of the train by the well-meaning fellow passengers who had earlier established where they were going via an ingenious mixture of smoke signals and Morse code. The blueberry woman pointed Sam towards a distant church tower glistening in the bright morning sun. That was where the memorial service would be held. Samuel thanked her politely in his well-practised *Queen's English for Foreigners.* As he was expressing his gratitude, the door closed with an ominous hiss and the train jangled away at a pace very nearly approaching walking speed.

Maggie and Sam proceeded along a cobbled road in the direction of the church. As they plodded on, they were overtaken by a cavalcade of black limousines, probably carrying the more affluent mourners to the service.

Sam suggested finding a taxi, but Maggie declined, asserting that the walk would be a pleasant one. She clearly didn't trust any of the modes of transport on offer in this hostile world. She was more than happy to walk. The village was picturesque and idyllic: detached houses bathed in greenery, roses and hollyhocks in front gardens, and only occasionally would a mongrel fix them with a watchful stare from behind broken fence pickets. In her severely disturbed state of mind, Maggie went on muttering discontentedly under her breath, extolling the advantages of Bishops Well and frequently repeating her new mantra, 'I wish I'd never left home!'

'It isn't that bad, Maggie. You may be milking it now. Man up!' Sam interjected at one point, only to be sternly chastised with one of Maggie's *looks*. She had mastered those looks teaching unruly children in Bishops Primary. Sam recoiled and swallowed his next observation about the charming woodlands in the distance.

If the village and its surroundings were idyllic and understated in their charm, the church was a scream. It was opulently baroque: dripping with gold, shouting in a symphony of vivid murals and stained-glass windows, and bursting with fresh flowers.

The church was full, but there was hardly anybody that Sam knew. Perhaps the tricky travel arrangements to this distant location had something to do with it. Maggie pulled his sleeve and whispered into his ear, pointing to a small and shrivelled male figure in the front pew, 'I swear that's Roman Polanski!'

'If you say so.'

They found two seats in the back pew and let themselves be enveloped in a haze of frankincense and rather beautiful organ music, which sweetened the fact that the service was excruciatingly long. The priest went on and on. For a minute Sam had the strong impression that even the priest had nodded off halfway through a sentence as his eyes remained closed and his mouth moved mechanically as if of its own accord. Half of the congregation was definitely asleep.

The coffin was carried out into the cemetery. It was crowded with gravestones as showy and elaborate as the church itself. The procession of mourners arrived at the Ruta family tomb. It was formidably large and made of polished black marble. The inscriptions were in gold. Most of them were old. The gold leaf had peeled off the engravings. The oldest ones at the top were illegible, expunged by time and the elements. The first name that could be read belonged to Beata Ruta, who died in infancy in 1961, at only three years old. Richard's little sister, Sam guessed. Bogdan and Adela Ruta followed. Their names were etched into the stone in

211

quick succession, Adela in 1966 and Bogdan in 1967. They must have been Richard's grandparents. Following them in chronological order was Tadeusz Ruta, born 1928, died 1991. Next to his epitaph was one for Teodora Ruta. This one displayed a year of birth, 1927, but the year of passing was left blank. Sam assumed it was Richard's mother, who already had her resting place reserved for her. Apart from Richard's entry, stating his date of birth and his date of death sixty-eight years later to the day, there was another one that appeared very recent. The lettering was still golden-bright and the date of death was 13 January 2018. It was a young man, born in 1982 – only thirty-five at the time of his death. He didn't bear the family name – his was Adam Topolski. Samuel surmised he was the son of Richard's other sister; probably Topolski was her married name. It must have been a harrowing experience – losing a child. Had it been an accident or prolonged illness?

As soon as Sam and Maggie placed their wreaths on Richard's grave, a man approached them. 'You Richard friend? From England, *tak*? OK?' he said in broken English. 'Please come to house. Like party, OK? Remember Richard – familia and friend.' He nodded encouragingly. 'I – Henryk. Richard cousin.'

Sam shook the man's hand which he proffered alongside a pat on Sam's back and another nod.

'I'm Samuel Dee, Richard's friend from England, and this is Maggie.'

'Hello, Henryk. Please accept my deepest condolences,' Maggie shook the man's hand too, 'but we have to be going now. We've a train to catch.'

Henryk didn't understand. He showed them the way, 'Come, please, to party, this way.'

'He means the wake,' Sam said. He was surprised at Maggie's mulish reluctance to accept the invitation.

'I don't think we should, Samuel. It's just the closest family and friends.'

'I was Richard's friend, a close one, I fancy. Can you see anyone else from Bishops?'

'Well ...' Her face crumpled. It was an unintended pun, but Bishops Well had indeed forgotten poor Richard in record time.

'Let's go! It's just a gesture. It'd be rude otherwise. I'm sure they'll have a nice cup of tea and a slice of cake on offer.' Sam really didn't look forward to another train trip so soon after the last one.

The Rutas' house wasn't nearly as ostentatious as their tomb, but it was pleasant and spacious. Space, it seemed, was something Poland had plenty of. The house had a sloping, red-tile roof, walls built from thick pine logs and a wooden balustrade wrapped around the ground floor decking, all of which gave the house a distinctly rustic feel. In the front garden fragrant roses bloomed and the backyard was an orchard-cum-veggie patch, full of buzzing bees and rather large and murderous mosquitoes. These were beginning to make a real nuisance of themselves as they relentlessly buzzed overhead like a squadron of bloodthirsty Messerschmitts.

Inside, the house was an eclectic assortment of high-tech and modern blending into an array of relics of a bygone era: chairs with crocheted mantilla-type wraps on headrests, leafy pot-plants on windowsills, pictures on the wallpapered walls depicting idyllic and religious scenes, framed in gold, Turkish rugs on the wooden floors and padlocked coffers blackened with age. The curtains were heavy dark velvet. Exquisitely elaborate lace nets hung in the windows.

Maggie watched mesmerised as the man she was almost sure was Roman Polanski walked to Richard's mother, Teodora, and reverently kissed her hand. He held it for a while, telling her something as she wept. She was tiny and gnarly, not the robust, no-nonsense woman Sam had pictured her to be. She looked every inch the ninety-plus years that she was. Next to her sat a younger woman. Sam assumed she was Richard's younger sister. There was something of him in her eyes and the contour of her mouth. She looked a good ten years younger than Richard. Dressed in black, she held herself with elegance and poise. Her hair was in a short bob. She looked up and her eyes met Sam's. She approached and extended her hand to him.

'Hello, I'm Grazyna, Richard's sister,' she said. 'I want to thank you for coming and for the beautiful flowers.'

Sam and Maggie introduced themselves. Sam said, 'We are very sorry about your loss.'

'Thank you. I didn't really know Richard that well. He left when I was away from home, at university, in Krakow, and before that, he had been away studying in Lodz, then working on his famous films . . . We weren't that close when he lived in Poland. After he left for England, we didn't hear from him, for many years – not a single word. He has become a new man there, in England. Of course, we are proud of his success,' she didn't mean it, Sam could tell from her tone, 'but we lost Richard a long time ago. Now – this is just his funeral. That's all. I don't feel the loss.'

'Ah, I didn't mean Richard, though of course Richard, too,' Sam stammered, feeling foolish for not making himself clear in the first place. 'I meant your late son. I couldn't help noticing the epitaph for Adam. Died so young! Thirty-five, tragic . . .'

'Adam Topolski?' she was taken aback. 'No, you are wrong! I never married. No children. No, you are mistaken. Adam was not my son. He was Richard's.'

'Richard had a son? I never knew!'

'Neither did Richard. Neither did we! Not until Adam was dead. We only found that Richard had a son after Adam's death. Renata – his mother – contacted us just over half a year ago – for the first time in thirty-five years. She visited in winter – how do you say it? – out of the blue . . . She just turned up on the doorstep to tell us that there had been a child, Richard's child, and that the child was now dead. She came back because she wanted Adam buried in the family tomb. Mother agreed, of course – we knew Renata. She had been Richard's fiancée – before he defected. We knew her well. Mother loved her like her own child.'

'So . . . how . . . how, I mean . . . How did you lose touch with her? So many years!'

'At first, we thought she joined Richard in the West, followed him there . . . that perhaps he had made arrangements for her to join him.

She had vanished soon after he defected – it made sense. We thought she was with him. We only discovered that she wasn't when he came here for Father's funeral, in 1991 it was. He was asking after Renata – everywhere, looking for her high and low. We thought that was odd, but then we came to think that she must have left him and came back to Poland to start a new life for herself. Probably didn't want to have anything to do with us . . . No one had the sense to ask. Then he went back to England and we went back to our normal lives. No one thought of Renata as a missing person.'

'So Richard never knew he had a son!'

'He did find out. Renata went to England to tell him. He knew in the end.'

'When?' Sam already knew the answer to this question, but he wanted to make sure. It all made sense at last. 'When did she tell him? When did she go to England?'

'It was . . . if I remember well, it was three months after Adam's burial here in Katynice. Renata had stayed with us after the funeral – she was very, very sad. Depressed. She couldn't pick herself up for weeks. And then she decided she was strong enough to go and meet with Richard, after all those years – to tell him about Adam.'

'So when was that exactly?'

'I would say it was the end of April or beginning of May,' Grazyna replied. 'But you can ask her yourself. She is out there in the garden, on the bench.' She pointed through the window, towards a slight figure sitting stiffly on a makeshift garden bench.

Sam squinted to take a look at the woman. There was no mistaking her: she was the mysterious woman from the airport. He whispered to Maggie, 'The love of his life . . .'

But Maggie wasn't listening. She had already darted off, heading towards the woman in the garden, as if she were hypnotised.

Chapter Thirty-three

There were two of them: two devilishly handsome men in their mid-thirties, looking deceptively like one and the same person: Richard Ruta in his prime, the famous young director I remembered from the peak of his career in the eighties. Even after death, Richard remained as flamboyant and vain as in life, and wanted to look his best. That wasn't surprising. But I was intrigued to encounter his ghostly presence here amongst the living for the first time since his death two months ago. I had not seen him keeping Penny company, or Frank, or anyone else back home, but here he was: watching over Renata Topolska, *the true love of his life* – there was no doubt about that. The clone version of Richard was obviously his dead son, Adam. He looked just like his father. They were sharing the garden bench with Renata, looking joyous and at peace, like one happy family. It didn't seem to bother Richard in the least that, after all, Renata was his killer. He had forgiven her. Maybe he loved her that much. Maybe he knew she had a good reason to put an end to his life. But it was strange, considering he had been planning to start a new life with Renata. That was why he had asked Penny for a divorce. There was a future, there was hope, there was a happy-ever-after on the cards for Renata and Richard, so why – why did she kill him?

I had to know. Samuel was as keen as I was, and he followed me to the garden to meet the woman who murdered Richard.

We levelled up with her and, for a minute or two, we just stood there, wordless like two mutes, staring into the soft and gentle face of a killer. Everything about her contradicted that notion. She was small and delicate, someone you would want to take care of. Her lips were full, heart-shaped, her face smooth, with high cheekbones and large, dreamy eyes. Her long hair, picked up messily into a bun had once been dark, but now it was laced with silver. Despite the lapse of time, I recognised her instantly as the young actress in Richard's short film, *Death Becomes Her.* That title, I mused ruefully, was proving quite ironic. She was still a beautiful woman. It was said Richard liked them young but the truth was he had simply liked them beautiful.

We introduced ourselves, offered our condolences about Adam, and asked if we could talk to her about Richard's murder. It was Samuel who put it so bluntly, but she didn't flinch. She rose from the bench, smiled somewhat defiantly, and invited us for a walk in the fields. She assured us it would be a pleasant walk and, yes, she would be happy to chat with us if that's what we had come for all the way from England. So we left the garden through a back gate and followed her into the fields – barley or wheat, I couldn't tell the difference. The crops were waist high and swaying lazily in the breeze. We walked around and across them, following tractor ruts imprinted in the dry soil.

She started speaking without any further prompting. 'I killed Richard, but you already know that. What you don't know is why. Here is why: it was payback. He had passed a death sentence on my son when he left me to fend for the two of us on my own. He left me for the wolves, to take the beating for his defection – literally.' She spoke in strongly accented English, throwing into the mix Polish words and phrases we had to interpret and second-guess so that the whole story finally made sense. At no time did she try to explain anything away or to justify her actions. She just relayed the story as if it had been somebody else's life. She struck me as someone who had died inside a long time ago.

To the best of my recollection this is her story and her reasons for murdering the father of her son:

She came from a good family, old Polish nobility, which was a

217

serious disadvantage in communist Poland. Her ancestry alone was a reason for punishment, so Renata Topolska had to tread very carefully whatever she did with her life, watch what she said and how she said it and generally be on her best behaviour. Any false move and she could end up in a gulag in the depths of Siberia. So, she stayed as far away from politics as possible. She became an actor.

At twenty-one she scored a small part in an historical film, *The Invaders,* directed by the young but already acclaimed director – Richard Ruta. This would be her breakthrough. Though her part was tiny – the tormented daughter of a perfidious aristocrat – Renata had instantly caught Richard's eye. And he, naturally, caught hers. He was her idol.

It was a whirlwind romance. Within days of concluding the shooting, as soon as they came back from location, she had moved in with him, to his flat in the old part of Warsaw, affordable only to the luckiest few. She appeared in every film Richard made, notably in *Death Becomes Her,* which earned him the award he went to collect in London. He never returned. But that was later. For the time being, she lived her dream. She mixed in high circles. The whole thespian world was at her feet and the top dogs of the political establishment treated her with reverent adoration. After all, she was with the poster boy of Polish cinematography, the pride and joy of the regime. She was untouchable, and began to believe that she had escaped the curse of her birth.

But most of all, she was hopelessly in love. At the time when Richard left for London to collect his prize at an international short film festival, she had discovered she was pregnant with his baby. She was going to tell him on his return. Only, of course, he never returned.

She knew nothing of his decision to defect to the West. At first, she thought his flight back was delayed by the state of emergency declared by the regime in December 1981. She waited. And so did *they.* They watched her every step and tailed her wherever she went. They weren't even particularly discreet about it. There was always a black figure in the shadows, hovering under the windows of the flat despite the sub-zero temperatures of that terribly cold winter. She could hear their steps crunching the freshly fallen snow as they followed her in the streets. She could feel their breath condense on the back of her neck. They were waiting for Richard to make contact with her. She was waiting too, but Richard had disappointed them all. He was gone, never to be heard from again.

When the rumours about Richard's defection became common knowledge, they came for her. In the early hours of the morning, when it was still dark outside, there was an urgent knock on the door. Two men stormed in and took her as she stood, in her night-dress. They packed her into an unmarked police car and drove off. She dared not look where they were going. Shivering, she sat between the two henchmen, staring right ahead, too afraid to glance at their faces. The driver wore a police uniform.

Nobody spoke to her. No charges were brought against her. She wasn't offered legal representation. Or a cup of tea. Or anything to eat. She was led down a flight of echoing metal stairs. A heavy metal door was opened for her and she was thrown into a windowless cell. The door shut behind her and, with that, every last glimmer of light had gone from the room. The darkness was oppressive. It wrapped itself around her and squeezed her throat. She struggled to breathe. She could not see her hand in front of her. Her wrist was on fire; when they had pushed her into the cell, she fell. Protecting her pregnant belly, she had extended her hand and it collided with the hard stone floor; something clicked in her wrist. As she felt it in the dark, she could tell it was beginning to swell. The pain was excruciating. She was afraid to call for help. She curled up in the corner of her cell, drew her knees up under her chin, strained her eyes into the dark and listened to the hollow silence.

It was hours of sleepless vigil, if not days, before they came back for her. She had begun to think they had forgotten about her, and she urged them to remember. She was thirsty. Hunger had come and gone. She was worried for the baby she was carrying. She would do anything they wanted her to do, if only they came. She would do anything to see light.

She saw it. It shone in her face. The man behind it was stocky – just a thickset black silhouette. He shouted at her, loud and incomprehensible. She remembered nodding, saying *yes, he was right,* and asking for some water. He slapped her with the back of his hand, a powerful slash across the head. She fell backwards on impact. The back of her chair cut into her spine. Her head hit the floor. He pulled her by her shoulders, and yelled in her face, spitting in it. She focussed as best she could. He wanted to know how Richard contacted her. She said she had not heard from Richard. They took her back to her cell. No water.

The cell became her coffin. She had died in it a thousand times. Every time, they dragged her out, it felt like being raised from the dead. She would tell them anything, agree to anything, do anything, but she simply couldn't answer their one and only question: how did Richard contact her? Because he did not.

She told them she was pregnant. She needed water and something to eat. Not for her, but for the baby inside her. They brought a huge metal bucket full of water. She was so happy to see it. She would drink from the toilet if that was the only water on offer! They held the bucket over her mouth, and poured. A powerful gush of water. She captured and drank some of it, but then began to choke on it. It was going in her mouth and her nose. She was coughing, drowning and fighting back. They took the bucket away when it was empty. A puddle of wasted water stood still and black around her chair. They pointed to the puddle and told her she wouldn't get anything to drink if that was how she chose to behave: to waste every last bit of water they gave her. Unless, of course, she told them how Richard kept in touch with her. She didn't waste her breath explaining all over again that he had abandoned her.

She couldn't tell how long she had been kept prisoner in that place, but the day had come when they shoved her into a police van, alongside four other silent, battered and broken people, and transported them to a new location. It was a very long and arduous trip. For the most part she was ill and hallucinating. She remembered being moved from one van to another and at some point her captors stopped speaking Polish and started speaking Russian. It was colder, too. Much colder. She and her fellow prisoners gravitated towards each other and huddled together for warmth, thus becoming intimate with each other, skin-on-skin, before they even got to know each other's names. In the end, she landed in a nameless place near Novosibirsk, the capital of Siberia. She was in a gulag. She thanked God for her good fortune. Anything – anything at all was better than the coffin of the black cell she had left behind.

Her pregnancy was now beginning to show. She had to be at least four months pregnant. Though she had survived the incarceration, the memories of it burned a hole in her head. The night terrors started. She would wake up in the thick of the night, gasping for air, in the grip of the worst fear of all – that she was dead. The fear of death was so real that they had to put her on medication to slow down her heart rate and save her from losing her mind.

That medication contained aconite.

By the time she gave birth to Adam, she was stabilised. She had even made a handful of friends – other detainees. They helped her through the ordeal of discovering that Adam was unwell – very unwell. He was mentally and physically handicapped. His prospects were very poor. He was given ten, maybe fifteen years to live. He lived to the age of thirty-five.

One of her fellow detainees used to be a pharmacologist in his previous life before his deportation to the gulag. It was he who explained to Renata that the probable cause of Adam's motor-neurone disease was the medication she was put on during her pregnancy. The components affected the baby's development in her womb. She had later studied all those enzymes and components. She had learned about the properties of Aconitum. It was then that an idea of revenge took root in her mind: Adam's disability wouldn't have happened if it hadn't been for Richard. It was Richard who had sentenced Renata to torture and months of incarceration, panic attacks and the medication that would harm her baby. She didn't blame the Security Forces or the KGB – she blamed Richard. And she had sworn that he would get the taste of his own medicine – the same medicine that she and Adam had been poisoned with because of him.

Adam lived longer than expected and he had a decent go at his short life. With time, Renata was free to settle in Novosibirsk and to find employment. Arts and drama were supported and funded by the authorities as communism began to crumble. She and a couple of other enthusiasts started a small drama company, and in no time, received huge subsidies from the City Council of Novosibirsk. She did well for herself and for Adam. He was happy there in Novosibirsk. He knew no other life. But he had to die prematurely. There was no escape from his death sentence. It had been coming from the moment his mother had been arrested and tortured.

Renata returned to Poland and arranged for his body to be repatriated. She contacted Richard's family to bury the boy where he belonged, in the family tomb. Her own parents were long dead, never knowing what had become of her. Her brother lived in France. Richard's family was all that Adam had.

Once the burial was completed, she knew she had to deliver on the promise she had made to herself all those years ago. She had to honour that promise and she had to honour Adam's memory. It wasn't right for Richard to outlive his son, but it was also imperative that he paid the price of his son's tragically early death. Richard was still in England, and it was down to her to contact him. He had never bothered to contact her.

It was at this point in her story that Sam decided to interrupt and said, 'But he did try to find you, Renata. He tried ... in 1991 he –'

She laughed. It was a bitter laughter. 'He was ten years too late – ten years into Adam's death sentence. No, he had to die. It was fair that he died.'

After that unequivocal statement, she went on to finish her story:

Even before she met with him, she was in no doubt that he had to die. Richard's death was so many years overdue. She didn't hesitate for one second, and she still wouldn't hesitate now. She gave him the poisoned bottle of his favourite Tokaji and showed him pictures of Adam. Richard cried: at first, tears of joy, then when she finally told him Adam was dead, it was tears of loss and great, great sadness. Richard hugged her and wept, and between his sobs came promises of making it up to her, recapturing what they had lost, realising she had been the one and only love of his life, the mother of his one and only child. To the end, he did not understand anything. He did not understand that there was no going back, no mending broken lives and no bringing Adam back from the dead. There was no remorse, no redemption, and no hope for Richard. He had to die like a dog infected with rabies – beyond a cure. It was justice.

Renata had made her peace and was now ready for whatever came next. No matter what it was, it would be nothing compared to what she had been through – a tiny aftershock following her catastrophic life.

Chapter Thirty-four

Our forty-minute trip back to Lublin was the longest silence that I had ever had to endure in my life. Samuel sat with his head hung down on his chest, his eyes closed. The judders of the train had no effect on him. He would let his body shift to adjust to the perilous trajectory of the train. He appeared to be sleeping, but I knew he wasn't. A deep frown crumpling his forehead told me he was thinking.

I was doing the same. Pretending to be looking out of the window at the monotony of passing flatlands and thick forests, I was thinking of what we were to do with Renata's confession. The good citizen's instinct directed us to relay everything to the police, but I cringed at the mere thought of it. Delivering this woman into the hands of the police after the inhumane incarceration she had already been through seemed inexcusable. She had already been punished ten times over, more than her crime justified. Any more punishment would amount to gratuitous cruelty. But then she had murdered a man – in cold blood and with ruthless premeditation. She had exacted her own justice. It was a prime example of natural justice, but we live in a world where justice is man-made, and in this world, she had committed a serious crime for which she had to answer. It was up to the courts to find mitigation in her actions, maybe to let her go free on the grounds of insanity, but it wasn't up to me. And yet . . . She was no threat to the public. She had already paid her dues. And at the end of the day, it wasn't my job to bring killers to justice.

I shut my eyes. I shouldn't have done so: darkness took me back to Renata's coffin. I inhaled sharply and stared at Samuel. 'What are we going to do?' I asked him.

'The right thing,' he said, as if that had an unequivocal meaning.

Our rickety train came to a screeching halt, wheezed and died. With its last breath it opened its pneumatic doors. We were in Lublin, our decision put on hold.

'We have a train to catch. It's leaving in five minutes.'

I picked up pace and followed Samuel. We dashed up the stairs, two at a time, which is something I hadn't done since I was at school. It felt precarious. We crossed a couple of platforms and then broke into a tumble down the stairs. The train was waiting for us. To my relief it wasn't the same suicidal train variety we had left behind us. This new train looked like it meant business. We were in good hands. The conductor blew the whistle just as we forced open the door and the train jerked into motion. That was the only jerk of our entire voyage.

We had seats booked in the first-class compartment on this train. We found them with some help from a smartly dressed ticket inspector, who was friendly, very obliging, and spoke our language. We flopped into our pristine seats, breathless. There were only two occupants – just us – in the compartment for six. A waiter wearing a bow tie rolled in with a trolley and offered us a choice of beverages. A lovely cup of tea was God-sent. We sipped silently and with all due reverence. The taste of home in exile . . .

Our next stop was Warsaw, with no intervening stops, hisses, or judders. We could relax and put our feet up. I took off my shoes; my feet were killing me. You would know how that felt if you ever tried sprinting on stilts.

When we finished our tea, the question returned. 'What are we going to do with Renata's confession?'

'Is there any doubt in your mind, Maggie, about what must be done?'

'I've been thinking. After all she's been through, is it really our place to denounce her?'

'We cannot protect her. It's up to the courts to look into her culpability, and I am an officer of the court –'

'A retired one,' I pointed out.

'You never retire from your ethical duty!'

'I'm sorry, I just can't bear that poor woman being put through extradition, trial, and prison in a foreign country. That is exactly what she's already been through! We could pretend she had served her sentence in advance, and forget all about it.'

'I can't believe we're having this conversation.'

'She is mad with grief!'

'It will be taken into consideration as an extenuating circumstance, I'm sure of that. She may even be found not fit to stand trial. But we have to report what we know to the police.'

The train came to a halt so softly that we wouldn't have noticed we were in Warsaw had it not been for an announcement from the loudspeakers above our heads. Next stop was Berlin. We didn't have a hotel booked there. We headed for the exit.

A woman with a large piece of luggage was battling to dismount from the train. She was young and good-looking. Chivalrously, Samuel went to the rescue. 'Let me!' he said, jumped off the step ahead of her and landed on the platform. From there he offered her his hand to guide her off the train. Then, leaving me to wait my turn, he reached for the suitcase, one foot on the train step, the other on the edge of the platform. He heaved the suitcase and suddenly both Samuel and the suitcase vanished into the gap. No one was there to tell poor Samuel – a Londoner through and through after all – to mind the damned gap! The handsome woman and I raised the alarm. For different reasons, of course: I was worried about my missing neighbour, she about her missing luggage.

Our ticket inspector appeared, huffing and puffing. An immediate search was carried out while the train waited, with all the passengers hanging out of the windows to see what the commotion was all about. Within seconds, Samuel and the suitcase resurfaced to everybody's applause.

Samuel wasn't amused. He wiped his face, leaving a smudge of black engine oil or some other such substance on his face. He looked like Rambo on a jungle mission. His chivalry had been abandoned under the train. 'Ask her,' he grunted, 'what the hell she's got in that suitcase! A cut-up corpse, is my guess!'

Ungrateful for his efforts, the woman retrieved her suitcase and tottered off, pulling her luggage behind her with little effort. I thanked our inspector, who promptly boarded the train, and waved to us from the window. As did the rest of the passengers.

Never before had I seen my neighbour this ungraceful. He swore under his breath, but I could hear it. It was unrepeatable. It seemed that Samuel now had an issue with the female race as a whole. Still fuming, he pulled out his mobile phone and dialled a number.

'Alec? Hi! It's Sam Dee.'

I froze. I knew he was calling the superintendent to report Renata Topolska. There was nothing I could do to stop him. He wasn't prepared to debate it with me any longer. I stood there, on an empty train platform, listening to his side of the conversation.

'We, Maggie and I, we're in Poland and we have ... we've run into Richard's killer. She actually confessed to killing Richard. Her name is – Yes, that's correct. How did you know ...? OK, that's fine. There was no need for me to call you, I see. You've got it well under control.'

He rang off and gazed at me, looking uncomfortable.

'Well?' I prompted him.

'They already know Renata's identity. They're having a European Arrest Warrant issued for her apprehension. Apparently, they tracked her down through their *"good old-fashioned police work"* – scrutinising hours of CCTV footage until they came across her and Richard in a restaurant in Bristol. They matched that against the database of passenger passport photos. Painstaking but effective, that's what Alec said.'

I shook my head but didn't openly gloat. Deep down, I always knew that we should have kept our noses out of it and left the investigation to the police. At least I wasn't a big-mouth tell-tale, like some. My conscience was clear.

Chapter Thirty-five

It was a sunny but breezy day in August. I was feeling rather optimistic: Mum had her medical check-up after the series of radiotherapy sessions she had been through and received the all-clear – for now at least, as you never know with cancer. Sometimes it packs up and leaves for good, sometimes it comes back to wreak more havoc. I crossed my fingers that our cancer was a goner. I say *our* because it did feel like all of us had been affected by it.

Samuel invited me for a small get-together in his garden to celebrate his birthday. He didn't say how old he was.

'I hope you don't end up like Richard,' I commented flippantly, 'I couldn't stomach another death in Bishops.'

'I'll try my best not to die, but with my mother around, I can't make any firm promises.'

I didn't have to wonder for too long what he meant. His mother, Deirdre, was a presence to reckon with. She was one of those larger-than-life individuals who knew everything better than you and didn't mind reminding you of that fact every chance she got. She was of small stature, but that didn't stop her from claiming centre stage and filling it with her overwhelming persona. She arrived dressed to the nines in her finery of a feathered hat and a red silk shawl that flapped belligerently, pulled every now and again by the erratic breeze. She had been driven by Samuel's son, Campbell – a good-looking young man with traits of his father evident in the mane of his thick black hair and an endearing smile.

Deirdre climbed out of the car with a scowl, cursing and spitting bile, 'Has nobody told the boy that speed kills?'

'Gran, I was going extra-slowly! As soon as you told me your stomach was in your throat –'

'You see what I mean,' she shook her head and the feathers in her hat rippled ominously.

'I was going no more than fifty, even on the motorway. I thought I'd never make it here with Gran screaming blue murder next to me.' Campbell looked spent. I could tell from his pained expression that he had been to hell and back delivering his gran to this event.

Clearly, he had drawn the short straw. His twin sister, Abi, appeared sympathetic but relieved. She had arrived by train at Sexton's and Samuel collected her from the station. She, I must say, looked just like Alice (who, naturally, was hovering around, more radiant than ever in her ghostly form). Abi's hair shone with golden highlights, long and lustrous, and untamed. It seemed like she didn't care very much what she looked like – she had this air of effortless elegance about her.

I couldn't help but like her. I took an instant liking to all of them, in fact – even to Dragon Deirdre, as I had christened Samuel's mother quietly in my head. I had adopted them all and taken them into my heart. Sitting there with them in my grandparents' old garden with my favourite childhood swing and with the big cedar tree that Andrea and I had climbed as children, I felt at peace. I had sold that half of my grandparents' garden to Samuel Dee with a heavy heart and lots of trepidation. That trepidation was now gone. The garden, the swing and the cedar were in good hands. Soppily and tearfully, I conceded that I had lost nothing but acquired a friend as well as a good neighbour.

Author's Note

Although Bishops Well is a fictional village situated near the fictional town of Sexton's Canning, it is typical of many such villages scattered across the beautiful county of Wiltshire. It hasn't entirely moved with the times and remains steeped in its proud history with medieval and Tudor buildings dominating its cobbled alleys. Its wider setting is even older than the village itself, featuring such prehistoric gems as a Neolithic stone circle, an Early Celt settlement and Bronze Age burial grounds. These and many other ancient mounds and chalk hill carvings scattered amongst its rolling fields and grazing paddocks are the very landmarks of Wiltshire.

Bishops Well and Sexton's Canning are an amalgam of real places where I have lived, worked or passed through when exploring my locality. The reader will find references to Bishops Well's Market Square with a stone cross in its centre. Its prototype can be found in the town of Malmesbury. It was built in the late fifteenth century using rubble from the partially destroyed Malmesbury Abbey. I spent over a decade teaching in a village school near Malmsbury and frequently travelled past the Market Cross on my way to sporting events.

Sexton's Canning has been modelled on the historical town of Devizes. The county's police HQ is situated there. I once lived in its close proximity. Behind the police HQ is Quakers Walk, a greenbelt footpath that leads to a hill adorned by one of Wiltshire's several White Horses. Beyond Quakers Walk is a wood that gave inspiration to Sexton's Wood and Bishops Swamp.

The main street of Bishops Well, full of graded buildings, some thatched, some with the distinct criss-cross of Tudor framing, is a fusion of the old towns of Market Lavington and Potterne, and the villages of Sandy Lane and Lacock near Bowood. The Stables Tea-rooms in Lacock gave inspiration to Bishops' own Old Stables Café. It is a perfect place to meet up with friends for cream tea and a natter. Notably, it is dog-friendly. With their opulent grounds and stately homes the Weston and Forget-Me-Not estates featured in 'The Shires Mysteries' owe their style and design to Bowood House.

Geographically, Bishops Well lies somewhere near Trowbridge, with Bath ten miles to the north-west and Salisbury to the south, some thirty miles away over Salisbury Plain. On a nice day, when I walk my dog in the fields, I can see the Westbury White Horse in the distance. Unlike the White Horse of Bishops Well, it is the real article and the oldest hill carving of its kind in Wiltshire.

Priest's Hole, Maggie and Sam's home, is based on my house, which is part of a historical church enclave and borders an old cemetery with some of the tombstones so ancient and weather-worn that one can no longer read their inscriptions.

The places in 'The Shires Mysteries' replicate the rich landscape and landmarks of Wiltshire, however all of my characters are entirely fictional and any similarity to persons living or dead is, as they say, purely coincidental.

Acknowledgements

First and foremost, my heartfelt thanks go to my husband, Steve. Without his encouragement and belief in me, none of my books would ever get off the ground. He is steadfast and honest in his critique and advice, keeps meticulous records of names, places and dates, and holds me to account whenever I stray into incomprehensibility or get my facts muddled up. He is the man I go to with my first draft for a robust, but always kindly imparted, verdict.

I must also offer my gratitude to Greg Rees, my indefatigable editor. He has been unrelenting in keeping me within the boundaries of the cosy mystery genre. At his behest, The Shires flourished and developed into a self-contained world and their inhabitants have formed a pretty tight and cohesive community. Without Greg's timelines, some of the plot would have warped and events jumped into multiple alternative dimensions.

I would like to say a big *thank you* to Frankie Edwards and Bea Grabowska at Headline for holding the reins of the entire publishing process. Their expertise has been invaluable in understanding readers' tastes and expectations, polishing my titles to shiny perfection, ensuring cohesion across the whole series, and finally putting 'The Shires Mysteries' in front you, the reader.

And last but not least, I am forever grateful to you for choosing to read this book, and hopefully those that will follow in the series. I hope that you enjoyed solving this mystery with Maggie and Sam, and came to like this pair of West Country sleuths. Your reflections and views about the book are priceless. Many thanks for sharing them and for reviewing *Death Comes to Bishops Well* if and when you get a chance. I would love to hear from you. Visit me at www.annalegat.com, on Twitter @LegatWriter or Facebook @ AnnaLegatAuthor.